THE REVERENT DEAD

BRYAN NOWAK

Editing by Kelly Hartigan, XterraWeb;
http://editing.xterraweb.com

Bryan Nowak – Sterling, VA
www.bryannowak.com

First Edition

United States of America

1

CALLING ALL CARS ... CALLING ALL CARS

Carrie tried to remember the old saying about sailors and skies as she drove toward the police station. Something about red sky in the morning and red sky at night. While the meaning escaped her, certainly the red sky at night stood out as the better of the two. If that was the case, the delightfully pink evening sky suggested the next day would be a gift.

Too bad I am destined to spend most of it sleeping after the night shift.

Following in the footsteps of her father, Carrie Pettygrew made her way through the police department with the encouragement of her friend, boss, mentor, and now police chief, Melonie Dixon. Every step of the way, she proved a quick study. Smart and quick on her feet, she was well liked on the force.

Only recently achieving the rank of acting detective, she threw her heart into the work. As the new detective, she drew the short straw and had to cover the dreaded night shift, an assignment no one ever took willingly. Still, Carrie wanted to make a good impression. Not one to mind the work, it gave her access to all the city's stranger late-night cases. She hated being away from home at night far less than her longtime boyfriend Dirk did, as he preferred to have her home at night.

While waiting at a red light, she checked her reflection in the rearview mirror. Her mother used to comment that her gray eyes looked troubled and stormy upon first glance and softer after you spent time with her. She once wanted to be a model, but being several inches short of the minimum ensured the runway was not a suitable career choice. Growing up in a cop family almost guaranteed her a spot at the police academy.

Crossing the intersection of Central Avenue and Fourteenth Street, she rolled down the window and breathed in the night air. It was intoxicating.

The police scanner had been eerily quiet while she dressed for work that afternoon. Any cop worth their badge allowed a sixth sense to inform them something was about to happen.

Dirk sensed it too. He seemed extra clingy this afternoon. She admonished him to stop pestering her so she could get on with her day, unwilling to admit to herself that she wanted him as close to her as possible. Without an active case to work, Dirk Bentley, in his role as private investigator, would not be allowed to ride along.

Carrie tried to calm her unsettled nerves. Outside the car's window, a light breeze rustled the autumn leaves. The smell of decay played in her nose forced thoughts of Dirk to give way to ideas of caramel apples and spiced cider.

The radio broke in with the calm, sardonic voice of the county dispatcher. "Attention, all cars in the vicinity of

Central and Twentieth, Center Point Security is reporting an intrusion at twenty-twenty-eight Central Avenue."

Reflexively, Carrie reached for the radio while glancing up at the street sign indicating she passed the intersection of Seventeenth Street and Central Avenue. "Fifteen-seventy-one to base, responding. You can show me on duty and on scene. Will wait for backup. Advise, no lights or sirens." Carrie, being the on-call detective, was the ranking officer by default on the night shift. Lights and sirens spooked criminals, and she did not want to chase someone down a dark alley, at night, on the first few minutes of her shift.

"Affirmative, Fifteen-seventy-one, I show you on scene and on duty." After a brief moment she continued. "All units responding to twenty-twenty-eight Central Avenue be advised no lights or sirens."

A block away, Carrie brought her car to a stop several houses from the address. The building, a gothic church built in the early part of the twentieth century, dominated the area. Sodium-vapor bulbs bathed the front of the church in an eerie yellow glow. The light breeze sent leaves whirling along the sidewalk to undeclared destinations. Nothing living moved, and there was no sign of anything amiss beyond the morose night scene of the urban landscape.

A few minutes later, a crackle erupted from her radio. "Detective Pettygrew, Officer Collins and Sergeant Davis here for backup. What's your play?"

Davis, a veteran on the force and someone you wanted to have your back in a fight, stood out as the model of a great cop. The executive officer of the National Black Law Enforcement Officer Association, local scoutmaster, and chairperson of the PTA, his call sign on the department was All American.

Carrie's nerves steadied slightly, knowing the caliber of her backup.

Officer Collins, in sharp contrast, glowed goth-white, loved grunge metal music, and weighed in at about one hundred and fifty pounds soaking wet with rocks in his pockets. The patrolman struck Carrie as someone in constant need of more food, more exercise, and more time in the sun. With an uncanny inability to fill out any uniform, no matter how tailored the fit, the kid looked perpetually like an intern on his first day. However, the young patrolman's reports showed him to be a competent officer, and when not working, Collins spent much of his leisure time studying police procedure, and Davis trusted the rookie.

"Davis, I think there are two entrances. Have the new guy keep an eye on the front while we check around back. You head around your side, and I'll cross the front. Meet me at the rear entrance." Carrie had reservations about taking a new cop into a potentially dangerous situation. She and Davis understood the layout of the building. After the all clear was given, she planned to take Collins through to check the place out.

"Ten-four, Detective," Davis replied.

She watched the light inside their squad car turn on and both men step out. The patrolman crept to the front of the church, avoiding the illumination of the streetlight and ensuring no one looking from the windows would see the wiry officer lurking in the shadows. Davis, also avoiding the light, turned down the alleyway opposite the one Carrie now made her way down.

Drawing her weapon, she took careful steps as she picked through the broken bottles and abandoned shipping boxes left to rot. The last thing they needed was noise to scare off any would-be suspects. Clearing the side of the building, she scared a cat and almost disturbed the peaceful slumber of a homeless man snoring inside an old children's sleeping bag.

In the darkness, she breathed a sigh of relief, making out the form of the sergeant standing behind the church. Someone had broken the streetlight covering the entrance, giving Carrie a good idea where they would begin their search for an intruder.

Sergeant Davis pointed down a short flight of stairs. Carrie could just make out the steel basement door of the church. Its metal frame had been pried open like a tin can, dispelling any hope she had of a false alarm. Approaching the steps, pricks of moisture broke out on her skin while her heart raced like it wanted to jump out and run away from the scene of the crime. *Not exactly how I wanted my workday to start.*

Sergeant Davis, the consummate gentleman, motioned for Carrie to cover the door while he went in first. She nodded and said a silent prayer. The last thing she needed before her vacation was to get shot or beaten up.

Through the open door, the ambient light from the alley cast a rude glow into the church basement. The aroma of dust, rotting paper, and mothballs assaulted Carrie's sense of smell. It reminded her of her great-aunt Tilda's house. Nothing moved inside, and the door remained blissfully quiet as Davis opened it.

As Davis covered the hallway, Carrie entered and made her way into the darkened room. Carrie had attended a dozen or more weddings, baptisms, and funerals in this church, so she knew the layout well. The kitchen featured pots and pans either hanging on hooks or stashed away in cupboards where they belonged.

After sweeping the room, Carrie moved to the next, a small library doubling as a youth room for the younger kids. Small plastic chairs and beanbags presented the largest impediments. The tiny chairs momentarily made her think of the children she hoped she and Dirk would someday have. *Focus, Detective.*

The next room on her end of the hallway stood empty, save for the stacks of chairs waiting to be used in the large banquet hall. Although she hated to give away her position, she removed her small flashlight and scanned the darker corners of the room. After confirming she was alone, Carrie put the light away and let her eyes readjust to the darkness.

From upstairs came a thud. It sounded like a pile of hymnals being knocked to the floor.

"Would you watch where you are going?" a voice cried out.

Sergeant Davis appeared at the end of the hallway, locking eyes with Carrie. They stood in silence, listening to the conversation taking place one floor up.

"Shut up, asshole." Another voice pierced the darkness. Neither of the men seemed to realize that a whisper inside a church sanctuary carried a considerable distance.

"Hey, needle dick, leave that shit. We need to go. We're taking too long."

Another loud crash, followed by unrestrained yelling, would have seemed comical if they were not trying to apprehend burglary suspects. Something moved across the floor, making a strange shuffling sound suggesting an object heavier than either man could lift.

Carrie risked a whisper, knowing the racket the men made

would conceal it. "I may not be super cop, but I'm pretty sure the guys we' are looking for are upstairs. I'll go to the main stairs at the front. Take the rear steps. I'd like to try boxing them in."

Davis, who until now looked calm and collected, chortled lightly at her joke. A sudden gleam in his eye made him appear less like a police sergeant and more like a Labrador in a tennis ball factory. He beamed at the idea of collaring a criminal.

Carrie gave Davis a minute to reach the back stairs, which led up to the small room behind the altar where the priest changed out of his robes. Now, it served their purposes, ensuring one of them moved in coordinated fashion on either side of the church sanctuary. She ascended to the first landing, which would take her up to the coatroom near the church's entryway.

The shuffling of items along the floor stopped, and the two voices murmured to each other.

Carrie pulled out her cell phone and texted Collins: Two suspects inside. Davis and I moving to intercept. Be ready in case they bolt.

Collins responded with smiley face and thumbs-up emojis.

God, I hate millennials.

She climbed the rest of the stairs, pausing long enough to discern two figures moving around the dimly lit sanctuary. For the moment, the two were staring at a pile of items on the floor. Carrie backed away, doing her best to avoid the light streaming in from the doors.

A loud crash rang out from behind the altar, alerting everyone in the building to their presence.

Davis broke radio silence. "That was me. Sorry."

At once, the reverent silence became a chaotic tumult. The two suspects bolted in separate directions, tripping over everything in their path. Carrie reached the door to the sanctuary just in time to see one of the men bolt out a side door with Sergeant Davis giving chase.

Carrie flipped a light switch on the wall, the luminescence jumping to life just in time for her to see the second man lunge past her and crash through the front doors of the church. She followed the would-be burglar and was rewarded by watching Officer Collins execute a perfect roundhouse kick, putting the man firmly on his back, his head bouncing off the curb. Before Carrie even processed what she just witnessed, Collins turned the suspect onto his stomach and cuffed his hands behind his back. The lanky officer had not uttered a single word during the seemingly fluid action.

"Holy crap, Collins. That was friggin' awesome." Carrie detected the slightest smile from the lanky youth as he bowed to his bested adversary.

Carrie grabbed her handheld radio. "Davis, what's your location?"

"On my way back, boss. Perp got away." Disappointment seeped from Sergeant Davis's voice. "Understood, American Dad. You'll get him next time. Come on back." Standard protocol in a chase at night was to pursue the suspect until it was no longer safe to do so. Dark alleys presented the most unsafe of all scenarios. Charlottetown was not a dangerous city, but it retained bad elements like any other.

Carrie made a quick call to inform dispatch what happened. She directed the crime scene unit and four other squad cars to help control the growing pajama-clad crowd exiting their homes at the sight of the handcuffed man on the sidewalk fronting the church. Sergeant Davis made his way back along the side of the alley to rejoin Carrie and Collins.

"That little ... idiot ... got away from me. I was literally six inches from grabbing him. He flipped over a fence and kept running. Too dark back there for me to keep up." He sighed. "I'm not as young as I used to be." Davis injected a humorous tone although Carrie knew he took losing a suspect personally.

"I think you mean that little shithead, but I hear you." Carrie put her hand on the large man's shoulder. "You did fine. More importantly, you came back in one piece. Too bad you missed your little buddy here karate kicking this guy and hog-tying him in what had to be record time. It was amazing."

The suspect, regaining consciousness after EMTs administered a smelling salt, wore the ubiquitous low-hung jeans and torn T-shirt of any garden variety dirtbag one would find on any city street. His appearance was marred slightly by the fresh slick of blood from an abrasion on his face.

"It was kung fu," Collins said.

Carrie cocked her head to one side. "What was?"

Collins straightened up. "Oh, forgive my insubordination. It was kung fu, Detective."

"No, that's not what I meant." Lights of the crime scene truck and several responding patrol cars lit up the sides of the buildings in a wash of red and blue. Uniformed officers swept the building looking for other potential suspects hiding in crevices the trio had been unable to search. "What I meant, Collins, is I'd like to know how you were able to perform that kick."

"As I said, kung fu, Detective," Collins said, shoving the

suspect into the back of their patrol car and slamming the door.

"Oh, sweet Jesus, never mind." She shook her head and smiled. "Congratulations, Officer Collins, you go on record as making your first arrest. Now you get to fill out the paperwork. You two take Prince Charming for a quick examination at the emergency room to make sure you didn't scramble his brains too much. If he's all right, lock his ass to a table in an interrogation room. We can find out where scumbag number two got off to."

The parish priest, a fat little man with a nervous disposition, arrived and repeatedly attempted to enter the premises against the instructions of the officers present. Officers kept him out, insisting it remain untouched while the crime scene investigators finished collecting evidence, taking pictures, and dusting for prints. Davis and Collins left with the perpetrator for the hospital.

Carrie entered the church with the pudgy priest, systematically inspecting the first floor, looking for anything missing. Although the burglars appeared to linger in the building long enough to raid the refrigerator and make a pile of brass fixtures and expensive crystal, the alarm system did only half its job as the outside annunciator and the lights did not perform their critical tasks.

The priest reviewed the items the suspects compiled to remove, opining the brass and crystal religious items fetched a premium on the black market. The chubby cleric also mentioned other similar churches in the area reported a rash of burglaries focusing on high-end items resalable to other unsuspecting churches. This particular church took the extraordinary step of installing a security system on their building at the behest of the archbishop of the diocese.

Punctuating this point, a large brass cross lay on the floor where the burglars dropped it. The brass figure of Jesus stared up at Carrie, begging for someone to replace the cross and allow him to continue dying for the sins of the world.

Sacrilege aside, the massive fixture could be melted down for its metal alone and make quite a profit. Brass offering plates, communion serving utensils, and other metal objects were tidily piled in a few places, waiting to be loaded into a car or truck.

Oh well, I guess it is just another of those silly little crimes that take place in any town.

The odds of this small-time burglary taking up more than the minimal amount of her workweek were slim. As far as crime went, this was nothing too spectacular. With a light caseload, Carrie thought this case offered an interesting distraction and an easy win but little more.

Leaving the scene to the other investigators, Carrie drove another few blocks to the newest location for The Beanapse, open twenty-four hours a day and catered to people working nights and college students.

"Mocha latte, please. Also, can I have an extra shot, Trudy?" Carrie asked the thirty-something-year-old barista behind the counter.

Trudy smiled in recognition. "Sure thing. Late night, Carrie? I was getting used to seeing you a little earlier, on your way to the office." Trudy took over as the night manager shortly after the store opened. The petite brunette would talk endlessly about either her two year old daughter if you let her. Recently she also hinted at a crush on their mutual friend Keith.

"You could say that. I didn't even make it to the office before being called to an alarm. I hate days like that."

Trudy grinned while the extra shot of espresso filtered through the machine into a shot glass. "You know, one thing I'll say about working here, at no point do I have to worry about responding to police calls."

Carrie pulled her card out of her wallet, eliciting a frown from Trudy. "Your money is no good here, Carrie. But, you can do something for me. Tell Keith I said hello. If you see him, of course."

Carrie threw three dollars into the tip jar. "Thanks, you guys are the best. I will although I can't help but wonder if you are a little sweet on him." She took two napkins from the dispenser and smiled at the logo of a coffee bean jumping the synaptic gap in a brain cell.

After the first surge of caffeine kicked in, Carrie's mind started processing the crime scene.

That cross must weigh at least fifty pounds. The other metal and glass came in at a hundred or two hundred pounds. They needed a truck or a car to get away. They must have been waiting for a wheelman, who suspiciously never showed up. Who knows, this could blow up into something interesting after all.

2

THE ARCHBISHOP OF CHARLOTTETOWN

"Oh, come on, quit sitting around like a sour puss and focus." Keith maneuvered his pickup truck down onto the county road that led to the driveway of Bentley Motorcycle Repair. The exchange reminded him a little of trying to convince his nephews to put down the video games and go outside to play. "I know, you have a difficult time getting past these things, but you of all people need to regain your focus here. We have cases to work, pulled pork sandwiches to eat, and worlds to change. I can't do it alone."

Keith knew that on the other end of the phone, Dirk sat with a cup of coffee and a scowl on his face. Dirk Bentley, owner of Bentley Detective Services and Bentley Motorcycle Repair did not suffer defeat well.

This defeat, or rather the perception of defeat, hounded him.

Scratching a whiskery chin, Keith thought about the old nun who approached them about finding her missing friends.

Dirk accepted the case and dove into it with his usual gusto. Just coming off a high from having solved the case of a serial killer, he was on top of the world.

Several dead ends and a roadblock at the church itself sapped any remaining enthusiasm.

Four weeks after Sister Sophia visited, Keith arrived at the shop one morning to find Carrie sitting in Dirk's chair. They sat quietly inside the office, watching Dirk pace back a forth across the parking lot, occasionally picking up a handful of rocks and throwing them at an old stack of tires left by the previous owner. She looked over at Keith and shook her head. They both understood this was Dirk's special version of self-deprecation. He'd become so frustrated with the lack of movement on the case that he pushed himself into a spiral of self-pity and anger.

Now, a full six months later, Keith determined to drag Dirk along, kicking and screaming if need be, to a case Dirk decided not to work. Dirk and Keith had known each other their whole lives, and no one knew Dirk better. Keith suspected his old friend was just having a difficult time accepting the reality that not all cases were solvable.

"Keith," Dirk said, "I really don't feel like it today. I mean, I know we have a case to work, but I'm not feeling up to it. Why don't you go by yourself?" In the background, the repetitive sound of Dirk kicking the aluminum file cabinet repeatedly made a vague gong noise. It was Dirk's standard go-to move at times when overly frustrated.

"I'm not asking, Dirk. You're the boss, and this is a very important client." Keith had scheduled a meeting with the archbishop of the Catholic Church who had retained them to investigate an odd rash of burglaries at their warehouse.

Although the police department tried to be helpful, the case was too small to devote enough time to find out who committed the crimes. The archbishop knew Dirk had investigated the case on behalf of Sister Sophia and decided to give them a call.

"You need to come out because they're asking for you, and I am no reasonable substitute." Keith was telling a little fib. The archbishop had not asked for Dirk. It served as a convenient white lie to make Dirk feel needed and push him out of his current funk. Although a functioning security system protected the warehouse, it seemed worthless in catching any thief coming or going. So far, only furniture went missing, and the church worried the problem would grow if left unattended.

"I really don't like this, Keith. I looked over the case and couldn't find any way they are getting into the warehouse. This is just a waste of our time. The police need to solve this one." A long slow sigh on the phone pierced the relative quiet of his truck. Dirk's intransigence seethed through the earpiece.

"Okay, Dirk, you've left me no choice." Sitting outside the motorcycle repair shop in his truck, Keith held down the horn. Through the cell phone, the sound of his own horn blared through loud and clear, picked up from Dirk's receiver. "Get your ass out here now and quit being a big baby." Keith continued to lay on the horn without letting up, resolved to continue making noise until Dirk either relented or the horn gave out.

"Okay, okay, stop. Thank God, I don't have neighbors. I'll come. Why are you such a pain in my ass?" Dirk stood from his chair, flung open the office door, and glared at Keith who wore a self-satisfied smile.

"I'm only a pain in the ass when I need to get my best friend to pull himself up by the boot straps. Jump in, buckle up, and hang on, cowboy."

"Fine. You owe me a beer," Dirk yelled, crossing the parking lot.

Keith pursed his lips as Dirk climbed into the truck. "Why do I owe you a beer?"

"For being such an incredible pain in the ass."

Forty minutes later, Keith turned into the parking lot of the rectory at Saint Mary's Cathedral. The sprawling campus housed the modest Saint Mary's Cathedral, the offices of the archbishop, and various support offices for the massive administrative functions of the church. The offices of the archbishop dominated the landscape, towering over four stories. The building held over fifty various church offices, storage rooms, and a large mail and distribution center. Made of stone from a nearby quarry, the building would have blended in nicely on the Irish countryside as well as it did the wooded property in Virginia. Four stone chimneys rose from the peak of the roof, and a weather vane, directly in the center, looked like it had seen better days.

After Keith and Dirk checked in with the security guard at the front entrance adorned with the image of Pope Francis and a painted reproduction of the iconic *Jesus at the Door* painting, the guard pointed down the hallway to the third door on the left. Keith wondered how terse and jaded the world became that they needed a security guard to keep an eye on things in a place dedicated to humanity and the soul.

However, the rise in gun violence against churches did portend difficult times ahead for people of faith.

The third door along the hallway sported a meager sign declaring "Office of the Archbishop of the Greater Metropolitan Catholic Region and Director of Saint Mary's." Keith opened the door and pushed Dirk inside. A woman stood from behind a large desk and looked at Keith and Dirk with a twinge of disdain. "Hello, gentlemen, can I help you?"

Keith spoke up while Dirk plopped into one of the leather chairs against the wall in what made up the archbishop's waiting area. "Yes, we are here to see Archbishop Weebley. My name is Keith Marvin, and this is my associate, Dirk Bentley. His Excellency asked us to stop by."

"May I ask what this is in regard to?" The bookish secretary stood five-foot-four and only just broke one hundred pounds. On her right arm, a bandage suggested a recent injury. The black-rimmed glasses and the graying bun on the top of her head reminded him more of a librarian, admonishing the patrons to lower their voices, than someone working for one of the more active Catholic archbishops on the East Coast. Something about her was off-putting and yet not outwardly offensive. For a secretary, she exuded a commanding presence.

The door to the archbishop's office opened. "Carolyn, I need these faxed over to the—" The archbishop stopped mid-sentence, and a huge smile broke out across his face. "Pastor Keith Marvin, it is so great to see you again. I'm so glad you came."

Carolyn stuttered like she'd swallowed something wrong. "I beg your pardon, Pastor Marvin, I had no idea. I did not mean to be so cold to you when you walked in. You see, I try to run defense for the archbishop during the workday. Please forgive me."

"Don't worry about it, Carolyn, he's out of uniform now anyway." Dirk spoke up, saying more words than he had since they walked into the building. Rising to his feet, he offered a hand to the archbishop.

The archbishop took his hand and gave it a shake. "Well, thank you both for coming. We should talk in my office. Carolyn, please fax these papers off. You know where they go. Then, please have housekeeping bring up coffee and a few sandwiches. We have much to discuss."

"Yes, Your Excellency."

Archbishop Weebley ushered the two into a large office and pointed to a leather couch centered under a huge bookcase featuring everything from holy books to works of fiction by contemporary authors. He sat across from them in an overstuffed leather chair.

A tall man, in his late fifties to early sixties, he either made good use of a gym membership or spent a lot of time doing manual labor outdoors. His gray hair and deep brown eyes put you at ease the moment he looked at you, but there was something in his aura commanding respect without needing to ask for it.

The archbishop spoke after furtively ensuring the door closed completely behind them. "Gentlemen, I will refrain from beating around the proverbial bush. As you likely know, we have a large warehouse. We store everything from Christmas decorations to the personal belongings of nuns assigned to regional convents or anyone off on temporary assignments. Our priests make use of the warehouse as well."

"Actually, we didn't know about the warehouse. However,

from our previous conversation, it sounds like things are going missing?" Keith interrupted.

"Indeed, they are. At first, you understand, it was nothing major. We thought it was just a clerical error and the things would show up eventually. We scoured the shelves, looking for the missing items. I thought there was a problem in the way we bar-coded things for storage. And then everything changed."

"I didn't think nuns came to the order with furniture and personal belongings. You mentioned that everything changed, how so?" Dirk asked.

"Nuns sometimes receive items as other family members die off, and we store them until they decide what to do with those belongings. Mostly things like large pieces of heirloom furniture, family photos, and the like. In a few rare cases, we rent space out to organizations or family members of our staff. Until recently, it was only low dollar things. Now, whoever is behind this seems unhappy and has moved up to larger items."

"You haven't reported any of this to insurance?" Keith shot the archbishop a questioning glance.

"No, we haven't, I—"

The intercom crackled to life, and Carolyn boomed, "Your Excellency, I have the coffee and sandwiches."

"Fine, bring them in, please." As soon as the intercom went dead, the archbishop added, "Carolyn doesn't know, and only a few of the staff are privy to this information. I want to have solid answers before I create a panic. People know things are missing, but they don't know about the break-ins."

The door opened and Carolyn pushed in a cart. Keith

found himself surprisingly hungry and took several bites of a ham on rye.

"Thank you, Carolyn," the archbishop said.

"Yes, Your Excellency."

After she left, he poured three cups of coffee. "As I was about to say, the insurance claims were never filed as the nuns took it upon themselves to donate those items to the church ex post facto. It is as if they are allowing the items to be lost by us, and therefore, they need not be replaced. However, you can understand that I have a responsibility to all who serve the region to ensure this doesn't continue. After all, nuns have comparatively little, and preying on them is unconscionable. The value of most of these things is in the memories they provide. I must protect those meager possessions as best I can. Mostly, I think I just want to know why anyone does something like this."

"If you don't mind me asking, do you have a list of things that went missing?" Dirk asked, leaning forward and putting down the coffee cup. Keith smiled at his old friend taking an interest in the case. This was precisely what Dirk needed to refocus himself.

The archbishop reached over to the desk and picked up a stapled pile of papers and handed it to Dirk. "I anticipated your question, so I printed off the list. I hope you understand that I need to ensure privacy is protected. The information must not be shared outside our circle."

Dirk gave the papers a cursory glance and handed them to Keith. "Where is this warehouse? I'd like to take a look at it."

"Naturally," the archbishop said. "I've arranged for someone to give you a tour of the facility, someone who knows about the thefts. He'll show you around and familiarize you with places from where things have gone missing.

"About the sisters, is there anything we should know about them? Anything in common?" Keith asked, glancing at the papers Dirk handed him.

Archbishop Weebley rubbed his hands together and cast a glance toward the floor, searching for words seemingly evading him. Keith noticed the slight glance toward the door and gave a nod to Dirk. The question obviously struck a nerve.

"Anything at all," Dirk said. "Help us help you, Your Excellency. We need your full cooperation, or this will not work."

"Okay, I hesitate to tell you this. It must be kept in the strictest of confidence. I can't let it be known that I told you this or the bishop will be all over me. Every one of the sisters who lost something of any value suffered from a terminal illness. As if the perpetrator knew their time on earth wore thin, as it were."

Dirk raised an eyebrow. "Every one of them?"

The archbishop shook his head. "I am afraid so. Even Sister Sophia, who I believe you know."

Keith watched his friend's eyes fly open wide with the shock. This information hit him hard.

The archbishop read the shock across Dirk's brow. "I'm sorry, I thought you knew. Initially, we thought she could work through it. However, she is no longer responding to treatment. I drove her to the hospital and checked her in myself. The doctors aren't sure she has more than a week or two left. I don't know when the last time you spoke to her was, but you'll want to go over and see her."

"We will. Thank you for the information," Keith said. "My

understanding is that you are not supposed to know that information. How did you find out about their medical conditions?"

The archbishop straightened in his chair. "You are correct, I'm really not supposed to know this under normal circumstances. However, with nuns, it's a little different. They sign a confidentiality clause stating they will keep the church informed of any and all issues affecting their ability to meet their calling. Each one of the sisters came to me and voluntarily disclosed the illness."

Dirk cocked an eyebrow up. "Okay, that kind of begs a follow-up question then. How long after the nuns told you they were sick did the thefts occur?"

The archbishop leaned back in the chair and squinted as if looking at a far-off database in the back of his mind. "That is an interesting question. It was certainly within a few days."

Dirk spoke up, "Who knew of the illnesses?"

Once again, the archbishop squinted his eyes and furrowed his brow thinking through the answer. "Really, only I knew about it, and I made a notation in their personnel files. There are only a handful of the staff having access to that information."

"Okay, it would be helpful to know who has access to the information. Also, Your Excellency, can you provide background information on everyone who had something stolen? Perhaps there is something in their backgrounds of interest, something binding them all together?"

"You understand, I am hesitant to provide you with this information. Essentially, it lays bare everything we hope to keep out of public scrutiny. If anyone had reason to doubt the security of the Catholic Church, this could cause quite a bit of trouble."

Before Dirk answered, Keith interjected, "Don't worry, Stephen, I'll make sure he is damned to hell for not keeping his word."

Dirk looked shocked at the use of the archbishop's first name. Both men laughed at what constituted an inside joke Dirk was not a party to. Keith's clerical credentials had proved a valuable asset over the years.

"You know, the only reason I am even contemplating giving this to you is that I know Keith. I'd be far less ready to hand it over to someone I didn't know." He went to the computer, and after tapping into his database, the printer sprang to life.

Three full pages of names of people having something go missing from the warehouse spat out of the printer. Ten more pages provided basic background descriptions on everyone. To Keith, it looked like an unusually large assortment of things to end up just vanishing. "Your Excellency, forgive me for saying so, but this sure does seem like a pretty big list. How much is even left in your warehouse?"

"Well, those are everyone who had something go missing. They are sorted by the value of the item missing. Most of the people at the beginning only lost things of relatively low value. But, let us show you the warehouse, and then you'll understand. Many things could go missing from that place, and no one would ever notice. People could go missing in there, and it would take a while to find them. Every church in the region sends things here for storage."

"I see," said Dirk. "Well, you sure have given us a lot to sift through. If you don't mind, I'd like to see this warehouse of yours."

Archbishop Weebley picked up the phone and dialed three numbers. "Edwardo, can you pick up the visitors I told you about and give them the tour of the warehouse?" He listened to Edwardo for a few seconds. "Sí, déjalos ver todo. Muchas gracias." Hanging up the phone, the archbishop nodded to Keith and Dirk.

"Wow, impressive," Dirk said. "I only learned how to say lewd things to girls in Spanish. Basically, enough to get smacked."

The archbishop chortled. "Edwardo is our operations manager. Spends almost all of his time working in the warehouse, and there is no one who knows it better than him. The guy could find his way through there blindfolded."

Keith leaned forward. "I hate to sound indelicate, Your Excellency, but I have to ask—"

"Yes, I trust him implicitly. Out of all the staff, ordained included, his seniority is uncontested. Started out here cutting the lawn as a fifteen-year-old kid. Please check if you like. Trust me, he understands why you might suspect him, and me for that matter. However, we pay Edwardo well for running things around here. To be honest, a man with his skills easily commands a better salary at a private company. He likes serving the church. He'll meet you outside the building to take you to the warehouse when you are ready."

They left the archbishop's office and closed the door behind them. Carolyn stood from her desk and nodded to the men. "Good luck. Be careful down by the warehouse. It is pretty creepy down there."

"Thanks, we will. And hope your arm gets better." Keith

pointed to her bandage as he opened the door to the outer hall.

"Ah, it is nothing. My dog scratched me. Have a nice day, Pastor Marvin."

Moments later, they faced a smiling man who proudly wore a sewn-on name tag declaring him to be Edwardo.

"Mi amigos. It is a pleasure to make your acquaintance. My name is Edwardo. Let us be on our way, please." Edwardo sat behind the steering wheel of a small utility vehicle. Keith remembered it was called a Gator.

As they made their way down the driveway past several of the buildings, Edwardo gave them an impromptu tour of the facility. "This building, to the right, was originally built as a horse stable in 1874. Burnt down twice, it was rebuilt last in 1910. His Holiness, Pope Pius the Tenth, stabled horses there when he visited the convent and cathedral. And you see that little out building back in the woods, the abandoned thing? That was the original springhouse. Sometimes, I sneak down there and fill a jug with the fresh water. The spring still is as fresh and clean as ever, mi amigos." As they whizzed by each building, Edwardo provided unsolicited, and yet interesting, factoids. He even pointed out his own personal quarters on the property where he slept if work required him to stay on site.

The small utility vehicle crested a short hill and descended into a small valley out of eyesight of the main buildings. Sprawling out, at the bottom of the valley, a huge warehouse complex appeared out of place surrounded by a forest of green. The building looked formidable with a ten-foot-tall fence adorned with strands of barbed wire.

Edwardo, in a somewhat more professional tone, continued, "In addition to the barbed wire, we have bars in the middle of each culvert providing drainage for the property so no one can go through the concrete tunnels. We have thirty-six cameras, all being run from a central security desk. We don't have very many inside. We never really needed them."

Dirk asked, "But you are installing more then?"

"Si, but it will take time. After getting His Excellency's blessing, if you will pardon my pun, it takes weeks to get them installed. All of the paperwork is handed into Carolyn and then approved by someone else whose job it is to approve papers. Aye, God called me to this place, and I have no right to complain. However, the bureaucracy can be a little overwhelming at times."

Edwardo brought the Gator to a halt at a panel at the fence. After he swiped a security badge and typing in a pass code, the large metal gate opened with a lurch. Keith examined the operation of the door as it opened. Smooth and efficient, the gate and the rest of the fence stood in good working order. It would not be easy to move something large in and out of here without anyone noticing.

Dirk pointed to Edwardo's badge. "Who has access to the warehouse?"

"A few people. Anyone can obtain a temporary pass from the secretary and come into the area. We will catch you on camera, but the resolution isn't very good, and likely we won't recognize the people coming and going."

"Who comes and goes most often?" Keith asked, picking up on Dirk's question.

"Me, the archbishop, Carolyn, and I have one full-time and three part-time staff persons here during the week to help around the grounds. The archbishop, Carolyn, myself, and the staff all have cards that mark their coming and going. It will show up on the logs. Sisters of the order arriving and leaving will come and get things from time to time. Not too much else goes on down here. It is pretty quiet."

The Gator came to a halt in a space labeled Edwardo, and all three got out.

"Can you think of anyone who would want to steal anything from this facility?" Keith asked.

"No, amigo, I really can't. I know you might find this hard to believe, but nuns really don't possess much of worldly value. The only things worth stealing in here are a few pieces of furniture and personal collections placed in here for safe-keeping." Edwardo seemed sad after uttering safekeeping. "Señors, the archbishop and I go back a long way. I was here before him, and I treat most of the people here like family. Please stop this. I don't want to see another thing go missing. I feel responsible."

Keith put a hand on Edwardo's shoulder. "Edwardo, I can promise you this, we will try to do everything within our power."

Edwardo seemed a little more upbeat with Keith's reassurance. It was evident to Keith this man took his work seriously and the thefts were very personal.

The compound sprawled out along a hillside. A small pass in the hills led to a valley on the other side, where the warehouse dominated the valley floor. Several smaller outbuildings sat just inside the fence line and suggested the storage of garden equipment and other machinery.

Inside the large warehouse structure, Edwardo showed them a large safe for holding anything of value over a thousand dollars. Only he and the archbishop accessed the safe, and he could not remember the last time they used it.

Completing the tour of the facility, he showed them the security office where one of his men dutifully watched security cameras for eight hours a day ever since things started disappearing. Edwardo admitted, they lacked the staff to monitor them twenty-four hours a day. Edwardo explained the cameras also fed into the main office, accessible on the two computers in the main office. They could also change the main view of the security cameras to focus on one area if the need arose. A precaution in the event no one was at the warehouse and someone needed to control the cameras remotely.

Dirk watched as the man at the terminal switched through a few of the feeds. They mostly focused on the front of the building. "How many different views do you have to switch through?"

"Eight total, we have issues with cameras we have not resolved yet."

Dirk continued to watch the scenes flash through until they started all over again. Curiously, none of the images caught anything other than small portions of the back of the building.

Keith and Dirk looked around the warehouse. Most of the items stored fell into the category of general household goods or bulk items waiting for shipment to churches. Treasured old desks and boxes of personal collections adorned the shelves. Each box carried a bar code Edwardo scanned on a handheld reader, bringing up the relevant information such as the owner of the item, weight, and allotted storage section in the warehouse.

Although no security expert, Keith thought the warehouse

carried better security than many small-town banks. He wondered afresh about pilfering a warehouse dedicated to storing the scant belongings of clergy. The most nagging question of the day plagued his mind. Something unshakable and irreconcilable.

If Bishop Weebley really kept all of this information from Carolyn, then how did she know they were going down to the warehouse?

3

CRIMINALS MAKE THE WORST BUSINESS ASSOCIATES

Interrogation tables featured unnecessarily long stretches of stainless steel designed to give the impressions of cold institutionalization. Directly in the center, a ring of steel welded into the metal served to keep a suspect's hands in place. It also made it impossible for the suspects to move more than four inches in either direction. The chair the inmates sat on was bolted to the floor and sat just far enough away from the table that any possibility of sitting comfortably while being handcuffed to the ring proved impossible. Before an interrogation ever began, an inmate sat that way for at least thirty minutes in the cold and uncomfortable room with their thoughts and fears centered on contemplating life inside a prison cell.

By the time Carrie walked into the interrogation room, the object of the interrogation, previously rendered unconscious by Officer Collins, fidgeted in the stainless-steel chair. The youth tried to exude as much machismo as possible and failed miserably as he glared at her. He was likely from a

Latino background, and his long hair carried a lighter brown shade that suggested a mixed heritage. The criminal record spoke of minor crimes. Mostly drug related and petty theft. Nothing violent to suggest someone unredeemable in her mind. Just a kid who took a wrong turn and needed help getting back. Underneath the exterior lay a scared and quivering little child. So far, the boy didn't ask for a lawyer, so she could press any way she wanted to.

Digging into the criminal mind made Carrie's day. Psychological gamesmanship in the extreme, she left suspects dressed in a ubiquitous jail-orange jumpsuit for the interrogation. It ensured the prisoner understood their lives were essentially over unless they cooperated.

Today she needed him riled up while also ensuring he thought getting out of this situation remained a possibility. The effect of providing both hope and despair at the same time manifested on the boy's forehead.

Carrie loved to just sit and stare suspects down. She'd used this technique on Dirk a few times, and it always worked when she wanted to get her way. Pulling two paper cups and a metal thermos from a bag, she poured two cups of coffee. Drinking one of them, she left the other just out of reach of the kid who still tried to look cool.

After five minutes of just sitting, he finally erupted. "Look, bitch, I don't give a fuck about you. Either put me in a hole or let me go, either way I don't give no shit!"

Carrie took another sip of the coffee. "You know what? I talked to the chief tonight before I came in here, and she told me I could rack up all the overtime I want sitting here with you. I am in no hurry, and I have a vacation coming up, so I need the money."

"Fuck off, pussy lips!"

Carrie calmly put the empty coffee cup down. "Aww, flattery will get you nowhere. Do you talk to your momma that way?"

The door to the interrogation room opened, and a patrol officer handed a file to Carrie. It was a pre-arranged interruption designed to give the impression of a more weighty case against him. Carrie already knew everything she needed to know to make the little worm squirm in his orange jumpsuit.

Carrie pretended to read the printout and then smiled at the inmate. "So, Mr. Alvarez. Wanted in New York for some pretty minor stuff. Breaking into cars, huh? You must have been a big man in New York, working with Solntsevskaya Bratva, still nothing too impressive. You know, you did all right until we caught you breaking into our church here in town. An extradition to New York would probably not end well for a pretty boy with connections to Russian organized crime."

"Congratulations, Dick-sucking Tracy, you figured out my name. Now how about you go get me a sammich, bitch!"

To someone not in law enforcement, this bravado easily passed as confidence. Carrie read the twinge of fear flashing across the youth's face when she brought up his connections to Russian organized crime. Never much more than just a foot soldier, Mateo Alvarez served under the organization nevertheless. According to the New York Police Department, the Russians took out a hit on the kid for skimming money off the top. Spending any time behind bars likely meant the organization could take him out at will. Mateo was nothing more than street rabble anyone could find on any corner in the seedier parts of a large city like New York. Kids from the streets like him were a dime a dozen. Right now, the thought of facing his former masters scared him shitless.

In one fluid movement, Carrie crossed the steel desk and pulled out a baton. She put it against his throat and pressed down, and a raspy rattle escaped his lips when he tried to breath. "Listen here, you little shit. I want nothing more than to put a knife through your eye socket, but you have a date with some of your homo-boys in prison. How do you think it will feel with someone making you their little bitch? Then a fat ole oligarch is going to piss on you while someone slits your throat, so you better start—"

The door to the interrogation room burst open, and Chief Dixon entered the room with a concerned look on her face. "Whoa, whoa, Detective. What do you think you are doing?"

Carrie stepped back from Mateo and looked sheepish. "Just having a nice conversation here in the room when you came by, Chief. Mateo and I just started understanding each other."

"Detective, you and I should step outside for a moment." Standing just on the other side of the door just close enough to ensure Mateo overheard every word, they continued their conversation.

"Chief, just let me do my job, all right? Every time I try to do anything around here, you give me a hard time. Now I've got numbnuts here, about to confess, and you're stepping in the way."

"All I'm saying, Detective, as your boss, is that you can't rough a suspect up again. You remember the last time? You almost killed that guy. We can't have that happen again. The internal affairs investigation itself cost this department nearly half your salary. You need to learn to control your anger."

"Chief, if we play by the rules, this guy will be out the door. You know that and I know that, and likely he does too." Carrie paused a moment for dramatic effect. "However, we get this guy to confess to murdering a priest, and we can give the prosecutor the perfect perp."

"Fine, Detective, you do it your way. However, if this gets out, you are on your own."

Carrie walked back into the small interrogation room. Mateo's face had taken on a sickly color since Carrie and Melonie staged their drama in the hallway. The staged conversation accomplished its mission.

"I didn't murder anyone, I swear. Me and that other guy only take brass and stuff. Find Julio Rodriguez, he was there when we got the orders."

"So, Mateo, only there to steal the valuables in the church? Do you think I'll believe that?"

"Yes, I was only there to steal the brass and crystal. This was an order from Jimmy. I swear, I didn't kill anyone. Ah, shit!" Mateo held his hands together, pleading with Carrie.

"And this Julio Rodriguez will back up your story? Why should I believe you, dirtbag?" Carrie knew it was probably over the line to call him that. She enjoyed playing the bad cop character to the hilt.

"Yes, find my amigo Julio, and he will back my story up."

"Who is Jimmy?" Carrie hit the side of the desk with her baton for effect. "And if you lie to me, I swear I will ... "

Mateo struggled to regain any composure or normal facial color. "I don't know who he is. I do know he gives the orders though. Told us to only take what we could pawn easily and make off with the goods."

Carrie smiled inwardly, knowing full well that Chief Dixon stood only feet away, just on the other side of the interrogation room glass. Their well-rehearsed and fine-tuned play in the hallway had worked on more than one suspect. By having a conversation in the hallway and not mentioning any names, they ensured there was no way a defense attorney could stand up in court and definitively say they talked about him.

Carrie flipped open the folder and glanced down. "Oh geez, I'm so sorry. You are not a murder suspect at all. Wow, can you imagine my embarrassment? Thanks for telling me all of that though."

"What?" Mateo shook his head in disbelief. "Oh man, you played me. I ain't saying no more until I get a lawyer."

"Fine with me, I got what I was looking for. Let me ask you a question, Mateo. How long do you think you'll go into the can for? I mean, let's be realistic here. You'll probably only spend a little time in jail, but you *will* be in jail. Sitting with all the MS-13 shitheads sitting in cells waiting for deportation. Do you really think they have time to tolerate a two-bit thug like you who lack the imagination to break into anything other than a church? Yep, those cells are filled with not-so-good Catholics who will be less than happy to hear you stole from God. You really want to go into a jail where they are going to know you broke into a church?"

Although clearly going off script, Carrie knew Chief Dixon, likely still listening in the other room, would go along with her line of reasoning.

"What's the deal, Detective?" Mateo asked, no longer sounding like a two-bit thug and more like a businessman.

"Not as dumb as you look." Carrie shook her head at the young man who reached the conclusion to cut his losses. "You're not exactly Charles Manson. Still, with your priors, you are going to have to make it a great deal, and I'm happy to let you walk on this, provided you promise to stay out of the burglary business. We call a prosecutor in here to draw up the agreement. You cop to the burglary charge and tell us where to find your buddy who ran from us. Answer a few questions right now, and the worse you'll be for the wear is having breakfast in the holding cell and have to check in with a probation officer. I'll even buy you a breakfast burrito from Ernie's Deli if you want. One of those good ones with chorizo."

"Home by lunch, huh?"

"If you're square with me and sing like a canary, then yes."

"What questions?" Mateo tried to relax a little.

Carrie sat down and pulled out a pen and a small pocket notebook. "You are a lot smarter than I took you for. First off, I don't buy you were carrying all that stuff out of there tonight. You look like a strong fella, not Hercules though. Who was coming to pick you up?"

Carrie knew Mateo was a little fish in a much larger pond. If they tracked down who fenced the stolen goods, they netted a bigger fish in this ocean.

4

JUST LEAVE IT TO VICTOR

Standing a few feet from the door, Dirk saw the telltale sign of lights bouncing off the interior walls of his office—something that did not make him particularly happy. After inserting the key and pushing open the door, the noise of a blaring television assaulted him relentlessly. Grabbing the remote and snapping off the television set, Dirk plopped down in the office chair, annoyed that the television was left on in spite of frequent warnings.

The building served as home to Bentley's Motorcycle Repair. With three bays, each with space to work on two motorcycles simultaneously, it served the business's purposes well. A small outbuilding stored motorcycles waiting for servicing or personal projects of the staff. Dirk's office took up the front northern quarter of the building, and behind it was a large locker room for men and a smaller one for women since his niece, Claire, recently became a certified motorcycle mechanic. Carrie also occasionally used the facility when the need arose.

The sign outside unceremoniously read "Dirk Bentley's Motorcycl Repa r." It once read "Dirk Bentley's Motorcycle Repair." However, someone thought shooting out a few of the letters of the neon sign made for a rewarding past time. Dirk considered ordering a new one and simply never bothered. Locally, Dirk's shop remained the last unaffiliated motorcycle repair shop in the area. In the corner of the front window, a relatively new sign indicated this also served as the home of Bentley Detective Services.

Dirk did not have to think long about who left the television on. The perpetrator of that crime repeatedly violated the rule. If possible, Dirk would wring his neck. Unfortunately, few consequences carried any weight for Victor other than repeatedly yelling at him for wasting electricity. As Keith once put it, Victor essentially carried the ultimate form of immunity.

Dirk had bought Victor a new television for the office after his help in the last case saved a girl's life. A small price to pay and Victor certainly earned it. Out of the members of the little detective team, Victor cost him the least. However, Victor's needs were few as the deceased seldom ate, needed a bed to sleep in, or wasted utilities outside of the electricity for the television.

"Victor, where in this great green earth are you?"

A small wisp of smoke puffed from under the door connecting the office to the three motorcycle bays. It snaked up the wood door, looking slightly riverine. Dirk watched the white vapor make its way up the door and past the knob in a continuous stream. With intention, it made a right turn and wandered toward the television set.

Three inches from the remote, still sitting on the small filing cabinet under the television, Dirk waited until it almost closed the gap. "I turned it off already."

The small snake stopped in its tracks, frozen for a moment in indecision. Dirk continued his paternal lecture. "Victor, I know you don't pay the electric bills around here, but I do. And I don't mind you watching the television. Can you please not leave it running?"

Mist poured through the bottom of the door and coalesced into feet, a torso, and midsection. In a few seconds, it manifested into a man dressed in full Confederate military uniform, looking like a statue of Robert E. Lee.

"I am always here and never here!" the specter said.

"Save me your philosophical bull crap. Just turn off the damn television."

"You know, it ain't easy being round here all by myself. While you and that goofy-looking best friend of yours are out hitchin' yer wagons to any dang fool investigation, I have to divide my time between here and the afterlife. You try answering to the almighty sometime! Ain't going to be so judgmental when you have to answer for your sins."

Dirk turned the coffee pot on. "Really, Vic, you are going to equate me wanting you to turn off the television to a mortal sin? Where do you come up with this wonderful comedic banter?"

The ghost came with the property and no one bothered to inform Dirk of the haunting before he bought the place. According to Victor, the last owner wanted nothing to do with a haunting and tried to exorcise the stubborn ghost from the building once or twice. Victor finally left until the building sold and reappeared soon after Dirk opened the business.

Victor once explained his role in a battle, which took place on the hill the motorcycle repair shop now inhabited. Forgotten by time, records were unclear on the battle since it only had one human victim, Captain Victor Rutherford Buckner of the First Virginia Reserves. The battle, locally called the Battle of One Shot, ended abruptly when Victor's rifle went off, killing him while he negotiated the terms of surrender.

Victor elongated a hand and touched the television, which snapped on in response. He hovered over a worn chair in the corner in a sitting motion. "So, I see you got your thinking cap on tonight. What's the situation? Or as kids say these days, what's the sitch?"

"Oh geez, Victor, don't use slang. It is bad enough Claire and that new mechanic she is all doe eyed over talk that way. I swear to God, if I catch that kid laying a hand on—"

Victor interrupted. "You humans love to throw that swearing word around an awful lot more than you should. I can tell you the big guy takes that seriously upstairs. You want to make promises and break 'em, fine by me, but don't swear to the big general on the other side."

Victor acted, on more than one occasion, as Dirk's go between when a little insight from the great beyond provided crucial information. Although Dirk asked several times, Victor only spoke about the afterlife in vague references. The stubborn ghost explained that it was almost unexplainable and he just had to wait his turn to find out, just like everyone else.

Dirk's niece, Claire, was the closest thing he had to a daughter. After his sister's husband, a soldier, fell in a battle with insurgents in Afghanistan, Dirk took over the father figure duties. He loved Claire and would do anything to protect her.

"Don't get your britches all wrapped around your ankles, Dirk. Been keeping an eye on those two, and I can tell you he's about as gentlemanly as they come."

"Thanks, Victor. Continue keeping an eye on them, will ya? Feel free to hit him in the head with a wrench if it looks like he needs it." Claire had known Victor since the days of diapers and preschool and loved the specter the way someone did a beloved uncle.

"Speaking of yer drawers, what in tarnation are you working on anyway? Bit late for you to be hanging out here. Carrie's gonna get worried."

"She's on night shift. We have these printouts from the church. A bunch of nuns had things stolen from them. You can see the names of each one and what was stolen." Dirk figured it wasn't really a breach of the bishop's trust since Victor wasn't technically a living human. "I am trying to figure out the pattern. Right now, I am missing something, but not sure what."

"I reckon you are just toeing the mark a little too long and a little too closely that you just can't see the forest for the trees."

Dirk frowned at the apparition, who now floated upside down and behind him. "I swear, Victor, I'll never understand you."

"I reckon it's like staring at your horse's mane so long you forget she's a horse."

"You had a horse?" Dirk looked at Victor a little surprised.

"I am a proud officer in the Army of Virginia, I brought my horse from home. May Bell, a beautiful nut-brown Morgan sired from my daddy's stock. Great horse, and not the point, you cotton for brains! Step back from the paper and think it through a bit. Go get some sleep and start fresh in the morning."

Dirk pushed himself back from the desk and looked at the papers once again. As he scanned each of the names and items stolen, it made even less sense. "Do ghosts sleep?"

"Are you kidding me? Why would you ask such a dang fool question? No, you don't need to sleep after you're dead." Victor shook his head. "Dirk, take it from someone who has seen a fair share of time pass, go home, and in the morning, this will make a lot more sense."

Victor was right. Time and a little rest might allow the thoughts to coalesce in his mind. "Victor, I can't believe I am about to say this." Dirk took a deep breath and shook his head at the translucent man hovering in front of the desk. "You are right. I'm taking your advice. Time to head home and grab dinner. I'll see you tomorrow."

VICTOR WATCHED Dirk pull out of the drive and off into the distance. Touching the television again, Victor changed the channel to a station that ran a constant stream of old war movies.

Floating over to Dirk's chair, he reclined into a seated

position and watched John Wayne give a lecture to a bunch of soldiers in a tent. The young troops looked convincingly like his own soldiers. Nothing more than just kids at the time, he took it as a Christian duty to do everything he could to ensure their wellbeing.

With the Duke preaching in the background, Victor glanced down at the papers. Dirk left them sitting in a way that all the names lined up perfectly forming a list of all the names and items missing. Continuing to watch the movie, he glanced down every once in a while and scanned the names. Having done it a half dozen times or more, the process began to feel boring. *Well, I'll be, maybe Dirk's right. I reckon this is a dead end after all.*

A loud explosion on television caught his attention. Glancing up, he saw two soldiers lay in a crater, both obviously injured. Each man, an American and a German, suddenly were forced to look into the eyes of their adversary. While the German died, the American tried to comfort his enemy. It made Victor think about humanity and the lack thereof in today's world. His own war experience included striking examples of incredible compassion and depths of depravity. Often from the same people.

How could anyone steal from a nun? He looked at the papers again and something sparked a different memory. A nun who'd visited the office looking for advice. Victor hid while she was there and listened intently to every word she said.

While being dead did nothing to improve your memory, Victor's memory had an almost eidetic capacity. The names were Mary Sophia, Mary Rebecca, and Mary Ruth. Each one of them appeared on the paper, almost one right after another. "Well, I'll be a son of a Yankee." Without another word, Victor vanished.

THE AFTERLIFE, as Victor commonly called it, was a fascinating place. Infinitely wide and infinitely long, it could be anything to anybody. He once tried to describe it to Dirk and Keith and decided the living simply lacked the conceptual basis to understand the indescribable.

Spirits in the afterlife for a while tended to not hop back and forth like Victor did. When he did, it was usually out of an obligation to help Dirk and the others. Moving back and forth took a lot of energy and left him drained, so trips needed to be kept to a minimum. Victor tried to stay in the motorcycle shop as often as possible in case he was needed.

The landing pad for the afterlife was a large field of green grass. Lush and enormous, if you passed on, it allowed for a place for the deceased to meet up with those who preceded them in death. Parents, aunts and uncles, grandparents, or others who knew them in the living world greeted the recently deceased and lessened the shock of being dead. A system in place ensured those arriving before any immediate family members received support. Victor played a role in welcoming people with no one to greet them when called upon to do so.

Victor trudged across the field of green. Time normally did not mean much to people in the afterlife, as the rest of eternity essentially meant time became irrelevant. Since Victor helped those on Earth, he kept one eye on the clock to ensure anything he found out made its way back to Dirk in time. He needed to find out if the names on the list had already passed on, and that meant doing something he hated doing—searching for missing people in a place full of an almost infinite number of people.

The living incorrectly assumed finding someone in the afterlife should be a simple matter. It was, if you were related to the person or knew them in life. Finding three nuns in the afterlife full of nuns presented an impossible task.

5

OH YEAH, DUDETTE!

Carrie took notes while Mateo continued to suffer from diarrhea of the mouth. Not only did he meet the intent of their agreement, he also closed several unreported crimes. A font of knowledge, he told them they all belonged to a new crew in town belonging to a guy simply known as Jimmy.

"Who is Jimmy again? Can you give me a last name?" Carrie asked this question several times over to see if the kid might let more details slip. So far, he swore he did not remember, and after a while, it looked like he was telling the truth.

"I don't know. I've only seen him twice. He is tall and skinny. Got dusty brown hair and brown eyes. Kind of unremarkable for a dude." Mateo was now uncuffed and sipped a bottle of soda he'd asked for.

"Would you say this Jimmy is taller than you?"

"Oh yeah, dude is probably six inches taller than me, at least. Skinny as hell. You know, the chicks go for a guy like that, but if you throw a punch, he'd fold. An entitled coward, not scrappy like me, yo."

Carrie chortled at the ridiculous comment. "Sure, scrappy. This tall piece of beef jerky have a scar or anything?"

"Naw, man, nothing like that. Well, wait. There was this weird tat. I only saw a little of it. Big boss man wore a T-shirt. A nice job too, not a jailhouse job."

"What did it look like?"

"Something like the bottom part of a boot kicking a deflated ball. Lend me the paper and pen a sec."

Carrie handed him the pen and paper, and he sketched out the bottom of a boot and what looked like a smaller triangle. The crude artwork suggested to Carrie something familiar. A knot formed in the pit of her stomach.

"Where the hell have I seen this before?" Carrie squinted at what Mateo scrawled out. "I just feel like that is something I should—" Carrie's eyes grew wide, and she pulled out her cell phone. After a few moments of typing, she turned the screen toward Mateo. "Is this what you saw?" She held the phone up.

"Hellz yeah, dudette. That was the tat."

Carrie put the phone back in her pocket and made a few notations. The quality tattoo Mateo noted on Jimmy's arm represented the lower half of Italy, with Sicily making up the triangle.

"Wow, okay. So, tell me, what did you do for this organization? Did you have titles or anything?" Carrie wrote a brief note for someone to begin researching the tattoo immediately and handed it to a patrol officer standing dutifully by. He took the note wordlessly and then left the room.

"You know, I was like the guy in charge of running around

town and getting stuff. My own crew, and they did what I told them. If they knew what was good for them."

Mateo's sudden burst of bravado convinced Carrie anything after the phrase you know was likely crap. "So, if I interview the other members to check out that portion of the story, they are going to back you up, right?"

"Dawg, why you got to be like that?"

"Mateo, I will throw you into the drunk tank and you can take your chances with the guy going through heroine withdrawal. Right now, he is about to become really agitated and convinced everyone is a girl who wants to fuck, so I advise you to keep your ass cheeks clinched. Or quit fooling around with me." Carrie understood the attempt at bravado and found it endearing. She mused about turning the little worm into a reasonable informant after this. Of course, only if Mateo reformed into a halfway decent human being. The constant need to be the big man made her want to kill him.

"Fine, geez, lady, this is like talking to my mom. I was a foot soldier. Me and the other guys sat around at an abandoned house on Fifth and waited for orders. Our crew was part of something larger, and we just handled the stuff we could turn easily. Never got to see the other parts of the group though."

Carrie suspected he returned to the real story although embellishing a bit. "So, what do you do with the stuff after you steal it?"

"Got a guy, Sully I think they called him, who picks it all up and takes it to a place where they buy it. Sweet deal. Another guy came around once a week with our cut. Once the stuff got loaded, we walked off in different directions so no one knew we were together. Our motto is no fingerprints, no evidence left behind."

Carrie instantly knew who he referred to, any cop in the city knew that name. Sully was a well-known wheelman in the underworld of Charlottetown. Far from a hardened thug, Sully mainly served as a delivery driver for bad guys. With his nasty habit of getting drunk at roadside bars and orchestrating drunken brawls, they stood a good chance at rounding him up easily. She knew he would be down at The Riverside Bar, drinking beer and playing pool. Unofficially, it served as his office, and he stayed there waiting for any jobs to come along. Mateo admitted he only knew the name because they waited at the bar for him to sober up one afternoon to take a bunch of stolen cigarettes to a distributor.

"Who was the guy you were with? You know, the guy who ran out the door?"

"Oh, yeah. Mister Personality himself. All high and mighty, some jerk named Deluca. That guy really chaps my ass." Mateo frowned at Carrie.

She knew what he meant and knew Deluca pretty well already, and she understood the guy's persona easily rubbed people the wrong way. Still, Carrie liked Vance Deluca. For a criminal, he proved easy to work with if you knew the right buttons to push. "What did Vance ever do to you?"

"He's one bossy son of a bitch, telling me how to touch things. You know, be careful with this, and be careful with that. I wanted to hit him with something."

Carrie found the description of Deluca spot on. Vance Deluca was another well-known underworld figure to anyone spending more than three minutes on the police force. An old-school thief from a time when burglary was an art form.

As far as his whereabouts, after a few clicks in her text message window, a police officer responded that he would go pick Vance up right away. Not a violent person, he would come without a fuss.

After getting Mateo a breakfast burrito and the final release paperwork, Carrie left Mateo with instructions to stick around town, stay out of trouble, and, most importantly, avoid Jimmy. After shift change, he would be let loose by the oncoming shift after the paperwork caught up with them.

At her desk, she brought up the database containing all the known criminal enterprises in the area. Contained in its circuitry, the information on the regular street thugs, newly arriving gangs, and older well-established organizations was laid out before her. Mostly, she was curious if any of the organized crime groups in town recently stirred up more than their usual amount of trouble. A few strokes of the keyboard revealed nothing telling. *As a matter of fact, if I didn't know better, I'd say they all went on vacation.*

Ordinarily, a steady number of threats, arrests, and racketeering operations graced the database. The research page showed only the slightest bit of crime going on in the city. Far less than normal, the reports painted an abnormal picture.

Carrie was pulled from her deep thoughts by a paper bag hitting the desk, sending a loud boom through the desk and startling her. She turned in her chair, and Dirk stood next to her.

"Hey, sweetie, I thought you might like breakfast," Dirk said with a smile.

Carrie glanced at her watch. "Shouldn't you be in bed? Kind of early for you." The darkened sky had only begun to lighten up slightly.

"You know me, I'm an early riser. Not really tired."

Carrie stood and wrapped her arms around Dirk. "Well, I'm not really in the eating mood, but you can keep me company."

Dirk released the embrace, pushed the food to the side of the desk, and sat down on the corner of the desk. "Sure, what's shakin'?"

She pointed to the screen. "Well, I'm not sure. We have this puke in lockup right now, and he gave us a ton of information. According to him, he works for a larger gang run by a guy named Jimmy who has a tattoo of Italy on his arm. Sounds vaguely organized, right? The organized crime reporting for the area tells a different story. Absolutely quiet lately."

"Want me to go downstairs and rough him up a little. You know, we can play bad cop, sexy cop?"

"Oh sure, and which are you supposed to be?" Carrie giggled.

"I'll let you choose, but you have the handcuffs, so—" Dirk's solicitous behavior was interrupted by the elevator opening and someone clearing their throat to announce their presence. Dirk wheeled around to see Melonie Dixon. "Good morning, Melonie, I mean good morning, Chief, how are you this morning?"

"Relax, Dirk, I mean Mr. Bentley. I'm doing well." She smiled back at him while glancing into the paper bag. "Why are you bothering my newest detective?" Chief Dixon, Melonie on their off hours, knew Carrie and Dirk quickly approached becoming more than simply boyfriend and girlfriend. Since Dirk's private investigation company stayed on retainer for the police department, any time spent at the station must be declared or someone could reach the conclusion Dirk skulked the hallways looking for cases.

"Just delivering breakfast," Dirk said. To illustrate the point, he raised his hands in a gesture of capitulation.

Chief Melonie Dixon unscrewed the top of her travel coffee mug. "I hate these early days. These stupid reports are due on the mayor's office the end of the week." Walking over to the coffee pot, she poured the pungent liquid into the mug. "So, Dirk, any interesting cases?"

"Well, I am still working on the nun thing but hit a dead end. Really, there are no leads, and I'm just about to give up. Funny thing though, Keith is working another case for me right now. Again, church related. It seems someone is stealing things from the Catholic diocese warehouse. Bit of an odd coincidence, really. I'm not sure I can connect those dots."

Ever since working the case of a serial killer, Dr. Harmon Rigby, Dirk enjoyed a little more respect from the police department. There was a time they ignored private investigators and refused to help if a case came along. Chief Dixon saw Dirk's utility and retained Bentley Detective Services as an outside investigator. Since Dirk did not wear a police uniform, people talked to him when they refused to talk to a uniformed officer.

"Chief, can I tell Dirk about the case I am working?" Carrie said.

"What is your justification?" Carrie understood that pillow talk on any case could not be tolerated by the senior staff of the department. Any cases Dirk even put one brain cell toward needed official permission. Chief Dixon, a law enforcement officer her entire life, understood the connection immediately and still insisted Carrie justify the expenditure in a way her government minders appreciated. Any involvement of Dirk meant the activation of him as a private investigator, bringing an extra layer of scrutiny.

"If the bust today is connected to Dirk's case at the warehouse, then this could lead us somewhere. If not, we are no worse for the wear. No investigating anything until we know we have a connection."

Dirk didn't want to jinx himself. With the weather turning cold, the receipts at the motorcycle repair shop slowed to a trickle. He'd love nothing more than to log a few billable hours with the department. Since Sister Sophia, being a nun, could not be expected to make much in the way of payment and Archbishop Weebley was notoriously stingy with the church's money and would try to guilt Dirk into letting him pay as little of the bill as possible. Billing the police department at a set rate allowed him to recoup any of those losses.

Melonie took a long drag of her coffee. "Okay, you have my permission. Dirk, nothing gets billed until you two turn up solid leads to follow in the case. You are set at a thousand billable for now. And, as of right now, Carrie is on a flexible schedule until you can make headway." The chief maintained a close eye on the department's budget, and that made her especially good at the administrative part of her job. She knew what the budget allowed her to pay Dirk for and how much she needed to keep in reserves for any issues that came up. "On a less serious note, you know I trust the both of you. Be careful please."

Dirk smiled. "Thank you, Chief, and don't worry, we'll be careful."

Carrie briefed Dirk on the case. Although still skeptical, it sounded like the two cases might have a connection. At the very least, the possibility should be examined. Driving to the crime scene, not yet released back to the church, Carrie considered a few lingering questions left to answer. The most pressing being why anyone would go to as much trouble as they did to break in for such a relatively small payoff.

DIRK STOOD at the back of the sanctuary. The center aisle sloped toward the altar, giving the back center a commanding view of everything. Dirk was not necessarily better than the police detective, but his approach displayed an innate instinct to see evidence differently than most people. A police officer looked for clues to point to the perpetrator while Dirk took a different approach. To him, the totality of the evidence was what mattered. Dirk never formed an opinion until he had a chance to take it all in and process it.

In the alleyway, behind the church, Dirk examined the door. While the crime scene techs looked closely at the marks, he stood back and examined everything but. The job screamed of amateur hour, someone watching the clock or who just had better things to do. The person forcing entry into the building maintained more of an interest in speed than style points. Bent pieces of metal in multiple directions suggested a crowbar and several other pointed instruments gained access. Dirk knew Vance by reputation and questioned why a criminal who prided himself in burglary chose to pry a door open this way. Vance Deluca was an artist and certainly not that kind of careless. Sharing those suspicions with Carrie, Dirk suspected Deluca did not actually open the door at all.

The fact that they did not notice the burglar alarm was a lucky break as well. Although the central monitoring office of the security service got the call, the annunciator on the outside of the building stopped working. The wires to the large audible alarm were cut while the ones ensuring the company would get an alarm signal remained intact. An odd thing to have happen. In the recesses of Dirk's mind, too many puzzle pieces fit too well by mere coincidence.

"Carrie?"

"Yes, hon—Dirk." She smiled at her slip of the tongue.

"Look at the stuff they collected to take. What do you notice about them?" Dirk became laser focused on the collection of shiny items on the floor. The patterns and relationships to one another mattered to him more so than the individual items. Inside those relationships was where Dirk's investigative skills reigned supreme.

Carrie flustered at the question. Dirk wore a smug smile when he knew something others missed. "I don't know. Lots of brass and crystal. Items of higher value mostly. We dusted them for prints and didn't find anything interesting. The drop cloth on the floor is nothing special."

"I am afraid, my love, that is where you are wrong. That drop cloth is extraordinary."

"Okay, Hercule Poirot, tell me what I missed." Carry found her boyfriend's methods a little frustrating. Sometimes she really wanted him to simply make his point without his usual flourish.

Dirk turned to the crime scene tech in charge of the scene and asked, "Did anyone step on this cloth since it was laid out here by the criminals?"

"Nope, we cordoned it off and haven't set a foot on it since. We won't do that until inventory time."

"Okay, so"—he nodded back to Carrie—"if I took our bedsheets out of the drier and laid them out on the floor, what would they be?"

Carrie cocked an eyebrow. "Dirty, and I'd have to wash them again. And you'd be dead."

Dirk smiled at her. "They'd be perfectly smooth. Like fresh from a dryer smooth. No wrinkles. This sheet they used is perfect. No one walked on it after they laid the sheet out. Then, they put objects on it, carefully. This was done by someone exacting and careful."

"So, we are looking for a bunch of obsessive-compulsive burglars? Deluca is known to be pretty darn exacting when he works." Carrie still was not following.

"Every burglary scene you've ever been to, save for this one, has what?" Dirk asked, still staring at the linen on the floor.

"Dirk, for the love of God, whose home we are literally in, please get on with it."

Dirk stood and took her by the arm. Pointing to the altar, he made a sweeping gesture. "Knocked over things. Carrie, nothing is knocked over. The pads on the kneelers are all in place, the bibles, hymnals, and all of these other smaller things are perfectly in order. Do you really theorize the criminals crudely pried open the door and then became so careful once inside they wouldn't step on the cloth they used to transport the stuff out of here? That doesn't make any sense at all. No, Detective Pettygrew, Mateo and his buddy did not open that door. Go back and ask him. Someone else pried open that door, a third suspect. You just assumed it was Mateo and Deluca."

Carrie looked at the room. A pile of bibles lay neatly stacked next to the altar. A poinsettia plant sat untouched in between where the cross sat and the cloth they planned to drag the stuff out on. In the dark, no one could have seen them, much less negotiated around the stack easily, unless they knew it was already there.

"Someone cased this job to the point it was rehearsed." Not, as Carrie suspected, a simple case of burglary. There was no way the same people who took such careful precautions to ensure they avoided knocking over anything would pry a door open like that. A professional worked the inside and an amateur opened the door. Again, it begged the question why a professional would be so interested in things fetching a relatively small payday on the black market. "Dirk, don't let this flash of brilliance get out. All the detectives will want you for their cases."

A FEW MINUTES before the end of her shift, Carrie sat across from Mateo. He had finished breakfast in lockup and was about to leave, but she had stopped him. "Mateo, I need to know two more things."

"Then can I go?"

"Yep, then you can go. Who opened the door?"

Mateo sat back on a steel chair and sighed. "You aren't going to believe me."

Carrie leaned forward. "Oh yeah, try me."

"I have no idea who opened the door. It was open when

Deluca and I got there. Funny thing too, Deluca looked pissed when he got to the door."

"Believe it or not, Mateo, I actually do believe you. Second question. Did you guys rehearse the job?"

"Yes, but a different team took the pictures of the inside of the church the day before. Bunch of morons though. They gave us all kinds of unnecessary details, and we just sat there and took it all in. Like this was practice for something bigger. They even gave us lists of things to take and exactly how to take them out of there. It was really bizarre."

Carrie finally left the office. With Sully in custody, Deluca about to be, and Mateo on the way home, Carrie's fourteen-hour shift finally ended. They both drove back to Dirk's house, showered, and fell into bed. Dirk was already sleeping soundly. Carrie knew that afternoon promised more questions. For the moment, they stole away for much-needed rest.

6

I HEAR A RING. CAN YOU ANSWER THAT?

The light of the afternoon pierced through Dirk's window, forcing rays through worn-out blinds and underneath sleeping eyelids. Carefully getting out of bed, Carrie lay a few inches from him. Her hand had been delicately draped over his shoulder in a position that seemed like it would be uncomfortable if she was awake. Although a mountain of work faced her regarding last night's events, Dirk decided to let her sleep.

The last thing he wanted was for her to run around low on sleep. It probably wasn't fair to the criminal world of Charlottetown if Carrie pursued them in her current state. Plagued by lack of sleep, and then overcompensated on caffeine, Carrie became abusive and downright mean.

When she finally got back to the office, every ounce of sleep would help. Making coffee for them, he walked out the door to grab the newspaper from the box at the end of the driveway. Dirk wondered what the neighbors thought of their bathrobe- and boxer-short-clad neighbor wandering around at two in the afternoon. At this point, he didn't care much.

Over the past few months, Carrie spent more and more time at Dirk's place. He did nothing to stop her. Something changed in Dirk, and he found himself at a loss to describe it. After a particularly hard case, Dirk thought of mortality and wondered how long Carrie would wait for him to get his shit together. Waiting too long to be ready to make a formal marriage proposal was not going to work. Carrie was a patient woman. However, Dirk was losing patience with himself.

Carrie had progressively left more things at Dirk's house over the last few months until more of her things hung in his closet than at her own apartment on the other side of town. Although Carrie never asked to move in, she would eventually accomplish the same mission left to her own devices. She knew Dirk would do nothing to stop the process.

Dirk pulled out the newspaper from the box and then the mail which came while he was dreaming about a dancing bear and a small bunny selling life insurance. Dirk's dream life could be the envy of almost anyone, except when working particularly tough cases. Then it became a hellish nightmare of twisted horrors any psychoanalyst would love to delve into.

From the mailbox, he pulled out a series of letters—one card offering birthday greetings, the latest bank statement, and four pieces of junk mail suggesting an investment in new windows, gutters, or a new roof. Lastly, he pulled out a white and gold envelope. He glanced around to make sure Carrie had not woken up from her slumber and spied the curious scene from the living room window.

The envelope gleamed from the pile of mail as if announcing its own extraordinary prominence. The gold lettering and bands across the top suggested richness and class. Gaudy to the extreme, the first letter he received from the company he almost threw out as junk mail. In the upper left corner of the envelope shined the letterhead of Barrow and Carrington, Diamond Importers. For the last three months, Dirk wrote a hefty check, paying off an engagement ring the store held for him. Not wanting Carrie to catch on, he kept the letters and payments hidden like a secret agent with extraordinarily sensitive intelligence.

The moment for the proposal was still not quite right, and at the same time, he wanted to do nothing more. Tearing off the corner of the envelope, he pulled out the letter and read what he had already guessed. The letter confirmed the final payment on the modestly sized diamond, and they planned to send the ring via insured mail and gave the delivery date.

The only other person Dirk worried might figure out his plans was Claire. She carried his ability to sniff out clues others might miss. Twice she tried to broach the subject of the possibility of he and Carrie marrying, and both times, he found less than clever ways to wave her off the topic.

Walking back in the house, Carrie stood at the refrigerator looking at their meager selection. Since they were continually putting off grocery shopping, the pickings in the refrigerator slipped from only a minor to a major shortage of sustenance. "Hey, honey, good morning ... or afternoon. I am not even sure what time it is. When did you wake up?"

She pulled the milk jug out of the door and smelled it. "Yeesh, this should be arrested, it is so bad." Dumping the rest of the milk down the sink, she threw the plastic container into the recycling bin. "I dunno, probably three minutes ago. When the front door slammed, I tried to fall back to sleep, but the game is afoot, Watson! I need to get dressed and go back to the office. And we both need to grab something from The Beanapse on the way in." Carrie gave Dirk a peck on the cheek. "I think you should probably consider talking to the archbishop again. Find out if he has any ideas about the robbery. By now, he likely heard all about it."

"Good point. I can grab Keith, and we can head over there later. Right now, based on the milk comment, we should probably go out for lunch. Or early dinner? What time is it anyway?"

Carrie glanced at her phone. "1415 hours, we put in some good rack time, but we need to get back to this investigation. I forgot how much I like it when we work together."

Dirk glanced at her and thought about how nice spending the rest of the day in bed together might be. She did make a good point. This case needed attention, and the motorcycle repair shop needed attention, albeit a shop without much work to do this time of year. In the meantime, he would call Keith.

As he glanced at the cell phone screen, three little telephone symbols flashed in the corner. All calls had come from the shop's main number. Dirk must have accidentally turned off the ringer again. The fall and winter slowed, and normally, he did not have much to do aside from sending a couple of past due notices or playing cribbage with Victor. Occasionally, someone brought a motorcycle in on a flatbed for work, but that was rare.

He pressed the send button on the phone, and it automatically dialed the last number who called.

"Oh, Uncle Dirk, I've been trying to reach you, and we need—"

"Claire, what did I tell you about answering the phone at the shop with someone's first name like that. What do I always say?"

Dirk visualized his teenage niece rolling her eyes.

She sighed a heavy sigh. "Professional appearance makes a professional organization. Look, my dear antiquated uncle, you are placing a phone call sometime after 1990, and I can see that it is you calling on the caller ID. Now, if you are done with the life lesson, we need you over here. Victor found a clue to something, but that crazy specter is way too excited to tell me what."

Dirk scowled at his niece who likely knew she occasionally frustrated him. Increasingly, Claire became more and more of a teenager. Still, she got her wit directly from him. "Fine, I am on my way." Dirk hung up the phone and kissed Carrie. "Rain check on the lunch, love, I need to get to the shop. Irony of ironies, Victor apparently turned up a clue of some sort."

"A clue?" Carrie said. "How on earth did he turn up a clue to this case?" Her face froze in a scowl.

"Not sure, but I will see you later. I'll drop by the precinct." Dirk paused for a moment and looked at the love of his life. Amazingly beautiful, even fresh out of bed, Carrie never needed a ton of sleep. Dirk wondered how an amazing woman like her loved an average guy like him. Unconsciously, he stared at the ring finger of her left hand.

"What are you staring at? Do I have snot dripping out of my nose or something?"

Dirk leaned in again and kissed her. "No, I'm just amazed that I have someone so beautiful to say I love you to."

Carrie erupted into a wide smile, and her cheeks turned red. "I love you, honey. Now quit being such a damn sap and get to work. Let's catch us a bad guy."

"Or a bad girl." Dirk swatted Carrie playfully on her behind before heading out the door.

A few minutes later, Dirk drove down the street in the direction of the shop. His brain worked overtime trying to figure out how on earth Victor could have put some threads together with so little information on the case. At this point, Dirk didn't even have that much to go on, and he knew way more about it than Victor. He didn't even remember telling Victor about the case in any great detail.

CLAIRE STOOD in front of the open bay door shaking her head at her uncle. She'd come that afternoon to rebuild a transmission a client left in storage and wanted the shop to work on over the fall. Once you looked past the grease under her fingernails and the dirt in her hair, a beautiful woman, the carbon copy of her mother, with sparkling eyes emerged. Happiest with a wrench in her hands, she had the intelligence to attain any goal and only wanted to hang out with her uncle.

"Hey, kiddo, how's Mom?"

"She's fine but says you need to call her about Thanksgiving." Claire avoided their traditional hug since her overalls dripped with a combination of grease and transmission fluid. "Now that you are here, can you please get that insane ghost of yours under control? I got like a quarter way through disassembling the transmission and had to leave. I tried to talk him down, but he's off the hook this time. I would have hit him with something, but you know... the whole ghost thing."

"Fine. I wish they just scheduled Thanksgiving dinner and tell me where to drive and what to pay for. They should be talking to Carrie about Thanksgiving anyway. They ask me my opinion and then dismiss all of my recommendations." Dirk let out a groan and walked into the office.

Victor paced back and forth through the wall separating the office and the shower room. "Finally, there you are! I sent you home for a nap, and you take the whole week off. What in tarnation do you think you are doing? We have a case to solve, and I don't think you're taking this seriously."

Victor generally feigned disinterest about the living world, loving nothing more than to come across as the perfect misanthrope. His reality was far different. The moment Victor understood how the intricate threads came together, he went all in. Bringing just as much energy as anyone living, sometimes Victor's enthusiasm carried the team when the going got tough.

"Victor, did you get into the espresso beans again? Claire is ready to beat you to death with a wrench. Imagine her disappointment at finding out you are already dead."

"Oh, you are so funny. You should consider a Vaudeville act! Why, of all of the stupid comments I've heard, that is about the dumbest, most nonsensical, mudsill of tongue waggin'! Shut pan a spell and eyeball them papers! The answer was right in front of you and you didn't see it."

Dirk plopped into his chair and looked at the papers again.

They looked the same as before. He picked them up and moved them around just as he did last time. Still, nothing really stood out. "I'm not seeing it, I'm sorry."

"Really? How'd you miss it? Right there in front of you, cannonball for brains! Think to yourself, what are the names of those penguins the other penguin, you know, Sophia, was looking fer?"

Dirk found it amusing that the more worked up Victor got, the more Southern the specter sounded. Right now, the spirit was more annoying than endearing. Doing as told, he glanced down at the papers, which did not help. The names swam around like a pool of goldfish after someone dropped a few fish flakes in the bowl. Three of the names suddenly swam to the top of the jumbled mess. Sisters Mary Sophia, Mary Rebecca, and Mary Ruth suddenly aligned in Dirk's head. Sister Sophia lay dying in the hospital of cancer. The other two remained missing and no sign of either nun turned up.

Rearranging the papers on the desk, each nun's loss tidily summed up in one column. In each case, it was a piece of furniture valued at over a thousand dollars. The three were the only nuns on the page having losses of anything over a couple hundred dollars. Granted, possibly a coincidence, but a solid lead anyway. It spelled out a connection between the case Sophia hired him to pursue and the one the church hired them to solve.

"Victor, you crazy-ass ghost, I could kiss you right now if it weren't for you being dead and all. How did you figure it out?"

"I just looked at the papers, you danged fool. If you'd only done the same, you would have seen it too." Victor put his hands on his hips, physically reprimanding Dirk.

"Okay, I need you to get back over and—"

"Already done it. No luck, Dirk. I tried to find them nuns, and no one's seen hide ner hair. Ain't that easy to find one specific penguin, lots of them around. I scoured the place, and a few people reckoned they remember two nuns recently, it could have been anyone."

The news didn't wipe the smirk off Dirk's face though. A lead in a case developed where leads were of the sparse variety, and he itched to follow it. "Okay, try again, and see if you can come up with anything. I need to grab Keith and go over to talk with Sister Sophia before you end up having an easier time talking to her. She's not long for this world."

Victor turned around and headed toward the wall, "Just what we need up there, another of them penguins." He vanished into the wall with a puff, and Dirk realized poring over those sheets for days would not have produced a satisfactory conclusion. Victor had been right all along. Dirk became too close to the case to see the patterns. He took the investigation too personally, eschewing objectivity. Even an old ghost like Victor still taught new tricks if you let him.

Dirk dialed Keith's number. "Hey, Keith, what are you doing right now? What's that? No, I know the sermons don't write themselves, but I need you to come with me to see an old friend at the hospital."

THIRTY MINUTES LATER, Dirk pulled into the hospital parking

lot. Stepping out of the car, he silently questioned the wisdom of trying to talk with the nun again. She likely would not have too much to add to the investigation. Parked one section up, next to a huge planter, Keith stood sipping a bottle of water.

"So, I see we've gone from down-in-the-dumps Dirk to our regularly scheduled Super Dirk with the kung fu grip." Keith smiled at his friend. "I don't want to say I told you so about dragging you out on this case, but I almost feel compelled to."

"You know, arrogance doesn't suit you. Shut up, and take a look at these." Dirk put the papers on the hood of Keith's truck and lined up the names of the three nuns.

"Okay," Keith said. "Could just be a big league coincidence. How did you see this anyway?"

Dirk put the papers back into one pile and tucked them in a jacket pocket. "Still too good not to check out. I didn't see it at all. Believe it or not, this little gem is brought to you by ole spooky-butt himself."

"That ghost is going to be impossible to live with now," Keith said. Keith and Victor loved nothing more than to pick at each other until one or the other screamed at the other incoherently. Dirk watched the exchange go on so many times he suspected the afterlife would be a whole heck of a lot louder with Keith and Victor having nothing to do but sit around and argue well into eternity.

A few minutes later, they stood outside the hospital room of Sister Mary Sophia. Along the wall, cards and Mylar balloons for well wishes read "Get Well Soon" and "Be Healthy." One glance made it clear this hospital room represented her last stop in the physical plane. Dirk let out an unconscious gasp at the sight of the skeleton before him. An

IV hung from a pole, dripping fluid into the frail and gaunt old woman's veins. A heart monitor beeped out a rhythmic tone. Her eyes sunk into her skull, and her skin, pale and yellow, stretched across her face, leaving her a pained expression even while sleeping.

"Maybe we should come back?" Keith said.

"I'm not sure that is such a good idea. Victor says that when they cross over nuns tend to be scooped up pretty fast and they become really hard to find. I guess a lifetime of service gives you the right to privacy in the afterlife." Dirk advanced into the room and leaned against the metal frame of the bed.

Sister Sophia's face looked like a woman whose days on earth measured in hours. A nasal cannula pumped oxygen into her nose to improve the efficiency of her breathing. A morphine machine came to life and pushed liquid relief through the tubes into her IV.

Dirk was about to say something when a cold yellow hand grabbed his hand on the rail from beneath a thin sheet. "Dirk, it is ... nice to see you. Even with the Methodist in tow." Sister Sophia's voice came in labored breaths. Every syllable required immense effort for her now.

"Hello, Sister Sophia. You are looking well."

She smiled weakly. "Dirk, it is a sin to lie to a nun. However, I appreciate the attempt. I believe you might say I look like shit."

Dirk laughed. At their first encounter, Sister Sophia proved a whirlwind of a woman. Dominating any room, the wizened nun projected the image of a force not to be trifled with. The memory stood in sharp contrast to the present encounter where the emaciated corpse before him looked like a stiff wind could blow her away. "Sophia, I have to ask you a question, if you're feeling up to it?" Dirk said.

She nodded her consent. Dirk cursed himself for not bringing a police officer with him. A deathbed statement from a private investigator might not stand courtroom scrutiny as well as one from a police officer.

Keith sidled up to Dirk and asked, "Did your friends ever mention to you about anything being stolen out of the warehouse?"

"Pastor Keith ... good to ... see you." She took a few labored breaths in and continued. "I don't think ... wait... I think I remember that they said—" Her hand moved off Dirk's and fell to the bed. Sister Sophia slipped into unconsciousness.

"Do you think we can wake her again?" Dirk turned to Keith.

"You most certainly cannot," a voice commanded from behind them. Keith and Dirk turned around to see an older Indian male glaring at them. He wore the traditional dastaar headgear of a Sikh but spoke with a heavy English accent. Over a breast pocket, the name Dr. Ernesh Singh stitched into the fabric with dark blue thread added to the doctor's gravitas.

"Doctor Singh, I am sorry, we didn't mean to suggest we'd actually do something like that. Please accept my apologies." Keith grabbed Dirk by the arm and pulled him back from the bed.

"This is a hospice ward, gentlemen, not a place to harass the sick. We try to give our patients here as much peace as possible. The sister has certainly earned that consideration."

Dirk spoke up, "Again, we are terribly sorry. My name is Dirk Bentley, and this is my associate, Keith. We are investigating the disappearance of her friends. Again, we meant no harm. We will be on our way." Dirk took two steps into the hallway.

A thought crossed his mind as the door to Sister Sophia's room closed behind them. Something troubled him about the situation. A detail sat just out of reach of his mind. Then, like a flash, it pushed its way to the front of his cluttered mind. Hospitals kept perfect records. Turning back toward Dr. Singh, Dirk asked, "Doctor Singh, can you tell me if the Catholic diocese sends all the clergy here requiring medical assistance?"

Dr. Singh scratched at his thick beard for a moment. "I am pretty sure they do, why?"

"If I gave you names, can you tell me if they are or were ever patients here in the last year?" Dirk asked, unconsciously thumbing the papers in his pocket.

"What are you two getting at?" Dr. Singh now squinted at Dirk and Keith, communicating a developing mistrust.

Dirk pulled a business card out and handed it to Dr. Singh. "As I said, we are investigating a matter Sister Sophia hired us to look into. Unfortunately, she didn't give us a lot of details, and we hoped she could fill in a few blanks. She's obviously exhausted. Perhaps you may know some of the information we are looking for."

Dr. Singh put the business card into the breast pocket below the embroidered name. "What would you like to know?"

"Doctor, did the hospital treat any of these patients. Sister Mary—"

Dr. Singh suddenly put up his hand, stopping Dirk mid-sentence. "I'm sorry, without a search warrant, I can't really tell you anything about the patients here at the hospital. If you come back with one, then I will be happy to comply with that warrant. It is hospital policy."

Keith glanced at the sleeping corpse of Sister Sophia. "Doctor, can you at least check the names to see if getting a search warrant is even necessary? We can get one, but it is a waste of time if it is just going to yield no fruitful answer." The worry spread across Keith's brow echoed Dirk's feelings. They were running out of time.

Dr. Singh frowned at them. "Give me the names and wait right here."

Keith and Dirk stood in the hallway. A nurse, on shift and not having much to do, flirted with Keith for a while. Dirk watched his friend, forever on the lookout for the perfect match. So far, neither he nor Carrie had found him a suitable companion.

Their dastaar-wearing Sikh suddenly appeared around the corner of the hallway. He shook his head and handed the piece of paper back to them. "I'm sorry, gentlemen; there are no records of these women having ever visited this hospital at all. I don't think I am breaking any ethical guidelines or laws by telling you there are no persons in our database with those names. I'm sorry."

Dirk thought over the possibility of elderly nuns in such perfect health they did not need occasional trips to the hospital. A thought he found implausible. "Doctor, is there a possibility the computer systems from one part of the hospital won't talk to another? So, for example, are you only seeing the hospice ward patients?"

Dr. Singh chuffed at the idea. "Gentlemen, I have a lot of patients to care for, and I really must return to my duties.

However, if it will put your minds at rest, I will tell you that the records system covers the entire organization. If they spent any time in the hospital, or even one of our clinics, they would have shown up."

"Thank you," Keith said, grabbing Dirk by the arm. The two crossed the hospice wing, and Dirk pressed the button for the elevator. "Dirk, what do you think the odds are that those nuns never had a reason to go to the hospital? I mean, it seems—"

"Extraordinarily unlikely. Especially if the archbishop is telling the truth. Tell me this. Do you still think any of this is a coincidence?"

"I'll do one better," Keith said. "I think someone is lying. The only question is whom?"

7

FORMALITY IS UNDERRATED

Carrie tried not to stare, but it was hard not to. Officer Collins reminded her of a teenager wearing white face paint to pass as a ghost for Halloween, complete with dark eye makeup. Gaunt as a kid who lived in an impoverished third world country, he spoke about as much as a rock. Still, she couldn't help shake the image of the young patrolman round-house kicking Mateo to the ground and cuffing him with admirable quickness.

Driving in silence unnerved Carrie. "So, Patrolman, I've meant to ask you. Where did you learn to fight like that?"

Without turning toward her, he said, "I am not sure what you mean."

"You know," Carrie said, "that kick thing you did back at the church."

"As I said, kung fu."

Carrie remembered Collins said that. She found it hard to

deal with the youth because, in sharp contrast to peers, the young patrolman was quiet and never offered additional information. While waiting for the shift briefing to begin, she watched Patrolman Collins reading a book on Tai Chi or police procedure while the rest of the patrolman class sat around joking or telling war stories from their short time on the police force.

"So, you studied kung fu then, I presume."

"Correct," the statuesque police officer said.

"Not much of a chatterbox, are you?" Carrie liked conversation to break up the monotony of a call and was not ready to give up on getting him to talk.

Out of the corner of her eye, she made out the slightest of smiles on the young officer's face.

"Detective, I am, by training, very quiet. My master taught me to listen to all that is around me. Sight is but one sense. The fluctuations in sound and smell around me add to what I know. Talking is an outward action. Listening and appreciating the world around you is inward. It requires time and training to perfect."

That was the most words the boy had spoken in her presence to date. "So, you studied this then?"

"Indeed," Collins said.

Carrie waited a few moments for him to elaborate, but he didn't. Most of the martial artists and body builders she knew talked your ear off given the opportunity. "Have you studied long?"

An almost imperceptible sigh left his lips. She was obviously annoying him, but being far more senior, he would likely never tell her to shut up. "I have studied since the age of four. I spent the year prior to the police academy in Kathmandu, studying with legendary kung fu Grand Master Batbayar."

Carrie chuckled at such an official sounding reply. "Okay, Collins, I'll stop making you talk. Let me just tell you that you are pretty darn impressive."

With a smile, Officer Collins wrapped one hand around his fist and bowed. "Thank you, Detective."

Carrie wondered silently if he thanked her for discontinuing the conversation or the compliment. At that point, it did not really matter since they reached their destination.

Coming back from the church and clearing it as a crime scene, they left to speak with Sully, the wheelman. A contingent of officers found him, almost completely passed out, at a biker bar. Normally the police expected resistance from the band of notorious bikers but got none. One of the bikers suggested the police should consider keeping him. Sully proved more trouble than he was worth for the outlaw biker gang.

Entering the interrogation room, Carrie sat down while Collins took up a stoic position behind her. The perpetrator maintained a disinterested look about him. A small smear of blood discolored his mustache beneath a large Neanderthal nose and unkempt mane of dirty brown hair, suggesting he resisted arrest. "Sully, is it? Do you know why you are here?

"Nope, and I don't really care. All I know is that I was having a nice drink with a few of my friends and a bunch of cops came in and violated my constitutional rights."

Carrie expected abrasive individuals, so Sully's performance proved less than entertaining. "I need to talk to you about the events of last night. Maybe we can help each other?"

"Detective, if there is anything I know for sure, it is this.

The police are never in it to help me. I am exercising my constitutional right to have an attorney present at any and all interrogations, and I want one immediately. I need one appointed by the court, and you can't ask me anything until he or she gets here."

"Look, this will go a lot easier if you just—"

Sully held up a hand, and Carrie knew this signaled the end of the interrogation. He didn't have to say anything until an attorney represented his interests.

"Fine, I'll see what dirtbag public defender I can find hanging around. Sit tight."

After they stepped into the hallway, Collins asked, "Shouldn't we take Mr. Sully back to lockup?"

"First off, there is no mister. Sully is a piece of shit with legs, plain and simple. The best thing to do is let that bag of garbage ripen for a while, shackled to that table. We'll come back in an hour or so. He might be ready to tell us just about anything. Sometimes, we make them sweat.

"He did request an attorney."

Carrie nodded. "Indeed, he did, and we'll get him one. It just happens I don't have time to kick over rocks in search of a deadbeat ambulance chaser right now. Besides, there is no way the clerk is going to scare one up at this hour. All the public defenders are downtown in the bar right now, playing grab-ass with their buddies.

Collins nodded. Carrie thought she detected a slight twinge of disapproval. "Ah, I see."

"You have a lot to learn. Sometimes, if you let them stew in an interrogation room a while, they will get antsy and make a mistake. In the meantime, let's go see how our other friend is faring. For him, we take a different tactic. I warn you though,

Vance Deluca is so slippery he'll do and say anything to get out of any situation. But, I think I have something that will make him talk." Carrie patted a blue folder she carried in her hand.

Opening the door to interrogation room two, Carrie saw a man sitting there, hands folded in the center of the table with eyes closed. If Sully stood as the quintessential example of a thug at the end of his career, Vance sat in sharp opposition. With panache and swagger to spare, the man seethed cordiality. A little too cordial for the Charlottetown Police Department interrogation room.

As the door closed behind them, he opened his eyes and smiled. "Well, Detective Pettygrew, I'm delighted to see you got promoted. Congratulations, very well deserved. You are one of my favorites."

Vance Deluca recently celebrated a fifty-third birthday, and his graying hair and grandfatherly countenance belayed any thought he might be a master criminal. Coupled with a convincing British accent perfected while serving three years in a London prison, he disarmed you with a smile one moment and stole your wallet the next. Records suggested a life of crime well established before the age of ten, and he had perfected the criminal craft ever since.

"Thank you, Vance. How are you faring these days?"

He held up handcuffed hands shackled to the table. "Well, positively never better." Deluca looked up at Collins. "I see you are finally hiring vampires for the night shift."

"Vance Deluca, meet Officer Collins. He is working with me on this case."

"I am charmed and honored to make your acquaintance," Deluca said.

Collins did not move a muscle, seemingly staring at a corner of the small interrogation room.

"Might I inquire what our city's finest think I did?"

Carrie folded her hands on the top of the folder, lying flat on the stainless-steel table. "Vance, why don't you tell me what you were doing with Mateo the other night in the church?"

Vance pursed his lips and said the name Mateo several times. "Never heard of anyone with that name. Who is this Mateo fellow?"

Carrie answered, "This scumbag we caught running out of the church while you ran from my sergeant. I have to say, I am a little shocked to find you consorting with someone so unprofessional. Mateo is nothing more than a kid with a dismal track record. By the way, you outran the sergeant, not a small feat. I have to ask, cardio or do you do a lot of weights too?"

Vance shook his head. "My dear Carrie. You know I've turned a new leaf. I fly the straight and narrow these days. No one will find me anything less than honorable. Besides"—Vance paused—"you have no proof."

Carrie understood Vance wanted her to lay the cards on the table. Either she had evidence to confront or not. Vance, like Sully, knew the rules. Vance enjoyed the game too much and knew he would likely spend no real time in jail for the fairly minor charge. He essentially lost very little if convicted. Carrie knew better than to take the bait. She anticipated this move.

"You know, Vance, I think you're right. Perhaps I have nothing but the word of a dirtbag in lockup. Let's just say, for argument's sake, that I let it slip to the media that you broke into the church that night."

Vance frowned. "Carrie, you and I both know that would look bad at the acquittal. Plus, what are you hoping to gain by doing something so reckless? I mean, we must think of your new career."

Carrie flipped open the file folder and extracted three photos. The first photo showed the door where the criminals made an entry. The other two photos showed the items being stolen. "I have a little political capital to burn and too much time on my hands right now. Besides, it's not what I have to lose, Vance, it is what you do. It will only be a small reprimand. There is no reprimand in the world of organized crime." Carrie sat back in the chair and smiled. "What do you think? I am thinking we go with the picture of the door all pried open. The caption could read 'Vance Deluca arrested for burglary of the Catholic church.' Has a nice ring to it, but I'm no reporter."

Vance shuffled in his chair, a morose smile plastered across his face.

Carrie continued, "Do you honestly think anyone is going to hire you after we paint the picture you've turned into nothing more than a half-ass cat burglar?" She sat there for a count of five and then quickly picked up the photos and turned toward the door. "Very well, Vance. I am even going to let you go. But you'd better move out of town. No one likes a contract criminal who does such poor-quality work."

Carrie reached the door handle when Vance suddenly cried out, "Wait ... wait." Letting out a low growl, he hung his head. "Let's just say, for argument's sake, I was there that night. If I walk on the burglary charge, perhaps I can give you something much more interesting to sink those brand-new pointy detective teeth into." He sounded more like a New Yorker than a Londoner.

"You know that won't fly, Vance, you've been doing this long enough to know the prosecutor isn't just going to let you go. Not someone like you anyway."

"Fine, parole and you keep my name out of the papers. Keeping me out of this is not negotiable. Or we take this to trial, and you can deal with my plea of not guilty and spending all that precious time in court."

Carrie sat back down. "We can work with that, if the fish is good enough." She opened the folder and set out the three pictures on the table again. Vance recoiled at the image of the door smashed in with the metal of the frame peeled back. "Those morons. They have no respect, no art, nothing but brute force. I tell you, Carrie, I would never work with anyone like that had I known what they were going to do. That just isn't right."

Carrie knew a man of Vance's talents easily picked locks like the one on the church, stole what he wanted, and even locked the door before wiping down the door handle. Dirk's comment about a third person being involved screamed loud and clear. Thinking back to Dirk's comments about the cloth on the floor made more sense. A level of care only a seasoned criminal might take if time was not an issue. Or, possibly if they were waiting for something specific to happen.

"So, we are safe in assuming you were there that night. Again, I go back to my previous question, and this is partly professional curiosity. How is it that you came by working with someone like Mateo?"

"Yes, well. That is a sordid affair," Vance said. "You see, it was never my idea to work with that idiot Mateo and that drunk, Sully. Years ago, I did work with Sully, and he used to be the best. He's lost it though. I think one too many brain cells suffered death to his alcoholic hobbies. Anyway, I digress. The boss is a guy named Jimmy. I don't know anything about him, other than I suspect he has mafia links."

"Why's that?"

Vance pointed to his arm. "Tattoo of Italy. All these new Mafioso types are doing it. Stupid really, the nearest any of them ever traveled to Sicily is Virginia Beach."

Carrie remembered Mateo mentioning someone called Jimmy. "I suppose that could be right. Mateo said that was his new crew. It's totally out of character for you to join a gang, Vance. I always thought of you as a loner."

"I never joined, I was contracted to help out. Essentially teach, if you will. This Jimmy character wanted to breed a new type of burglar. In and out, nice and clean. But after the first heist, he told me I would just be working in the field with the new kids. It was stupid."

Collins spoke up. "I take it that didn't go well."

"He speaks." Vance smiled at Carrie. "He is right, though. Teach them to read books and all they do is chew the pages. Swine, nothing but swine. These thugs are children. No appreciation for art. Jimmy is trying to build something on the backs of spoiled little millennial brats." Vance glanced up at Collins. "No offense intended, Officer. Some of your generation need a good swift kick in the pants."

"No offense taken," Collins replied.

"Okay, why, in your opinion, are they targeting churches?" Carrie asked.

"I honestly don't know. I was forced to go along to help

teach that idiot Mateo. I do know that they consider the churches to be low threat targets for now. This was considered low-hanging fruit for them, and they wanted to grab as much cash as possible. Something far larger is cooking, but they won't let me in on it. I did overhear something interesting though."

Carrie pulled a set of keys out of her pocket and unlocked Vance's handcuffs. "Do tell."

"Thank you." Vance shifted to a more comfortable position in the chair and rubbed his wrists. "One night, I overheard this Jimmy fellow having a heated argument with someone addressed as uncle on the phone. Not sure to whom he was talking with, but it sounded like the uncle person tried to talk him out of the burglaries. Something about how the whole thing brings too much attention."

"How odd. How did you hear the uncle side of the conversation? "

"Oh, I didn't. Jimmy is incapable of an original thought. He literally repeats everything said on the phone. I did catch one thing though. Something about putting bullets into a couple of people."

Carrie scribbled a few notes feverishly on a yellow pad. "Why did he say those things? Any ideas?"

"Unfortunately, no. I do pay attention, but mindreading is not one of my talents. As you put it, I have a professional curiosity. I did see the name of a guy Jimmy wrote down while on the phone. More importantly, I know the name. A fence named of Carl Butler."

Carrie stood from the table. "A name we know well. Promise me that if you think of anything else you will let me know. I'll give the prosecutor a call. In the meantime, I need you to write down all the names, positions, and where I can find these fine fellows."

"I know where Carl is hiding these days. I will not only tell you where to find him, I'd be willing to arrange a meeting. Outside of Jimmy, I didn't know a ton of names. Mateo is just a stupid kid, and Sully is not only past his prime, I'm shocked that liver hasn't sued him for divorce. It would do some good to have him locked up for a while. Dry him out a bit."

Carrie nodded in agreement. "All right. Can I get you a coffee or anything while I make a few phone calls? You're probably going to spend the rest of tonight in lockup until we get a hearing in the morning. Pretty quiet down there right now, so you can get a good nap in."

"A coffee would be lovely. And, I meant what I said earlier. Congratulations on the promotion. I like to see good people ascend the ranks. Even if they are on the opposing team. I like a good challenge."

Carrie and Collins left the room. The young officer's forehead was up in confusion and his mouth hung open waiting to ask a question and fearing sounding clueless. "What is it, Collins? You have a question. Don't be afraid to ask."

"You just gave him a great deal. How do you know he isn't lying?"

"Like I said, you have a lot to learn." She detected the faintest hint of dejection in his downcast eyes. "Don't worry, you will. Vance is a unique criminal. If there is anything he values more than that fake accent, it's his reputation. To achieve success as a high dollar burglar, people have to believe he can deliver on promises. When I threatened to push a story to the press with those photos, I crossed a proverbial red line. He was right; most likely he'd walk, or at worst, he'd probably spend a week to a few months in jail for the botched burglary. Vance can do thirty to ninety days in the slammer on his head and probably make good use of the time to connect with more future clientele. I took a gamble he'd be far more interested in protecting his reputation over Mateo and Sully. Remember, this is not about locking up a burglar on a minor botched burglary charge. We want to find out what is really going on. Don't ever reach for a crumb on the floor when you know the entire turkey dinner is just waiting for you to reach up for it. The trick is always in knowing when to reach up.

"As far as the lying thing goes, Vance will tell the truth after we set the conditions. Before that point, he would have lied through his teeth. We reached an agreement, and he will honor that agreement. Unlike that shithead Sully, I can trust Vance to deliver after we have reached the agreement but never before."

Collins held up a finger, remembering something. "I got the impression he wanted to see the crime syndicate brought down."

"Now you're getting it, Collins. I noticed that too. Vance is a professional cat burglar who specializes in the finer things in life. He not only hates competition, he hates amateurs even more. I threatened to tarnish his reputation, and that's a step too far. Everyone has his or her price. Some people worry about money, and others worry about their precious reputation." Carrie smiled and pulled out her cell phone to call the prosecutor's office and explain the situation.

After the phone call, Carrie sat at her desk nursing a cup of coffee and examining an odd pen sitting on her desk. She tried straightening up the piles of files and notes lying there, but her thoughts continually ran back to something Collins said. He correctly pointed out how terrible the deal was for Vance. Taking the gamble with the judge might have benefited him more in the end.

A career criminal of Vance's experience only took a deal like that if something more tantalizing lay ahead for him. Something more basic than that. Perhaps he really wanted to hurt the organization. However, biting the hand that fed you only made sense if there was a larger meal out there.

Looking through Vance's confession, she noticed he mentioned the name Carl Butler as being his point of contact in the gang. A location he gave, at least the last known, was a bar over on Asbury Lane. His file in the police database suggested he was a well-known fence. Although not normally violent, he certainly had the skills, if cornered, to protect himself, so they would have to treat the situation carefully. Several units prepped to go over as backups. Carrie and Collins made a game plan to convince Carl to leave the bar peacefully.

Carrie kept a few outfits at the station in case she needed to change into a less conspicuous outfit than her normal blazer and long pants, an outfit sure to scream cop. After a few moments in the locker room, she came out wearing a black dress with a short blazer covering her shoulders. It also hid the specially designed holster, carrying her undercover weapon of choice, behind her back. Lipstick and eye shadow made her ready for a night on the town or an undercover operation at a seedy bar. The moments clicked by on the wall clock as she finished her coffee.

She wrestled with the suspicion Vance pulled something over on her.

Or maybe was pulling something over on someone else?

8

THE SCENT OF STALE BEER AND MISTRUST

The bar was located off the main road and down a poorly lit alley with only a few lights, and half of those were broken. In sharp contrast to other alleys, this did not have the normal collection of bums lying on the remains of cardboard boxes, looking for handouts from anyone dumb enough to pass this way. Perhaps the bar's bouncers kept the streets free of anyone who dissuaded patrons from entering the bar.

Carrie and Collins walked down the narrow alley past a few bags of garbage and ramen someone had vomited onto the street after a night of drinking. The pungent odor of cheap noodles mixed with bottom shelf liquor permeated the alleyway. They took solace in the fact that no less than a couple dozen cops currently watched the lonely alleyway. Maybe they would be lucky, and this operation would go down without a fight. It was doubtful since places like this were generally less than content to just let a cop walk off with one of their star citizens. Carrie said a silent prayer that divine providence allowed it all to stay low-key.

The door to The Smiling Orchid bar stood out as an imposing, solid metal slab, suggesting the place was not completely on the level. Either that or the decorator had odd tastes.

An ominous *bong, bong* noise reverberated throughout the alley as Collins knocked. A small window at the top opened, and a pair of eyes peered out at them. Before Carrie said anything, the owner of the eyes barked a question in a language she had never heard before.

Carrie stared back at the man with her mouth agape. Collins, sensing the awkward tension, calmly said something back to the man in whatever language he spoke, and the small trap door shut. A few deadbolts snapped back from their positions, and the door swung open.

Carrie glanced a wary eye toward Collins who appeared stoically unconcerned about this new development. She faced the possibility of having to either call the whole thing off, call in all the police, or let the situation play out. Melonie strongly encouraged any officer to follow their gut feeling, and right now, her gut told her to let the situation play out a little more before making any decisions about what to do. At the very least, she had a panic button in her purse if things went south. It would send the entire police force smashing through the big metal door.

They entered the room filled with the stench of stale air, sweat, and at least ten years of cigarette smoke, and her shoes instantly stuck to the grimy floors. To their right, a bar hunkered down under a waterfall of neon lights. Every bottle on the shelf behind the bar radiated back a dingy electric glow, as did the patrons, some of whom looked native to the bar or perhaps even native to the building itself. A quarter of the usable space featured illegal gambling of all kinds, and at the bar sat a half dozen prostitutes waiting for customers.

After a few inquiries, someone pointed to a young man sitting in the corner. It was not Carl Butler but certainly one of his men. A greasy-looking kid, probably no older than twenty, stood firmly with one foot in a pitcher of beer and the other in a shot of whiskey. Carrie wondered if he possessed the ability of speech or not.

"People tell me you are the guy I need to talk to if I want to get in touch with Carl," Carrie said.

"Sure, but you have to blow me first."

"Excuse me?" Carrie said.

"You heard me, suck my dick, you little whore."

Carrie snapped her fingers, hoping Collins got her meaning. To his credit, there was not a moment of hesitation. The little greaseball fell to the floor with a crash before he so much as raised a hand to protect himself. The table went sliding out of the way, and the patrons looked on with interest at the sudden commotion disrupting their slow march toward cirrhosis. Carrie knew they needed street cred to make this all work, and Collins delivered it.

"You will learn to speak properly to the lady," Collins said through clenched teeth.

Something in the way he said it made Carrie think he genuinely detested the little man and would be more than pleased if he chose to put up a fight.

A door opened in the wall next to where the altercation

occurred, and a man appeared in the doorway. "Please, don't kill Richard. An impudent swine, for certain, also my nephew. I would have a hard time explaining his untimely death to my sister. Although I doubt anyone would seriously blame you." The man motioned to the patrons who now took an intense interest. "A round on me." The room erupted into laughter and applause. Returning to his nephew, he added, "You shouldn't treat women that way, Richard. Especially when they come with hired muscle who appear capable of ripping your throat out."

The way he finished the sentence and lingered on the word *throat* gave Carrie the impression he either witnessed it before or generally accepted Collins could accomplish the task. Which she didn't doubt either.

"Please, come in." The man motioned inside. Closing the door behind them, he said, "I am genuinely sorry about my nephew. Not a bright bulb, so I gave him a job. Too violent to be of much use. I keep him drunk so the boy is of little harm to anyone but himself."

The telltale sign of the door latching in place suggested the only way out was for someone to hit a button hidden somewhere in the room. The metal on metal confirmation of Carl's security precautions meant the only way out of the room was with permission. In the corner, two goons stood by carrying MP5 submachine guns. Even if they made it through them, and got the door open, the booze-fueled mob would be inclined to help the man who likely served as the founder of the alcoholic feast. If they wanted out of this bar in one piece, they walked out with either Butler's approval or in a hail of bullets.

Carrie changed tactics on the fly. Asking him to come into the office for questioning likely posed significant lethal side effects. Quickly running through a few options in her mind, she concocted a story and an offer no fence would ever refuse. Carl Butler sold stolen goods, which meant he would never walk away from a good deal.

Carl motioned to two chairs in front of a large desk. He sat down in a large leather office chair and reclined slightly. "So, what brings you to my fine establishment?"

"It is nice to meet you, Mr. Butler. I need something done, and I need it done quickly and discreetly."

He waved his hand at her. "Whoa, where are the manners in today's America? Do you have a name?"

"My name is immaterial. What is material is what I have to move." Carrie did not want to overplay her hand, and providing a verifiable name ran the risk of him finding out it was fake.

In stark contrast to the exterior room, this room stood well furnished with deeply oiled wood and luxurious furniture. The air filtered through a large air cleaner having the unenviable task of cleaning whatever air came in from the bar. Behind the desk, a door led into a smaller room with a metal screen door. Farther on, a large bank-vault-style safe sat closed. In the corner, to their left, a small sitting area fronted a wall-mounted television sporting a layer of dust, the two apish goons, leather chairs, a coffee table, and a stuffed brown bear.

"I'm sorry." Carl stood behind the desk. "I don't work with anyone named immaterial. I'm funny that way. I like to work with people I know and trust."

Carrie's mind flashed back to an improv class she'd taken in college. "Okay then, I will find another buyer for my truckload of whiskey."

"What did you just say?" Carl stood up.

Carrie remembered reading about the amount of forged whiskey pouring into the U.S. with alarming regularity. She also knew that any fencer could move that shipment given the relatively low cost and high markup on the bottles.

"I believe the lady said—" Collins spoke up.

With lightning quickness, Carrie slapped Collins across the face. "I thought I told you to keep silent unless spoken to." She turned back to Carl. "I am sorry to have wasted your time. I will take my business elsewhere."

Carl held up a hand, begging them to wait. "I am a reasonable man and certainly understand the need for privacy. Please have a seat." Carrie sat and Collins dutifully stood behind her, trying to appear as subservient as possible while keeping an eye on the goons in the corner. "I believe you said something about forged whiskey. How can you be sure I'm not a cop?"

"A man with your reputation needs no further checking. You have your ways, and I have mine. For that matter, you don't know that I'm not a cop. So, we are both going through a bit of an exercise in trust."

"I'd like to see the merchandise before admitting I can move it." Carl said. In one hand, he held a small stone with the words "peace" and "love" engraved on it. It seemed ironic that a man, guilty of so much, flipped a novelty undoubtedly given to him by one of his children gingerly in his fingers.

Carrie called upon her dexterous brain to stay one step ahead of the man. "Very well, when and where?" Glancing up at the clock on the wall, she realized quite a bit of time had passed since the last check-in, and the entire police force outside likely discussed charging the door with battering rams and guns blazing.

Carl sat back in the chair and made a sweeping gesture across the room. "We seem pretty comfortable here. Why not bring a few samples to me day after tomorrow?"

Carrie seeing her opportunity frowned at him. "Come, come, Carl, as much as I love your office, I don't trust you, just as much as you really don't trust me. Somewhere neutral, maybe Jaytown Park. Let's say the day after tomorrow at three? Lots of people, lots of witnesses. I will bring you a bottle in a small bag and my terms. You and I can discuss things on the phone afterward. As nice as your office is, all of this dark wood screams male dominance. Besides, I prefer neutral territory."

Jaytown Park remained the lone harbinger of the old town square after chopping it up when downtown real estate became too lucrative to ignore. A commercial enterprise converted the remaining property to ensure economic viability by arranging a small children's carnival, pony rides, and an ice cream vendor. The rest of the park remained carpeted in grass where young couples with babies ate picnics from baskets. It also offered convenient locations for snipers and undercover officers waiting to arrest someone.

"Jaytown Park, then. Meet me on the park bench closest to the popcorn guy." Carrie stood and opened her cell phone, quickly dialing a phone number.

Had Carl looked a little closer, he might have noticed the slight shake in her hands. She'd bluffed her way through the situation and needed to let the team outside know they were all right. This whole deal could slide south if a dozen officers in riot gear rammed the door and arrested everyone. Responding to the voice answering the phone, she said, "I am on my way back. I need product for the client." She hung up the phone, hoping Captain Davies understood her.

9

DILECTIONEM VESTRAM, ET ACCUSAVIT!

YOUR EXCELLENCY, AND THE ACCUSED ...

Dirk woke to the sound of a cell phone buzzing on the nightstand. The thrumming of the vibrations sounded like something gone wrong with an old style stereo speaker. Dirk groped for the phone, catching it by its charging cord before it plummeted toward the floor.

"Yeah," Dirk growled.

"Up and at 'em, buddy, we have an appointment with the archbishop. Time to find our missing nuns." Keith's habit of being too cheerful in the morning always bothered Dirk. No one should ever be that cheerful.

"What time is it?" Dirk tried to find the clock on the nightstand. His shirt, hastily thrown across the room the night before, obscured its satanic digital glow. Dirk rubbed his eyes and then face, struggling to encourage his blood to move again.

"It's almost nine, you bum. Get up. Carl and Rico are at the shop taking care of things." Along with a nasty habit of being too cheerful in the morning, Keith also clung to a deplorable work ethic of never wasting a moment of the day. He likely already finished the weekend sermon, posted and answered in his advice column, and graded a few papers before calling over to the church for an appointment with the archbishop.

"All right, let me shower, then come over and pick me up." Dirk got out of bed and wondered briefly where Carrie was. No text message from her was out of character, and it likely meant her night went a little longer than expected.

As if the celestial powers answered his thoughts, the front door opened and Carrie walked in wearing a dress and carrying a black clutch. Wordlessly, she put her gun in the nightstand drawer and dropped into the pillows. Dirk began asking how her night went but thought it better to let what remained of his future fiancée sleep. Drooping eyelids and the lack of acknowledgment of him suggested sleep hit the number one position on her list of priorities.

He kissed her cheek, removed her shoes, and threw a blanket on her. Melting into the blanked the moment it hit her, she muttered, "Thank you ... love you." Carrie dropped into a steady rhythm of snoring like a woman who earned every single snore. She looked far worse for the wear, as if stress took her for an unplanned ride along the highway to hell. Still, she lay in one piece on the bed, in what hopefully would be their shared home. Exactly how he liked it.

Twenty minutes later, he stood in the kitchen, gulping down a piece of bread, when his phone buzzed the message that Keith waited outside. According to the plan, they were to head over to the church to find out about the three nuns and why they specifically were targeted. Sister Sophia, of course, lay bedridden in the hospital. However, the odds of the other two having never visited the good doctor sat between improbable and impossible. If a common thread presented itself, then it might explain everything else. Perhaps that little piece of knowledge would lead to who did the stealing and why.

Keith sat behind the wheel of his truck and held up a cup of coffee sporting the image of a coffee bean jumping the synaptic gap. A dirty move. One certainly designed to elicit some speed from Dirk.

His oldest and best friend never settled on one job. Keith knew a life of service to God was his calling from the time he was an altar boy. He also loved being a part-time college professor and anything else he tried to do. He ended up being talented at everything, which included an almost encyclopedic knowledge of motorcycle repair. Keith charted his own course in the world and decided to do it all.

Keith's truck, an old Ford F-100, shone at the curb. The color, something called Rangoon Red, was painstakingly applied layer after layer to get the right factory finish. Dirk knew this because Keith had told him the story possibly a thousand times. The truck had been restored from nothing more than a pile of rust, and his labors were both beautiful and functional. This truck demonstrated the depths and breadth of Keith's skill.

"See now, this is why I love you, brother." Dirk picked up the coffee and took a long sip, enjoying the sudden infusion of caffeine. "Oh God, that's good. Stopped by to say hello to Trudy, I see. Good thing. I had to keep the noise in the kitchen down to a minimum so no coffee. Carrie came home looking like beef jerky left in the oven too long."

"I think God knows how good the coffee is. And yes, I

stopped by the coffee shop and said hello to Trudy. I wonder if she is single?" Keith started the truck and put it in gear. "Did Carrie get any sleep?"

Dirk took another long sip of the coffee, being careful not to drip any on the fine hand-stitched leather of the seats. "Yep, fell instantly into dream land when she got home. I guess the big question we have to deal with is who is not telling us the whole truth. Do you think the archbishop has reason to lie to us?"

Keith took a sip of his own coffee and shook his head. "I've known Archbishop Weebley for years, and I doubt he's lying to us. He's a good person. I'm not sure we are barking up the right tree with him. Who else is there?"

Keith turned down a street and past one of five fire stations scattered around the city. Dirk waved to the fire-fighters washing one of the trucks along the street.

"I doubt Sister Sophia made all this up. What reason could she have?" Keith asked.

Dirk stared off onto the sidewalk up ahead of them before commenting, "You see, that's the problem right there. Dealing with clergy, it's easy to find someone who's good but not so easy to find someone who's bad and pretending to be good."

"Wow, both utterly profound and kind of dark. Despite our recent history, most clergy are basically decent people. As a matter fact, in this investigation, I'm not sure we are looking at clergy at all. If one of them were corrupt, then why bring all this heat on themselves?"

Dirk frowned. "Okay, Sam Sneed, where should we be looking?"

"Follow my line of logic here. We know that the bishop is likely not our suspect, not ruling him out completely. I also highly suspect that Edwardo, the operations manager, is too devoted to the parish to be behind the thefts, but that doesn't completely erase him from the suspect lists. I suppose it's possible he's covering up for them. It's a cinch that Sister Sophia and her friends didn't steal all the stuff. They're just too old for that. Besides, it's hard to steal furniture when you are also undergoing chemotherapy.

"Some of the items stolen are heavy objects and require more than one person to steal. This isn't a one-person job. Not at all. I think we're looking for someone who has an ax to grind or personally benefits from the thefts."

Dirk thought through the merits of the idea for a moment. The items stolen such as armoires and cabinets surely had sentimental value. He dismissed the idea quickly since he'd seen photos of the items, and aside from being nice pieces, they were essentially just furniture. The only similarity between the pieces was the age of the furniture and the age of the nuns. Yet that too could still just be a coincidence. Old nuns were likely have old things.

Keith turned the classic pickup truck into the driveway of the large church administration building and parked. Dirk and Keith made their way past the security desk and toward the archbishop's office, they found the outside door slightly ajar. Without knocking, Keith pushed into the room. Carolyn jumped upright from behind her desk. For a brief second, she gave both Keith and Dirk a dirty look. She quickly recovered and recognized Keith. "I'm sorry, Pastor Keith, I didn't realize you'd be here today."

"No, it's me who must apologize, Carolyn. I made this appointment with the archbishop himself. It doesn't surprise me he forgot to put it on the schedule, he's a very busy man. I know he is expecting us."

"I'm sorry, gentlemen, as you said, he is very busy this morning and I know he made the appointment, but I keep the schedule. Would it be possible to push this off to another time? Perhaps next week?" She opened the small planner on her desk and glanced down at the dates.

The door opened and Archbishop Weebley came out. He smiled the big, broad smile he was well-known for. "Gentlemen, it's great to see you. Please come in." Turning toward Carolyn, he said, "Please hold all my calls. These gentlemen and I have serious matters to discuss."

Carolyn gave Dirk and Keith a cold stare and said, "Yes, Your Excellency."

The three men entered the archbishop's office, and they sat at the couches surrounding the small table. Dirk glanced around the room. From the corner of his eye, he thought he saw a blip of light flashing on the intercom system.

"So, gentlemen, what did you want to see me about," Archbishop Weebley said.

Dirk dismissed the flash of light as a figment of his imagination. "Bishop, we've reviewed the print-offs you gave us, and something came to our attention. I didn't realize that Sisters Mary Sophia, Mary Rebecca, and Mary Ruth were all victims in the thefts. I wasn't looking closely at the documents, or rather, I was looking too closely at the documents to see the connection. Only after I backed off the papers did I see the pattern. These are the same two nuns that Sister Mary Sophia wanted us to investigate. However, when we went to the hospital to visit Mary Sophia, we found out, through another source, that the other two nuns never went to the hospital for any reason before. We found it a little interesting that two elderly nuns were never admitted to the hospital. I remember when my grandmother was their age and she was always in the hospital for something or another. It's possible but it doesn't seem likely to me. Can you explain that?"

The archbishop looked at Dirk and shrugged. "It is understandable you are accusing me of something. I know that if I were in your shoes I would likely suspect myself as well."

Dirk held up a hand. "No, Archbishop, not at all. Quite to the contrary. If Keith has faith in you, then so do I. However, you must admit it sounds somewhat peculiar. I'm wondering how this is possible. Is there someone who knows more about these nuns?"

The archbishop thought for a moment. Turning to the desk, he pressed the call button. It made a high-pitched screeching noise. Lifting his finger up and pressing down again, he said, "Carolyn, can you call Mother Superior in here, please? I need to ask her a question." Turning back to Dirk he said, "Stupid intercom has been acting up as of late."

Keith spoke up. "Look, Your Excellency, we are not accusing you of anything. Still, I'm not here as a pastor, I'm here as an investigator. If I can clear these questions up, I can move on and find the person who is doing this to you. I don't mind telling you that one of our theories, and it's a good one, is that the person doing this has a grudge against the church. And if that's the case, you, or any member of your staff, could be in danger."

"I'm sorry to sound defensive, boys. Sometimes, I feel like the church is in a perpetual state of defense. I try to run a clean ship, and I take it very seriously when anybody even sounds like they're accusing me of wrongdoing." The archbishop rubbed his hands together nervously. He was about to say something else when a knock came at the door. "Come in."

The door opened, and a nun dressed in a blue habit entered the room. She was in her sixties, short, and with the build of a woman who knew years of hard labor and had the life experience to go along with it. Dirk recalled it was that same divine presence Sister Sophia possessed. All three of them stood. Even the archbishop stood in deference to the commanding woman. "Mother Superior, thank you for joining us. I have a question, and I would like to ensure this discussion goes no farther than this office. It is of an official nature."

"Your Excellency, of course, you have my discretion," the woman answered.

"These men are Dirk and Keith. Keith is a Methodist pastor and private investigator, and Dirk is the lead investigator. You may remember they were in the newspaper last summer."

"It is my honor to meet you, gentlemen," Mother Superior said stiffly. "Forgive my bluntness, but I have much to do today, so brevity is appreciated."

Dirk wondered if she was always that much fun or especially surly just for them. "Mother Superior, I'd like to know if you can tell me when and if any particular nun went to the hospital for any treatments at all. I mean, really anything."

"This is most irregular. Your Excellency, are you sure I can share this information with these men?" The worry-worn brow of the old nun creased with concern.

The archbishop put his hand on her forearm. "Mother Superior, it is all right. Just don't share details. All they simply want to know is if they went to the hospital or not."

Her hands disappeared under her considerable robes for a few seconds and reemerged with a small electronic organizer. The old school nun negotiating apps on a cell phone made Dirk chuckle.

"What are the names?" She asked.

"Mary Rebecca and Mary Ruth."

After a few moments, the ends of the nun's mouth curled down into a frown. "Well, this is interesting. Why did you want to ask about these specific nuns?"

"Those are the ones we were hired to find," Keith offered. "Why, Sister? What are you seeing?"

"There are no records of them on the official calendar. I mean to say it's like they dropped off the map entirely. However, I maintain my own set of records on a different app that is easier for me to keep track of the sisters. I show them visiting the hospital at least four times in the last year. I also have the transfer orders, signed by the archbishop, sending them to a hospice center in upstate New York."

Dirk shot the archbishop a curious glance. "It seems odd you have no memory of them leaving."

"Indeed," the archbishop said. "As a matter of fact, that is quite impossible. I meet with every person in my charge personally when they transfer in and transfer out. I know, for a fact, I never met with them. I suppose I might be slipping. We have over three hundred clergy I am responsible for, and it's a lot of people, but it is my top priority to thank everyone for their service to God. The Mother Superior can attest to that."

The door opened and the secretary came in carrying a small tray of coffee, saucers, and small tea cakes. "I thought you might like these, Your Excellency." She poured cups of coffee and handed them out to everyone. "Mother Superior, I believe you are needed in the sacristy, and I have to remind you that you have an appointment at noon that you have to prepare for, Your Excellency."

"So I do. Carolyn, I have no idea where I would be without you. Please have the driver ready to take me over."

Carolyn bowed her head. "Yes, Excellency." Carolyn walked out of the office and closed the door behind her. It made a thick wooden *thunk* as it met with the doorframe.

The archbishop rubbed his hands together. "It appears our mystery has deepened and is less resolved than before."

Dirk glanced back over at the intercom and noticed a flash of light a few moments after the door closed. "Thank you, Your Excellency, and thank you, Mother Superior. Yes, this has made everything clear as mud, but I have a few new avenues I can explore."

"I really do have to go though. This meeting is important. As the saying goes, everyone has a boss, and this meeting is with mine. Going over résumés for the new mother superior."

"Leaving?" Dirk asked, turning to the woman.

"Well, not for a few months yet, but I am headed back home to Minnesota. I have family there, and it will be nice being closer." She walked out the door into the small outer office.

The archbishop looked away nervously. "You really think someone would intentionally hurt my staff?" For a moment, the old eyes of the wizened cleric focused on the tree line across the parking lot as if the leaves themselves whispered the answers they all sought. "I have served God for a long time. Have had a pretty good life too. Nearer to the end than I'd like to admit, most of my friends have retired or passed on.

All I have is my staff and parishioners when they let me preach. These people are my family. I worry about them more than you can possibly imagine. It is my utmost duty to ensure my staff is safe. If I can't do that, I'm not a very good archbishop."

Keith softened considerably—it was the pastor in him. "Your Excellency, it's one possibility. I don't really think it's you in danger, but we can't rule it out either. I'm going to talk to the police and have them keep a closer eye on you. They should be contacting you soon. This isn't just a simple matter of burglars taking a few things you left laying out on the patio. This has the markings of something much larger. If that's true, the people who are taking these things won't be happy with us trying to stop them."

Dirk leaned forward. "Your Excellency, is it all right if I go down to the warehouse again?"

"Absolutely. No problem, I'll give Edwardo a call and he'll take you."

Dirk waved the man away. "No, don't do that. At this point, it's only you and us that know I'd be going, and I want to keep it that way. I'd like to head down there all by myself. Snoop around a little bit. With your permission, of course. I'd like to crawl back through the woods and see if I can break into your warehouse without actually breaking anything. If it's truly as easy as I am beginning to suspect, I'll have a little more to go off of. If I'm wrong, Edwardo should call you when the alarm goes off."

Keith looked at his best friend and longtime partner with dismay. "Dirk, what are you doing?"

"Just ... humor me."

The archbishop gave Keith a dubious look before relenting

and nodding his approval of Dirk's plan. Keith and Dirk said their goodbyes to Carolyn and walked down the hallway. Outside the building, Dirk said, "Keith, did you happen to notice the intercom?"

"I did. I am not sure something is wrong with it as much as someone has listened in to the conversations. The bigger question is why?"

"Not sure old friend. I suspect someone inside those walls is keeping a very close eye on this investigation."

"You want me to hang around?" Keith asked.

"No, you go home, and I'll give you a call when I need someone to bring me home. Right now, I want to poke around a bit and see who suddenly appears. If I miss my guess, someone is going to take a keen interest in whatever snooping I'm doing. At least as long as they suspect we're not sure who is behind any of this."

"Okay, be careful." Keith walked to the truck, and Dirk made his way around the side of the building.

On one side of the property, the roadway that Edwardo drove them down before wound around the property and finally turned into the woods toward the warehouse. Walking from the corner of the main building, one needed only stumble through the forest and underbrush for ten minutes to gain the outer fence of the warehouse. Best of all, no one would see him.

After a few minutes of walking, Dirk crested the ridgeline and wound down into the small valley where the warehouse sprawled out from one end to the other. Unless he missed his guess, somebody had accessed this warehouse and not through the normal entrance. His guess begged the question of how they pulled it off. Edwardo had demonstrated how the logs indicated people checking in and out. So even if someone got in and out on a badge that did not have a name attached to it, they'd still have a timestamp of when they came in. Things went missing without anybody having badged in or out, providing the mystery.

Easy, all I really have to do is figure out the why and the how. No problem.

10

BAD COPS IN THE RECEIVING DEPARTMENT

Her phone buzzed out an annoying sound guaranteed to wake her up. Worried she would be late for the meeting with Carl and not get a chance to see Dirk, she rolled out of bed and planted her feet on the cold wood of the bedroom floor. A frown darkened her face as she realized Dirk must be long gone. However, the meeting with Carl, Carrie remembered, thankfully wasn't for another day. It was a good thing since plenty of small tasks stood in her way between now and then.

As she stared down at the dress she still wore, her mind rebooted with thoughts of the awful nightclub. Everything from the conversation with Carl and the disturbing sight of the inside of the bar played on her mind. The prostitutes would have to be dealt with, and a few of the men likely sold drugs, but no one moved on the place until her operation concluded.

A smile erupted on her face as she remembered slapping Collins. She owed him lunch for that. In retrospect, it was the right thing to do. Sometimes, being a cop meant you just rolled with the punches and did whatever came into your head. Freestyling it sometimes meant going off regulations, and poor Collins had paid the price.

Carrie slid on her slippers and went to the closet. In addition to three good outfits, her dress uniform hung on a hanger as well as her patrol uniform from days gone past. It hung there, untouched since she last wore it six months ago.

After selecting an outfit suitable for office work, she twisted the knob in the shower, bringing the reassuring hiss of warm water, followed by a spray of suddenly warm air. The water caressed her skin, removing the day like a bad suit. She'd have to remember to put on clean bedsheets after the shower. The stench of the bar followed her around, and it needed vanquishing as quickly as possible.

Carrie considered just asking if she could just move in. Unsure of herself and how to approach the subject, she continually put the idea off. Every impediment stood in her way in her own mind only. Neither of them was so overly religious that they feared the wrath of the church or their own familial opinions, but her hesitancy sprang from a little voice inside her head, raising concerns every time the idea of a more permanent situation danced through her mind.

And still, her patrol uniform hung from a hanger in the closet. Only worn for formal occasions such as department funerals, it served as a tie to the one thing in her life with permanency. Carrie chose to keep it here. Dirk's house contained the one thing in her life that made her whole, her identity as a police officer. The psychological implications suggested a deeper meaning, and the significance shouldn't be ignored.

Pulling off the bedsheets and throwing them in the washer, she briefly smelled the coffee in the pot. Dirk made her a cup, but it long since grew cold. Always doing things like that, Dirk continually put others before himself and tried to be the best boyfriend in the world. Definitely marriage material, Carrie's mother more than once pointed that out. The thought made her smile.

Dressed in the fresh suit, she combed out her hair and dabbed on a little make up. On her way to the precinct, Carrie made a quick stop at The Beanapse drive-through before hitting the desk. Based on everything that transpired, at least three reports awaited her, if not more. No one ever told her police work came with so much paperwork. Easily her least favorite part of the job.

The Detective Pit, as the patrol officers called it, took half of the building's third floor. The last time the open space of twenty desks had enjoyed any sort of remodeling effort Bill Clinton had still been the president. It retained a bit of an old musty smell of human refuse and stale toner cartridges of decades past. Every detective had a desk with a few left over that the patrol sergeants used for long-term projects.

Carrie sat, trying to refocus her brain on work. Still, that damn patrol uniform fluttered in the back of her mind, casting accusatory glances at her every time she thought of Dirk. Something in their relationship needed to change.

"Carrie, nice work."

Carrie jumped out of her chair at the sound of the chief's voice. "Oh, God, Chief. You scared the crap out of me. Whew. Don't do that again, or you are going to have to find another detective."

Melonie Dixon, a medium-sized woman with good skin

and an athletic build, leaned up against Carrie's assigned desk she shared with another detective. Melonie wore her brunette hair in a bob and almost never wore makeup. Carrie admired her mentor and friend and even stood in the wedding party when the chief got married to her life partner after the state supreme court voted to allow gay marriage to take place.

When Carrie joined the force, her father introduced her to Melonie Dixon. Already a seasoned detective, she made her way into the senior positions in the department all the while continuing to mentor Carrie. The frequency of the mentoring sessions diminished as they both rose in the ranks, but Chief Dixon always made time for her.

"Well, there is no way I could replace you. I put too much time into you at this point to kill you off. I was just reading your initial report from last night. Quick thinking. You gave me a good laugh though. I don't think I have ever seen anyone write in their report that they actually struck another officer to convince the contact of their sincerity." The chief threw back her head and chuckled. Melonie carried a feminine charm that always showed through. She was motherly when she needed to be, but those who disliked the female chief found out how mistaken they were in thinking her weak. Melonie told Carrie early on that if she built a successful career in the male-dominated world of law enforcement, Carrie could do it too.

"It's only fair that I owe the good patrolman lunch after that. I feel bad for him. Poor guy didn't know what hit him. Still, if he hadn't spoken whatever language that was at the door, we'd have never gotten in."

The chief walked over to a small coffee service on a table

next to the wall and poured a cup. "Actually, Carrie, that's what I need to talk to you about. Let's go into my office."

"Uh-oh. Do I need a notepad?"

"No," the chief said. "Actually, let's not take notes this time. We need to keep this on the down low."

A few minutes later, they walked into the chief's office. Melonie lowered the blinds on the windows and locked the door. "Carrie, I hate having to bring this up. Kind of a delicate subject. I had an interesting conversation about your report this morning."

Carrie suddenly got the impression she majorly screwed up. "I ... I'm sorry, Chief. Whatever I did wrong. I don't even know what it was. I followed procedure and—"

Chief Dixon held up her hand. "It isn't you. Actually, the senior staff and I talked about finding a detective sergeant spot for you eventually. Your quick thinking kept a potentially dangerous situation from exploding all over downtown. We need to talk about Collins."

"Collins? What did he do wrong? I was with the kid the whole time, and he did well, I thought."

The chief took a drink of the coffee. "That is the problem. He handled things a little too well. The senior staff made the point, and I think it has merit, that Collins never disclosed the ability to speak any foreign languages. He is supposed to tell us these things, and walking up to a dive bar and getting inside by a mere word is suspicious, you have to admit. To make a long story short, internal affairs is investigating him."

Carrie's mind flashed back to the night before. The discussion at the door was brief, but Collins undoubtedly carried influence, almost as if he knew the guy at the door. Carrie realized something sounded fishy, and after a while, she'd have gotten around to asking about it. At the time, her adrenaline overruled all other impulses. "Is this a fresh investigation or an ongoing one?"

The chief had no obligation to talk with Carrie about this. However, she knew the chief well enough that the something she was not explicitly saying compelled her to do it. Likely, since the chief talked to her, she cleared bringing Carrie into the conversation with the internal affairs investigator.

"Nothing is as bad as a dirty cop, Carrie. Except, a good cop wrongly accused. You understand my meaning?"

"No, I'm not entirely sure what you mean." Carrie squinted at her boss with furrowed brows.

"You are a great cop and quickly becoming a great detective. Use that instinct of yours and answer me this. Do you really think Collins is crooked?"

Carrie thought about everything she knew about the young officer. Always observant, always learning and listening. Something in the way the young officer carried himself suggested he was a cut above the rest. He clearly did not like misleading suspects into talking themselves into a corner. No one with that level of innocence contained a crooked bone in his body. Based on everything she knew of the kid, there was no way Collins was a crooked cop.

"No, Chief, I really don't see it."

Chief Dixon stirred a packet of sugar into the coffee and took another sip. "Holy crap, this coffee is horrid. You guys need a better coffee maker in the next budget. On another note, I agree. I don't think Collins is really a dirty cop. There is something about him ... something I feel—"

"In your gut?" Carrie interrupted. "I seem to remember

someone lecturing me about trusting their instincts once as a new recruit."

Melonie Dixon smiled. "Yes, in my gut. That's why we are going to have him side saddle with you for a while. The cover will be so that he can learn the ropes of detective work. You can keep an eye on the patrolman and report to me anything you see. Carrie, I have to caution you on one thing."

"Of course, Chief." Carrie leaned forward in her chair.

"I need you to promise that at the first sign of anything less than above board you back off. I don't need you getting dirt on yourself too. You know what a dirty cop can do to those around them."

Indeed, Carrie did. Her first year on the force, a dirty cop nearly destroyed the department in a scandal so large the department needed years to recover. Carrie's father had arrested the cop. He said that arresting another cop was the worst thing any cop ever had to do.

After the chief concluded the meeting, Carrie returned to her desk to prepare for the next day's undercover operation. Somehow, through the rest of her shift, she only thought about Collins and her nagging intuition about the young patrolman. As she reviewed her report from the other day, Collin's ability to talk their way into that fortress of a bar struck her as out of the ordinary. Although, her gut told her a different story which featured an honest cop wrongfully accused because of extraordinary circumstances.

THE NEXT DAY, Carrie made her way into Jaytown Park. The busy afternoon was made even busier by the unseasonably warm temperatures. This time of year, she normally needed some sort of coat, but not today. *Too bad,* she thought, *this day should be spent enjoying the sunshine rather than sitting out on a park bench waiting for a sleazebag fencer to show his face.*

The park, originally much larger, made up the town square. Years of renovation had changed its rectangular shape, and years of rebuilding and reclamation left it more pear shaped. The side of the park designated for the meeting made up the largest portion of the pear, and it was the part most frequented by the citizens of the town. On the other side of the pear sat a large fountain spraying water, a good-sized picnic area, and six concrete chess tables ordinarily occupied by old men and strangely a few kids from a Latin street gang who'd picked up an interest in chess while serving time in jail. The old men, at first wary of the kids, ultimately served as positive role models.

Behind Carrie's bench, a cover band played an obnoxious rendition of "Stairway to Heaven" on instruments ill tuned for the task. A popcorn vendor sat in an off-white plastic chair, reading a newspaper and waiting for customers desirous of his salty treats. A woman and man lay together on a blanket, behaving wholly inappropriately for a family park. Carrie thought how satisfying it would be to walk over, flash a badge, and give them a ticket for violating a hardly enforced public decency ordinance.

A couple of minutes early, she wanted time to walk the grounds before settling in for their meeting. People in Carl's line of work valued punctuality. Receivers, as the people who sold stolen goods were called in the underworld, fiercely protected their reputations. Efficiency and punctuality remained a hallmark of someone in his line of work. They viewed themselves as executives of the criminal world.

Carrie kept her plan simple. They would meet at the park and discuss terms. At the conclusion of the meeting, several undercover cops, posted on either side of the park, would come in as a group and apprehend the suspect. She carried a small sample of counterfeit booze from the evidence room. Recently, they had apprehended a shipment of five hundred bottles. Four hundred and fifty of those were destroyed, and the rest stayed in the evidence locker in case a need like this one arose. Carl must accept the bottle and talk terms to ensure an airtight case a prosecutor could close. Anything less left them with a flimsy case at best.

Like clockwork, a black car pulled up to the shoulder of the park and Carl stepped out. The hairs on Carrie's neck stood as her detective's intuition screamed warnings. The car pulled away and took the turn down a one-way street. That street led only to an on-ramp to the highway, giving the impression they did not intend to wait for Carl. Carrie wondered what his next move would be as his ride home just left. The question sent chills up her spine.

Carrie's earpiece jumped to life with officers discussing what Carrie noticed. She risked muttering into the hidden microphone, "Relax, keep it together. Maybe they are just running over for gas." If anything, the car leaving meant they did not have to worry about Carl summoning reinforcements in the takedown.

Within shouting distance now, Carl turned away from Carrie and approached the man selling popcorn. Carrie resisted the urge to steal a glance at him. A meeting like this should be low-key, and any loss of focus now would be a rookie mistake.

A moment later, he plopped down next to her. Reaching into a white bag with a few grease spots from the freshly popped corn, he pulled out a handful and threw some carelessly into his mouth. The crunching of his salty snack thundered in Carrie's head like jackhammers.

"Would you like popcorn, Detective?"

Oh shit!

11

AND THE HITS KEEP COMING

Dirk found a fallen log that made the perfect perch to watch the comings and goings of a virtually abandoned warehouse. With the exception of a few people going through the front gate, the warehouse looked largely abandoned.

Surveillance lost its luster after the snacks ran low and drowsiness ran high. Dirk especially disliked the task. Keith, being undeterred by boredom, was far better suited for such a mission. This time, an element of risk existed, and Dirk would never place any member of the team at risk if avoidable. Not necessarily worried about having someone call the police, he was concerned that someone might develop a violent dislike to his snooping. Deep in the back of his mind, although unpleasant, he actually hoped to see someone come around sooner or later and tip their hand.

From where he sat, the road that he, Keith, and Edwardo drove down to access the warehouse before lay just beyond the trees to his left. The structure stood in a large L shape with the front of the building facing Dirk and forming a right angle, turning to the right. That right-hand turn made up the bulk of the warehouse. He remembered a large office area occupied the front part of the building. A larger door, on the back of the building, featured a pole-barn-style door to allow large trucks to enter and exit. Edwardo indicated the door, usually padlocked, was only opened for special circumstances. Only a few people possessed a key. Another smaller code-operated door opened from the outside. Every time the door opened or closed, a log recorded the activity.

Dirk secretly suspected someone's version of the truth did not quite add up. If his hunch proved correct, someone had found a way into the warehouse outside of the normal doors. Through his binoculars, he made out the front side of the fence line. Small blue shields, evenly spaced, suggested Center Point Security played a prominent role in the installation. Dirk made a note to check on the name. Perhaps the company installing the fence could provide insight into any weak spots.

Dirk opened a text message and sent Keith a quick note telling him the plan. He wanted to make sure if something went wrong Keith knew where to look for his body. A grim but very real possibility when investigating the seedier underbelly of humanity.

Then again, how bad can things really get when you are investigating a bunch of priests and nuns?

After double-checking the building's parking lot to ensure no one stirred, Dirk picked his way through the underbrush toward the building and the impressive security fence surrounding it. Harboring suspicions about Edwardo, in spite of the archbishop's reassurances, remained logical as the man retained a position well-placed to be behind the thefts. While

Edwardo certainly boasted plenty of years working at the compound, it did not necessarily translate into reliability. Edwardo may have simply decided to pad his retirement.

Still, Edwardo and the archbishop did not fit for Dirk's idea of the culprits in this case. Aside from that, neither Edwardo nor the archbishop admitted to being security experts. No matter how proud of their security system they were, it was likely they only knew what the security company told them.

An eight-foot-wide stretch of river rock surrounded the outside of the fence. Pounded down flat before sloping off into a marshy area created by drainage from the hillsides, it also served as a security perimeter. The way the rock was tamped down reminded Dirk of the perimeter around military bases where security patrols drove in circles to dissuade would-be trespassers. Perhaps security such as this was overkill for a church warehouse. In the center of the path were two well-defined sets of tire tracks, one wider than the other.

Dismissing the perimeter for a moment, Dirk scanned the walls and the three sets of video cameras covering the major entrances and the corners of the building. From what Edwardo said, all three of these cameras functioned. Although, faking video feeds was easy enough. If the security cameras were controlled from either the security desk or the archbishop's office, it certainly presented a gaping hole in security. He also wondered how well the cameras behind the building worked. During their time with Edwardo, no security monitor ever graced the back of the building.

Dirk circled the hillside, scanning the fence as he went. The chain link fence and metal fence posts glinted in the sun, likely recently installed. Structurally sound, and in good repair, the bottom of the fence plunged below the ground, anchored to keep someone from pulling it up and crawling underneath. Strands of barbed wire menacingly graced the top, threatening anyone who dared to climb it. As he rounded the corner to the backside of the warehouse, little of additional interest caught his eye. In the back, the same fence lines and three sets of video cameras covered most of the area.

Dirk's mentor had stressed slowing down and taking in everything around him. The old detective had given a lot of advice like that. As Dirk got older, he appreciated how handy that wisdom came in. Now, while he stared at the security cameras, the realization hit that they were different from the others in front of the building. Every camera was connected to the building with a black wire leading from the camera into the building. None of these cameras featured the long black tether. He remembered Edwardo had said a couple of the cameras didn't work and Center Point Security planned to repair the cameras soon. Maybe the cameras were never designed to work at all.

Continuing across the back of the warehouse, he noticed another oddity. Directly in the center of the pathway around the building, a flattened path led off into the marsh area and crested a small hunting road that disappeared up the hillside. The trail narrowed and the woods widened only enough to allow a small golf cart to pass.

Or perhaps Edwardo's Gator.

Dirk looked over every inch of the fence line on the back of the building. Similar to the front, most of the sections appeared solid enough. Leaning against one of the poles, he felt it gave a little with his weight. Upon closer inspection,

Dirk observed this section's construction featured reinforced elements, setting it off from the rest, while someone had gone to great pains to ensure it mirrored the rest of the sections as closely as possible. The fence was set deeply into grooves in the post rather than connecting to it. Grabbing with both hands, he shook the fence back and forth while gritting his teeth against imagined noise. Much to Dirk's surprise, the fence lurched upward.

He took a few steps back in awe at the genius of it all. This entire section slid up and down on rollers like a window in a frame. Anyone knowing this section of the fence moved easily gained access to the facility in seconds without anyone likely noticing. Then, Dirk guessed, stealing anything after walking through the sliding fence line only involved moving whatever they wanted out of the warehouse and onto a waiting vehicle.

Satisfied he solved one of the most complicated mysteries of the case, the greater question of motive remained. The idea surfaced again that stealing the personal belongings of clergy could not be lucrative. During his short time in the warehouse, he found little of value. The most expensive things were the pieces of furniture, which still held only minimal value. If the criminals were willing to go to this much trouble, why not steal something worth far more?

Dirk pulled the fence up and let himself inside the perimeter. He still hoped the security guards might react to seeing an intruder, which would put his mind at ease about the fealty of the security staff to their jobs. It would put to rest a suspicion the installation of the cameras satisfied the need to appear like security without actually providing any. If Center Point installed the fence, that put two strikes against them.

Certainly not the first time a company became a prime suspect in an investigation.

The interior space between the fence and the wall measured about eight feet. Suspiciously large, it suggested a facility more in tune with high-level security than a regular warehouse. Dirk examined the side of the building for anything suggesting a secret entrance. If someone went to this much trouble to ensure they could easily walk into and out of the outer fencing, likely they also went to the trouble to ensure a door at the back of the building remained equally hidden.

Common pressed aluminum made up the outer wall, held in place by screws on metal framing. Two sections of aluminum covered the building from top to bottom. As he turned to leave, something caught his eye. A pinprick of light through one piece of sheet metal pierced through the shadow which engulfed this side of the building.

This particular piece of metal gave a little when pressed. Instead of the screws holding it in place, the screws served as decorative pieces for any onlooker who cared to look. Pulling at the seam, Dirk wasn't surprised when it came loose in his hands, swinging open as a door. Tripping over his feet and landing in the rocks behind him, he saw the large hinge, which was hidden from the outside. A perfect door into the warehouse. The aluminum sheeting reinforced with steel on the inside featured a heavier metal frame than the rest of the wall. The entire door was held closed by a series of rare earth magnets.

Dirk had learned enough. Someone had gone to great extents to ensure a supposedly secured facility lacked coherent security.

The door fell shut with a click, and an immense pain erupted from the back of Dirk's head. Stars overtook his vision as every fiber of Dirk's being cried out in alarm, and he had only a moment to process what had happened before blackness pulled him toward the depths of unconsciousness.

KEITH READILY CONFESSED his inner worrywart manner. When Dirk went out by himself, that inner voice spoke the loudest. His longtime friend's nasty habit of pushing things farther than they needed to often led to him having to extricate himself from needlessly difficult situations. However, having done this longer than most people in the business, he knew how to take care of himself.

When the clock read 6:30, the voice in Keith's head rose from a mere protest to screaming at the top of the register. Something deep inside of Keith felt, or knew, his best and oldest friend was in mortal danger. Out of the two people Dirk talked to the most, Keith sat at two, and he never could compete with number one. They never went this long without at least texting.

He dialed Carrie's number on the phone, and it rang a bunch of times before an unknown officer answered. "Detective Pettigrew? Nope, not here right now. I think she is out in a briefing or something. Can I take a message?"

"No message. Just have her give Keith a call when she gets back."

Keith tried to type Carrie a message, but every sentence sounded alarmist. Knowing Carrie, she'd drop everything and come running with a half-dozen uniformed officers to tear the town to pieces looking for the wayward Dirk. Thus far, no real evidence existed suggesting an emergency existed. Still, the feeling in the pit of his stomach refused to budge.

Without any better idea of what to do, he put on a coat and drove toward the warehouse. With any luck, Dirk's radio silence resulted from nothing more than a dead cell phone.

THE SOUNDS of tires humming against the pavement woke Dirk from his slumber. The smells of gasoline, motor oil, and the rubber compounds commonly found in vehicle tires assaulted his sense of smell. For a few seconds, Dirk wondered if he was in the shop. Those sensations vaporized, replaced with a searing pain of blinding intensity. With every bump of what he now knew was the road, his body screamed out in torment.

The searing sensation of coarse rope dug into his flesh and forced tears in his eyes as he tried to move his hands. His legs, although free, proved of little use. Scanning around in the dark, Dirk saw little pricks of light making their way through what he assumed to be the trunk of a car as it passed under streetlights.

Rolling over onto his back, Dirk found a small ice scraper. If he could slide the edge of the scraper under the rope and work at the knot, it might loosen. With each dig, the ropes dug deeper and deeper into meaty flesh. The slickness of blood covered Dirk's fingers, but it beat the consequences of arriving at their destination, which surely meant a bullet to his head. Whoever hit him obviously wanted to avoid discussion or negotiation.

The ropes continued to rend flesh, and blood now made it harder to hold onto the cheap windshield scraper handed out free with an oil change at any local service station.

One of the knots in the rope slipped slightly. Not much of a hole, but it was enough for Dirk to work a hand loose. Then he untied the rest of the rope.

Quickly checking over himself, he was pleased that all limbs reported ready for further instructions. Unfortunately, whoever thought to tie him up also thought to take his gun from his shoulder holster and the knife he carried strapped to his leg. In the dark, he groped around for something to use as a weapon.

A couple of more high-speed turns left Dirk grasping for something to hold onto inside the trunk. The car jerked from side to side like someone played a violent game of ping-pong. During one of these less-than-gentle turns, his hand rubbed against something metal. He grappled around the empty space until his hand came to rest on a metal chain. Not a perfect weapon, by any means, but it would work in a pinch.

All cars built after 2001 were required to have an internal release mechanism inside the trunk, and Dirk breathed a sigh of relief as his hand found the latch in the dark. The more pressing issue would be how to escape from a car while simultaneously avoiding being smashed along the asphalt road below. Jumping out of the car while driving at normal speeds, and the concussion surely following, presented its own set of problems. Just as troubling, any vehicle following might run him over. Waiting until the car came to a complete stop also carried certain risks as whoever drove might shoot him in the back before he made it to safety.

Complicating the matter, he was stripped of his pants,

shirt, and shoes, so the damp fall air made hypothermia a very real possibility. Dirk thought over the three ways to die in this situation. Neither the possibility of being smashed to bits on the road, getting a bullet wound to part of his body, nor hypothermia stood out as attractive ways to go out of this life. The thought of waking up on the other side and having to explain it all to Victor stood out as an embarrassing option.

Biding the time until his escape, he listened to the voices inside the car. From what Dirk could tell, a man and a woman sat up front. Both spoke with heavy New England accents. The woman's voice, Dirk swore, struck him as very familiar. Even with the buzzing of the road surface and constant jostling, which came from every pothole in Virginia, the voice haunted the back of his mind.

"Where should we do it?" the man said.

"Out by the dock. We want to make sure our private investigator here is found floating, facedown. Nowhere near the penguin nest. The last thing we need is any evidence that brings the cops back to the office. I don't need that. His girlfriend is a cop, you know." The woman's voice contained a hint of worry in it.

"Don't worry about a thing, I will—"

While straining to take in any intelligible part of the discussion, the opportunity for escape materialized. With the sudden application of brakes to turn a corner, Dirk stopped listening and pulled the trunk release. Dirk moved to seize the opportunity as it might never come again.

The trunk bounced open and Dirk rolled out. He protected his head during the fall, and the shock of his body meeting asphalt hurt less than he figured it would, likely a result of the adrenaline. His muscles would hurt like holy hell in the morning. Taking only a moment to find his legs, Dirk ran as fast as possible from the vehicle. A lake sprawled out to the right. Its mirror-like surface was dressed in wisps of fog common in fall. He opted for the woods, as it offered the best cover and concealment.

After he stumbled a few steps into the forest, a shot rang out and the bark of a tree next to him exploded, sending splinters of wood raining down on him. Behind him, above the sudden ringing in his ears from the blast of the weapon, he thought the woman yelled out something about the man going after Dirk while she took the car.

Dirk had learned years ago, from a self-defense instructor, that running was not necessarily your best option in a situation like this. Never believing he would ever have to use the advice of long since retired instructor, he thought that advice long since forgotten. Thankfully, the training came back like the rush of adrenaline surging through his bloodstream as his fight or flight reflexes kicked in. Sprinting through the trees, Dirk plunged under and over brush and fallen logs to put distance between himself and the pursuer. Although he guessed only one person pursued him, in the confusion of the run to the wood line, more people could have joined the race.

Halfway up the hill, Dirk made out the shadowy hulks of trees and picked out the perfect old oak dominating the landscape in the moonlight. Ducking behind the trunk, he flattened himself against the bark. In his hands, the balled-up chain hung menacingly at the end.

The pursuer stopped somewhere along the tree line, suggesting he or she understood the dangers of just plunging into the darkness. While Dirk certainly did not have any real advantage, the darkness allowed him to hide for the moment and make decisions about what to do instead of reacting to threats.

Only about twenty feet separated himself and the roadway. Little time to react to any of the assailant's movements meant the need for action came sooner than he wanted. Thinking he really needed to work out more, Dirk brought his breathing under control. The chain, with the lock on the end, hung loosely in his hands. With any luck, he'd be able to hit his pursuer without missing completely and hitting himself in the face in the process. Certainly, a risky move, but right now, he played the odds, and so far, he had beaten them.

The cold of the tree penetrated his bare skin as the chilly temperatures sunk through his underwear and socks. Dirk wondered why they would strip him of his clothes before abducting him. Likely no reason at all. Just something to humiliate Carrie and his sister when she went to identify the body.

Silence gripped everything in an oppressive hold. Wind, normally everywhere this time of year, conspicuously remained unmoving as if the air movement suspended itself voluntarily to watch the confrontation. A good wind would be nice to cover his tracks. Darkness only did so much to hide his actions.

Behind Dirk, on the other side of the tree, a stick snapped as an unseen pressure pushed it into the soil. He guessed the predator, or prey, stepped within reach. Out from around the tree, Dirk whipped the chain around in the darkness. Vibrations through the length of the chain and a satisfying thud suggested he'd hit the mark on something fleshy.

"Damn!" an unfamiliar voice rang out. Something heavy hit the ground and slid across the forest floor. Either way, darkness favored both the hunter and the hunted. Getting the gun in the dark proved a difficult proposition. Thankfully, the would-be assailant also faced that same difficulty.

Wasting no time, the man jumped out from the tree and into the moonlight just in time for Dirk to see his fist flying at him. Dirk tried to duck out of the way but only managed to partially avoid the punch. The punch connected with the side of Dirk's face, and the sensation of his brain bouncing around inside of his skull threatened a blackout.

Dirk wasted no time and returned the punch with an uppercut. Dirk connected with rock-hard abdominal muscles. However, the punch caught the man off guard, and Dirk managed to put a couple of feet between them before the man redoubled his efforts and punched at Dirk's head. A little better on his feet than his opponent, Dirk parried the punch and elbowed his assailant in the chest, sending him tripping over a log and onto the ground.

Counterattacking, Dirk lost track of his own thoughts, allowing animal instinct to take over. Wrapping the bike chain around his hand, he swung the lock over and over at the man's head. Dirk never thought about the idea of having to kill someone. He'd once fired his weapon in self-defense and wounded another man, and that was pure instinct as well. This situation stood in sharp contrast. As he kneeled on top of the man's chest, one driving sensation took over. Dirk wanted the man dead.

The potential to lose loomed ominously. Killing another man certainly was not something he wanted. However, if he wanted to live, the other man must die. The adrenaline took over.

Dirk was unsure when he stopped hitting the other, still

unknown, man, but it was after the other man stopped moving. Dirk blacked out and when he came to, the dead man lay in the moonlight. The corpse's open eyes gazed at the moon and stars. Dirk looked for a pulse, and finding none, he gave up. He examined the wound to the would-be assailant's head. The caved in cranium and the oozing mass suggested there was no possible way he survived.

The mix of adrenaline, running through the forest in the dark, and the exertion of killing the unknown man overwhelmed him. The emotions and the change in his body chemistry plotted against him while sitting there. A sound pierced the night. The pocket of the man's jeans glowed as a voice deep inside Dirk's subconscious told him the noise came from a cell phone.

Reflexively, he took it from the man's pants pocket and looked at the screen. The caller ID read unknown number, but right now, he needed a phone. Knowing hypothermia from the plummeting temperatures already effected his judgment, Dirk dismissed the call. He needed to make it back to the road and summon help.

As he stood, every sinew, muscle, and nerve in his body screamed out in pain. The bike lock lay next to the man, slick blood mixing with the dirt in a puddle appearing black in the moonlight.

Trudging toward the street, Dirk dialed Keith. Fingers went numb and confusion set in, all bad signs little time remained to save himself. Thoughts of Carrie entered his mind. If he did not gain the street and call for help, he would never see her again. Worse yet, he would never have the chance to ask her to marry him. That motivation became the most important of all.

"Keith." Dirk struggled for a clear head. His feet argued with him at every step, and the world around him blended into a blurry caricature of itself. "I need help. I don't know where I am. I see a boat dock, a lake, a Ferris wheel in the distance. I can see a pattern of lights up ahead. Looks like a town or something. I am next to a road. By a boathouse. I think I see a boat dock and a lake ... and ... and I ..."

In the last moment of melting sensation, the cool and moist dirt of the ground connected with his face.

12

LITTLE KIDS PLAYING GROWN-UP GAMES

A sinking feeling took up residence in the pit of her stomach. There was no way Carl should have any idea she was a police detective. Everything had gone so well in this investigation, and now the situation resembled a shit show so quickly she had no idea what to do.

"I can see you are at a loss for words, so let me start us off." Carl laid his hands flat on his jeans.

Coming to her senses, Carrie realized the SWAT team likely also made out what he said, and the trigger-happy commander of the SWAT team currently looked for any reason to cleave Carl's head in two. She said, "All teams to position one and hold. It seems my cover is blown. Wait for my signal." She took in a deep breath. "All right then, Carl, talk."

"You will notice, and anyone else who cares to listen, I am keeping my hands where everyone can see them. Doubtless, you have a team watching my every move and are more than capable of ending my life. So, let's make a deal. I will tell you everything I know, and you promise me the same kind of deal you gave my good friend Deluca."

"Aren't you mad at him right now? I mean he did rat you out." Carrie couldn't see an immediate threat, and if Carl had placed his own sniper, it might be too late to do anything about it. As long as he continued to talk, she indulged him. The question dominating her subconscious asked why both Vance and Carl plunged headlong into the pursuit of bringing down this organization. "I mean, he did rat you out."

"Oh, I know. But, the funny thing is that I'm not really mad at him. Sure, I am probably going to have words with him, but I am a receiver and he's a burglar. Neither one of us is cut out for jujitsu. I guess we'll have a good argument and settle the matter over a few drinks. You can say I have no hard feelings since this would have been the natural conclusion of this ill-conceived enterprise, no matter how you cut it. No, as they say, our interests in this little organization are aligned perfectly."

Carrie looked at him. "So, you are giving yourself up then? Just that easily?"

Carl chuckled. "Well, nothing has changed hands, so you don't have me for anything other than intent to purchase stolen merchandise. So, I am thinking a slap on my wrist is the most you are going to get out of this. Aside from that, you don't want me anyway. Small fish ... big pond sort of thing. No, you want the big fish on the end of this line. And I will bring him to you. Or, at least further along than you are now."

"Seems like a lot of that is going around these days. Look, I am getting tired of all this. I can't believe I am saying this, but

I prefer a good solid arrest to you bad guys turning on each other. It really is far less complicated."

Carl handed the popcorn bag to Carrie, who took a handful. "Well, Detective, I hate to break it to you, but Vance and I are not the only ones willing to turn over on this preschool type of criminal enterprise. Bring back the old days with the Bloods and the Crips. How about the old-school Mafia types? Now we have MS-13 and all these other kids out there trying to start trouble. I just don't know what is going on with this world, Detective."

"Are you really lecturing me about morality and the state of affairs in the underworld? You do know that you are in potentially a lot of trouble here?" Carrie tried to keep up a stern façade with the man but knew the futility of the threat. Part of her agreed with him. In the old days, there was honor among thieves. Now, petty thugs might just slit each other's throat for a twenty-five-dollar gift card.

"All right, Carl, let's just say, for argument's sake, you have a deal. I am not going to question you sitting on this park bench. Which is kind of a pity since it is such a nice day, but we need to do this all official. It does bring up a curious question though. You and Deluca are in an awful big hurry to turn on these guys. Did they shit in the punch bowl at the annual bad guys Christmas party last year? I mean, you should band together rather than want to bring each other down."

"The association is ... complicated, and I think it is better if we have the rest of this conversation at the station. The organization I work ... well, worked for, might be a bunch of junior varsity players, but they still have teeth and I cannot stand being in their crosshairs. I'd rather prefer to sit in a cell until this works itself out."

"Awww, shucks. That's sweet. Let's head over to the van, and we can drive you to the station. I can't say I have ever made a more pleasant arrest. You even brought popcorn."

"I can't say I've ever enjoyed being arrested more."

Two hours later, Carrie walked into an interrogation room with Collins in tow. Told to keep his mouth shut, Collins stood in the back of the room with his arms crossed. Carrie thought he looked less than intimidating, but she reflected on the more lethal capabilities of the boy.

"Okay, we are safe and secure in the interrogation room. No one here but us girls to chat now. So, let's start at the beginning. Who do you work for and what are they hoping to accomplish?"

"My dear Detective." Carl sat back. "I am not here for you. As you can imagine, I don't really give a damn if the good law enforcement community accomplishes their mission or not. I'm here for my own selfish ends."

Carrie folded her arms and shot Collins a confused look. "Okay, I guess I figured that out before we got here. Although, it seems strange that you want to bring it up right out of the gate."

Carl took a sip of the coffee Carrie gave him. "Wow, this coffee is tragic." He shook his head and put the cup aside. "It's simple, really. I need you to understand that although I am being completely honest with you, everything I say and do is for my own benefit, just like Deluca. However, I also want to make it clear the police department's interests and mine just happen to coincide."

"How so?"

Carl smiled at Carrie. "Theoretically, let's say another group decided to open shop in the organized crime world and fenced a whole bunch of low-level stolen merchandise. I only deal in the high-end stuff, and I prefer they were out of the picture as much as you want them out of the picture."

"But don't you benefit from having another source of items to fence? How does another potential client not work in your favor?"

"Detective, this is not simply a client. It is really a subset of another, much larger, organization. Initially, I wasn't going to help these nitwits. I hate to sound this way, but they are really beneath Deluca and I. Strictly bush-league stuff. Bring me a good shipment of stolen diamonds or minks, and I'm all in. This new group only dabbled in kids' stuff. Brass crosses, crystal, and old furniture are really not my style."

Carrie picked up her pen, twirling it in her fingers. She knew Carl's reputation, and the types of material they asked him to fence stood out as low-return merchandise to say the least. "Okay, then let's say I am willing to accept this idea someone forced you into this. Why not just walk away?"

"Detective, I am going to answer your question with a question. Ask yourself if you really believe Vance didn't know about that alarm? Vance is a master at his craft. He knows every system out there and can spot a wired building a mile away."

Carrie assumed it was just a glitch in the system. The police department alarm experts noted in their report someone tampered with the alarm making the outside annunciator go silent. The system should have gone off with a set of flashing lights and alarms outside the building. The noise, designed to bring the world's attention to the building, would have undoubtedly scared the perpetrators off. The alarm did trigger at the headquarters of Center Point Security who called the police department after a considerable lag. "Are you suggesting this was your way of walking away from all of this and that Vance knew that alarm would go off and they'd get caught?"

"Very good, Detective. To be fair, Vance hoped Mateo would keep his mouth shut about his involvement. I knew eventually that the scent would lead you to me. A small risk we decided to take. Let's just say there are a few of us who are less than fond of being told what we will and won't do. Forcing us into this is like asking Michelangelo to paint your living room robin egg blue and then paying him in beer and pizza. Go back and ask Vance about it. I'll bet, when you brought him in, he not only talked freely but very cooperatively?"

"But that doesn't answer my question about not just walking away."

Carl looked at Carrie. "Let's just say that when the Arrcados tell you to do something, it is usually best to do it."

"Wait ... wait. This is too much. So, you are telling me that Tony Arrcado, the hitman of the east side and crown prince of all crime, told you to go work with these two-bit thugs to steal petty cash?"

"For what it is worth, at first, I thought this whole situation had to be a joke. After a couple of jobs with these buffoons, I arrived at the conclusion someone wanted these buffoons out of the way. The same way you give a child a meaningless task when you want them out of the kitchen. Still, all of us were within easy grasp if they needed us. Tony ensured all the underworld remained tied up tighter than a drum right now. That's when Deluca told me he had enough, and I guess we reached a gentlemen's agreement to find a way out. Again, talk to Deluca about it. He'll be happy to confirm all I have said."

Carrie thought about the latest crime reports. Crime stood at uncharacteristically low levels, and it never crossed her mind the low numbers might be because someone, other than the police, wanted it that way.

Vance not only cooperated but unbelievably so. Almost like the entire encounter were scripted. All of it was designed to lead the police down a path like a puppy on a leash. Carrie glanced up at Collins who remained intractable in his demeanor.

"Collins—"

"Pick up Vance?" Collins answered without Carrie finishing the question.

Carrie hated being cut off by a subordinate. "Don't talk over me, Patrolman. I want you and the patrol sergeant on duty to head over to Vance's and bring him in for questioning. Make sure he knows I don't want him placed under arrest. Put him in protective custody for now. If our friend here is telling the truth, he'll be more than compliant."

Sergeant Patrick, a seasoned officer, knew how to handle himself and knew Vance well enough from walking the streets. Carrie still worried that if internal affairs watched Collins talking to Deluca, the investigator naturally would assume the worst. With the patrol sergeant by his side, the interaction came across far less suspicious. Although the idea of him being a bad cop still didn't fit.

"I apologize, Detective."

Carrie, more than a little annoyed, pointed to the door. "Go."

Collins, without saying another word, made his way out of the interrogation room and out into the main precinct.

"A little hard on the kid, don't you think?" Carl remarked, drinking the rest of his coffee.

"He needs to learn his place." Carrie dismissed his remark. "Okay, so you have it in for this minor league team you are being forced to work with. Why do you think Arrcado has such a hard-on to keep you working with them? I want you to walk me through it. Step by step."

"Detective, you know how things work in the underworld. Boy steals things, girl buys things, other boy buys things from the girl and sells the things on the black market. Then another girl buys stolen stereo equipment, computer, or counterfeit Coach purses."

"Yep, I'm following so far. The natural order of general scum-baggery. Still, I don't see what it is that you get out of having to work with these guys who are, I'll admit, beneath your skill set."

Carl leaned forward on the table. "You and I are on two different sides of a coin. You want me to stop what I am doing, and I want to keep doing what I do so I can make a lot of money. And, normally, we are talking about a shitload of money, Detective. I won't blow smoke up your ass. We have lots of people being paid off. We employ tons of people across the city. Ultimately, we represent a whole other economy."

Carrie looked incredulous. "Again, you think lecturing me about the virtues of fencing stolen goods is going to do something to improve your situation?"

"For our purposes, no. But, will you admit that there are people who put food on the table, pay their bills, and buy clothes with ill-gotten gains?"

Carrie, only one more snide comment from losing her temper, knew she must keep her cool and keep him talking. "Okay, I suppose I'll admit plenty of criminals feed their families. What does that have to do with anything?"

"I can see I am annoying you, so I'll get to the point. What do you think happens to our happy little criminal enterprise when a third party gets injected into the underworld and they have no idea what they are doing?" Carl folded his arms, waiting for an answer.

Carrie thought she understood the point he made. An entire economy, driven by illegal activity, suddenly turned up on its end by an outside force must be chaos in the underworld. "I suppose people stop making a shit load of money. So, they are really that hopelessly incompetent?"

"You said it, not me. And I won't say it. The Arrcado family has something up its tattooed sleeves with this group of incompetent buffoons. I have no idea what. Until something is done about this, I need to protect what is mine. Right now, I'm most interested in protecting my life, so I am throwing myself to your mercy. Something is going to go wrong some night and someone will get killed. I am a lover, not a fighter. I'll take protective custody over getting a bullet to the head, any day."

Vance and Carl worked in the criminal world for so long that nothing should have surprised either one of them. Both a high-end burglar and a fence so well-known their connections likely reached deep into city hall had sat in front of her and voiced concerns about whatever new development lingered just below the horizon. Carrie thought of her instructors at the police academy who had said "If you want to catch a rat, you need a rat. The best information often comes from the other rats."

At her side, her cell phone kept buzzing, but she ignored it while talking with Carl. She did not want to seem distracted. Right now, he gave her the best gauge yet on the underworld. A possibility rose up in Carrie's mind. Were things in the underworld shaping up so poorly they now laid their hopes on the police department to stop things before this criminal enterprise threw the balance too far out of hand? Something larger than either of them stirred the underworld pot, and that was never good.

As she glanced down at her phone screen, her breath caught in her throat. The normally reserved Keith called her twelve times in the last hour.

13

THE FIGHTING DEAD

Dirk woke up to the sound of an automotive engine purring down the road. Warm air blasted at his head from an unseen source, and he was no longer cold. Dirk remembered being cold and passing out but not what happened afterward.

Although unsure of where he was, the current situation suggested it might not be better than the previous. Since the gap in memory covered quite a bit of time, two questions stood out as needing sorting. The first question related to why his body hurt. The second, and possibly related, was who drove?

In the darkness of the back seat, the overwhelming scent of leather and automotive shampoo assaulted the senses. Like a leather store, the formerly living bovine flesh scent infused everything. The scent, while a little disconcerting, gave away who drove the car.

"Keith ... Keith?"

"Thank God, buddy. I was worried about you."

Dirk sat up and his head erupted in pain. "Where are we headed?"

"You need to go to the hospital. I figured something bad happened to you in the woods out there. You were laying on the shoulder of the street. Had you not thought to call me, I would have never found you."

"How did you find me?" Dirk still worked to clear the haze from his head and the conversation on the cell phone remained an abstract concept.

"You mentioned the boathouse. There is only one actual boathouse around a lake which also had a Ferris wheel. I took a guess but an educated one."

"Thank God for tha—Keith, you need to turn around."

"Look here, I know you are super detective and all, but take it from the advice of your pastor, you need a doctor to check you out. Unless you have forgotten, I found you unconscious along the side of the road. Also, I still have no idea what happened to your clothes."

Dirk became visibly more agitated. "You don't understand, Keith. I killed someone back there."

Keith brought the car to a halt along the side of the road. "You killed someone?"

Dirk lifted his hands and showed them. In the darkness, Keith likely could not make out the blood covering his hands. Pulling him into his car, he likely just threw his friend in and drove away. "Yes, it came to him or me and I chose me. We have to turn around now and call the police. We are fleeing the scene of a murder."

Keith shook his head and turned the car around, hammering down on the gas. Grabbing Keith's cell phone off the passenger seat, Dirk dialed Carrie. She did not answer, so he did the next best thing and called the police department's main line to report the murder. Thankfully, Keith would likely beat the on-duty homicide detective by about five minutes or more. He'd have to explain why they fled the crime scene. The body lay in the dark dampness of the woods, and Keith had no way to know that.

An hour later, Keith stood next to Dirk who sat on the back end of an open ambulance. Carrie, someone told him, had been held up interrogating a suspect but got the message and now made her way to the scene.

While the police mocked Dirk for conducting an investigation in his underwear, they let up upon seeing the unknown person in the woods with his head a puddle of blood, brain, and bone fragments. The paramedics tried to give Dirk fluids and meds, but Dirk waved off every attempt. Keith argued with Dirk, trying to convince him to accept the proper treatment being offered. The significant head wound he received at the warehouse could cause problems if left untreated.

After relating his story to the on-duty homicide detective, Dirk relaxed a little. "I really want to know what these scumbags thought they were doing. I don't know about this, Keith, but I have the sneaking suspicion someone knew I went to the warehouse and sent those two thugs down after me."

"Are you sure you don't want to go to the hospital and get checked out? You had quite a night, and no one would blame you. Don't forget, someone bashed your head in pretty good tonight. No telling how much damage they did to your noggin ... Who knows ... Maybe a few improvements?"

"You are so funny, you should get on stage, you know that." Dirk shrugged off the blanket on his shoulders. "Well, what do you say, old friend? We should probably start on that Harley Deluxe in bay one. Maybe order pizza while we work, what do you say?"

Keith cocked his head to the left and gave his friend a dubious look. "Dirk, if this is a joke, it isn't funny, given the circumstances."

"What? No joke. Fine, I'll head into the bay and start. You can order the pizza." Dirk took two steps forward and fell flat on his face.

DIRK AND KEITH had suffered a few narrow escapes over the years. They were shot at and had survived more than a few fistfights, and even a string of death threats had turned out to be credible. None of those instances scared Keith quite as much as sitting in the back of the ambulance with Dirk. Keith watched helplessly as his best friend's oxygen levels plummeted.

Whatever happened did significant damage. Muscling his way through the pain, Dirk managed to start the ball rolling to save his own life. However, the exertion came at a price. The paramedics failed to come up with a satisfactory explanation. One thought intracranial pressure the culprit. The other wondered if his brain chemistry fell so far out of balance his body shut down.

"Come on, Dirk, buddy. You have to make it. Carrie will never forgive me if I let you die on my watch." Keith wiped the tears from his eyes. Turning to the paramedics, he begged for more information. "What's happening to him?"

One of the paramedics, a young kid, turned to Keith and

said, "I don't know. All we can do is stabilize him and get back to the hospital."

The older paramedic, a parishioner in Keith's church and an old friend of Dirk's, looked worried and quickly glanced toward Keith. For a moment, the two mentally connected in a way few human beings could be. He just said simply, "Pastor Keith, now would be a great time to pray."

Dirk's face changed from the normal flesh tones to an ashen gray. The color faded from his lips to a disturbing blue, a condition Keith thought was called cyanosis. It never meant anything good. Keith simply would not accept his life-long friend quickly approached the moment of death.

Keith folded his hands and prayed harder than ever before. Squeezing his eyelids together, he begged God to come to their rescue. He brought up all the times Dirk faithfully attended services, how good he was to Claire, and finally how many people this servant of God helped.

His mind flashed through images of Claire. She would take it the hardest, not being able to understand why first her father and then Dirk were taken from her. She loved him more than it was possible to love an uncle. Carrie, of course, would be devastated. Keith thought, for a moment, of himself. He may never recover from losing Dirk, who had been at his side their entire lives.

The EKG machine barked out an ominous screech signaling the news that Dirk's heart no longer functioned in a life-sustaining way. The alarms bounced off the walls of the ambulance only amplifying the chaos to the point Keith wanted to jump out of the back of the ambulance and escape the horror.

The paramedics jumped to action, pulling out syringes

and tubes. They opened a dizzying array of bags and boxes, preparing for a pitched battle to keep Dirk alive or at least alive enough to do something more invasive at the hospital.

Keith opened his eyes and the surreal events playing out before him stopped his breath.

One paramedic sat on the bench next to Dirk's chest, and the other sat in a chair at the top of Dirk's head with his back toward the driver's compartment. Next to the paramedic on the bench sat, in a ghostly visage, the spectral image of Victor. Realizing that Keith could see him, he put his finger to his mouth and then wordlessly reached a hand into Dirk. Keith could not tell exactly, but to him, it looked like Victor reached directly into Dirk's heart.

Victor's face looked contemplative, as if listening to a far-off voice somewhere in the cosmos. The spirit's eyes darted around the room as if searching for something specific. Another few seconds passed, and Victor's mouth curled up into a smile. Keith was sure the specter never wore such a pastoral grin before. It looked reassuring, almost calming.

In a moment of oddly deafening silence, the machines stopped screaming in alarm, and the monitor reported a perfectly normal heart rhythm. Dirk's eyes even opened a little. Briefly, he looked at Victor and smiled before closing them again.

The young paramedic looked at the older one in disbelief. "You didn't do anything, did you?" His finger pointed accusingly at the more experienced paramedic.

The older paramedic pulled out a stethoscope and listened to Dirk's heart for a moment and checked on his breathing. "Nope, didn't do anything." He looked over at Keith. "I don't know what prayer you said, but if I am ever in the same situation, I certainly hope you are praying over me, Pastor Keith."

Keith still stared at the spot Victor previously occupied. Too speechless to respond to what the paramedic said, he looked at Dirk. The color was returning rapidly to his cheeks and lips.

By the time they got to the hospital, Dirk almost looked like his normal self again. Keith filled out Dirk's paperwork and made sure the police kept a guard on his room. As Dirk technically remained a suspect in the murder of a John Doe, likely they would have kept an eye on him anyway, but Keith insisted he needed protection since whoever did this would likely want another try as soon as they realized Dirk still counted among the living—unlike their compatriot lying cold in a drawer in the coroner's office.

A few minutes later, Carrie busted in the door of Dirk's intensive care room. She fell apart at the sight of Dirk unconscious with an IV in his arm and nasal cannula in his nose. Keith immediately took her in his arms. "It's all right. The doctor says he'll be fine."

Carrie stepped back from Keith and blew her nose on a tissue from a box on the small side table. "They told me he ... he ..."

"Coded?" a muffled, raspy voice replied.

Both Keith and Carrie turned to see Dirk looking at them from the hospital bed. He weakly smiled at them, and he'd only managed to one eye.

"Oh my God, Dirk." Carrie grabbed his hand and sat on the edge of the bed. "I don't know what I would have done if anything happened to you."

"I'm fine. And, Keith, tell Victor thanks. And no, I won't

buy him a larger television. That creepy son of a bitch's hand rummaged around in my chest," Dirk said, letting out a weak laugh. "He sure as hell can leave it on whenever he wants to after this though."

"Damn it, Dirk!" Carrie stammered. "This is all one big joke to you, isn't it? I threw up on my way over here worrying about you. I kept thinking about how to explain it all to Claire and how we never got the chance to do all the things we wanted to do and just ..."

Dirk held Carrie, now crying into his chest. "Not so rough. I feel like shit on a cracker. Thank God for a little help from the afterlife. Damn ghost is going to be impossible to live with after this."

Keith stepped over to the other side of the bed, opposite Carrie. "You knew he was there?"

"I did. If he hadn't come, the ambulance ride might have ended far differently." Dirk closed his eyes for a moment and winced suddenly.

"Are you all right? Should I get the doctor?" Carrie asked.

"No, I just have a massive headache. I'll be fine." Dirk shook his head weakly. "I need you to do something for me." Dirk exchanged glances with Carrie.

"Oh God, anything. Just, don't die on me ever again, okay?" Carrie leaned in close.

"Well, I can't promise I won't die ever, but for right now, I want you to find that asshole responsible for all of this."

"Babe, there isn't a hole deep enough on this planet for this scumbag to hide."

14

EVEN THE PERFECT MAKE MISTAKES SOMETIMES

In spite of his injuries, the doctor thought Dirk would be back home in a couple of days. They just wanted to make sure he ate and drank without issue and his oxygen levels stayed consistent. Twice during their visit, the doctor mentioned the oddity of having a patient just pop back into a normal heart rhythm.

Over Dirk's dinner of hospital food, Dirk, Carrie, and Keith talked about the two cases. Carrie shared what Carl told her. With Dirk out of commission, Keith took up the slack on the burglary investigation, which now turned into a case of attempted homicide.

Keith and Carrie spent the next morning at the warehouse, where they found it all exactly as Dirk said. Tracks in the stone told the story of where Dirk fell and was then dragged away from the side of the building. Little else of consequence revealed itself.

As Carrie climbed out of the car at the side of the road

where Keith found Dirk, her cell phone rung to the tone she assigned to the precinct. "Detective Pettygrew," she answered.

"Detective, this is the chief. I heard about Dirk. Don't worry, forensics is about to clear him. It was definitely self-defense."

A wave of relief washed over her. While she knew her boyfriend lacked the capability to commit cold-blooded murder, she also knew having evidence to support that theory was all a judge and jury cared about. "Well, that is great news. I still want a protective detail on him, if that is all right to call in a solid?"

"Carrie, I will expend every dime I can ferret out to protect him. He was working a case for us and got hurt in the process. At least, a case possibly tied to ours. And Dirk is one of our own."

"Thanks, Chief, I'll tell him you said that. He'll appreciate it. By the way, how did the thing with Officer Collins and Sergeant Patrick work out last night?"

"I don't know what you are talking about, Carrie. What do you mean?"

"I sent the two of them over to pick up Vance Deluca last night to put him in protective custody. I wanted to make sure no one could get to him before we sorted everything out."

"Carrie, I think we have a problem. I saw Sergeant Patrick last night before I left. He stayed at the front desk all evening and never left. Which means Collins didn't bother to bring the good sergeant because he thought he could handle it alone. Worse yet, it's possible he didn't want any additional prying eyes to see what he and Vance discussed. Either way, this doesn't sound good."

"Oh crap, I should have checked, Chief." Carrie realized

she potentially screwed up by putting a suspected dirty cop on the trail of a potential prosecution witness. "This is my fault."

"Carrie, you are better than this. Pull yourself together, Detective. First things first. I'll send a cruiser over to Deluca's and check that out. Stay in touch. I'll need you. Don't beat yourself up. I'll do that later. Right now, we need to circle the wagons on this." Sensing self-deprecation in Carrie's voice, she added, "Yes, Detective, you screwed up. But now you need to focus on getting back to work."

Carrie hit the disconnect button on the phone and stared out at the tree line. She'd made a couple of mistakes in the past, but this was a doozy. If Collins was a crooked cop, she sent the instrument of Vance Deluca's demise directly to his doorstep. Collins participated in the interrogation, listening to every word of the conspiracy unfold and impassively taking in everything to report to his handlers.

Carrie watched Keith examining the ground where he found Dirk. The reality dropped on her like a ton of rocks falling from an unseen cliff. She didn't want him to see her like this. She knew seeing her cry would pull his heart out of his ribcage, but it was too late to hide her emotions.

"Carrie, what's wrong? What happened?"

Tears streamed down from her face. She wondered for a moment if the situation with Collins or Dirk distressed her more. Perhaps a little of both, all rolled into one. It started so well with her interrogation and then ended like this. Maybe the lack of sleep had finally caught up with her.

Keith always knew what she needed and when she needed it. He stepped back and grabbed her hands. Lifting her chin, he stared into her eyes. "Believe it or not, I feel exactly the same way right now."

"No, you don't, Keith." She pushed his hands down. "I may have just gotten someone killed. Sure, a scumbag criminal but still a human being, and I am responsible for his death. I made the kind of mistake I can't simply undo, and I have no idea how to make this right. Dirk is in the hospital and I never told him all the things I needed to say. How did this go so wrong?"

Keith understood she wasn't upset specifically about the mistake. She more likely referred to how sideways the case went on its own.

"He died, Keith. Even for a few moments, we lost him. If Victor hadn't gotten involved, how do we go on after something like that?"

Keith let go of her hands and leaned against her car. Folding his hands on his chest, he let out a big sigh. "But, he was there to help. I don't know what motivations drive that protoplasmic weirdo, but he stepped in. I want to tell you something. Sometimes, I feel like a complete fraud. People come to me all the time for answers, and half the time, I feel like I have none to give. I can't even tell you anything to make you feel better because I am not sure what I can even tell myself."

"Oh, stop it. Of the three of us, you are the most together."

"I'm really not. I froze, Carrie. When that heart monitor went into alarm, I didn't know what to do. It felt like someone else sitting there. You'd think being a man of faith, actually knowing someone in the afterlife, would make my faith stronger than anyone. In that ambulance, for a moment, I doubted everything."

He took a deep breath. "Do you know why I never settled

into a full-time call? The synod has been after me for years to take one, and I have just kept them at arm's length. Every Sunday morning, I stand up there and do my best, but deep inside of me, I worry that I will never be good enough, have enough faith, never serve enough. I worry that I don't accept a full-time call because I can't accept the fact that if I fail that failure hurts infinitely more."

Carrie regarded her longtime friend and brother figure. She always thought of him as a proverbial rock. Unflappable to the point of being annoying, Keith stood out as the voice of reason when things came apart at the seams. More than just their pastor, friend, and fellow investigator, he made up the fabric keeping them all together. "Keith, I never realized you had those feelings."

Keith put up his hand. "I'm not done. Every time the three of us are together, I feel whole. Like pieces of me are missing until we come together. Alone, I have doubts. You and Dirk make up parts of who I am. Shoot, even Victor brings a piece to finish the picture. When we are together, I'm complete and can do anything. You guys are my superpower. I have to learn to accept the fact that I am not a full-time anything because that is not the plan for me right now, no matter how much that question bothers me. I can't tell you what happened to Dirk back there. Maybe that was exactly what was supposed to happen. I have no idea. Right now, we have a job to do, and this is exactly where I am supposed to be.

"I don't know what happened back there with your bad guy, but I do know this. You are a hell of a good cop. Yes, you made a mistake, but you are overworked and tired. You need rest and everyone can see that, not just me. You are being so hard on yourself because you expect perfection and hold yourself to an unattainable standard. What I am trying to tell you is that it is all right to make a mistake. Even a doozy like this."

"Thanks, Keith. I just hope the chief will see it that way." Carrie hadn't given any real thought to her own physical condition. She drove herself to the proverbial end while working this case.

For the rest of the morning, they went over the crime scene again. Other than the things the crime scene lab already picked up, little more of interest materialized.

Carrie called for updates on Dirk, and it sounded like his recovery tracked well. She wanted nothing more than to bring him home and take care of him. *His home,* she reminded herself. Hopefully, one day, it would be their home. Her mind wandered, not for the first time, to the idea of a wedding and a pregnant version of herself, standing on their front porch.

Later that afternoon, her cell phone rang again, waking her up from a catnap. Melonie Dixon sighed on the other line, informing her Vance Deluca's body had been recovered in his apartment, and he had been dead for some time. Officer Collins suspiciously vanished from the world, no longer answering his cell phone or texts. The patrol car signed out by the patrolman from the station sat abandoned in the parking lot of an equally abandoned department store. Officially, the chief signed the paperwork making him a wanted man. For the moment, she left it buried in the lower desk drawer, unwilling to accept Carrie's instincts were so wrong.

Carrie thought about what Keith said and found a modicum of solace, allowing her to drift off to sleep and combat fitful dreams.

15

THE WATER DEPARTMENT AND OTHER DANGEROUS ORGANIZATIONS

"All right, Dirk, let's sit you up." The doctor helped Dirk lean forward. "Tell me, how are you feeling?"

Dirk smiled at the doctor. "Actually, pretty well. I don't know what you put in that applesauce you insist on feeding us every lunch, but it is very therapeutic. And I tip my hat to the chef for making the meal taste less like shoe leather and more like leather still on the cow. Nice touch."

"Smart-ass. Hospital food isn't supposed to taste good. We don't want assholes like you sticking around too long." The doctor put a stethoscope up to Dirk's chest. "Take a deep breath for me and then let it out slowly."

A woman behind them cleared her throat. "Sorry to interrupt the witty banter, boys, are you having a moment, or can a lady join you?"

"Thank God, my savior has arrived. Carrie, I can't tell you what awful things the doc did to me." Dirk faked a pleading glance.

"Oh yeah, did he make you a eunuch or something?"

The doctor put his stethoscope back around his neck. "Worse, tonight the cafeteria is making meatloaf."

Carrie scrunched up her nose in obvious disgust. "Ewww, my cooking is far less likely to kill you."

"Dirk, as your doctor, I can't explain to you what happened. I only know that we are damn lucky you are still alive. I want Carrie to keep a close eye on you over the next few days. If anything seems out of the ordinary, you need to call me." The doctor scrunched up his forehead at Dirk. "In my twenty years of practicing medicine, I can tell you there have been a handful of times someone on the other side must be looking out for one patient or another."

"You have no idea how right you are." Dirk opened the small duffel bag Carrie brought with clothes from the house. "Well, let's see what she brought for me to wear. Honey, a leather dog collar and chaps? It's after Labor Day."

The doctor shook his head at Dirk.

"Yep," Carrie said, "he's fine, Doctor. Back to his same old self."

Dirk dressed. "How's the investigation coming?"

"Forensics is having a field day with this one. There is evidence all over Vance's apartment. Collins didn't go gentle on him."

"Carrie, you really have no idea if Collins did this or not. For all you know, it could be some other lowlife with a score to settle. Forensics can put them in the same apartment, but you have no idea who did whatever ass kicking."

Carrie frowned at his comment. "Well, either way, hair follicles place Collins in the apartment. I have to pull a few extra duty days for letting the boy out of my sight. The inquiry board pointed out that I screwed up by leaving him without adult supervision. My biggest task right now is to put the little ass weasel behind bars."

Dirk remembered Carrie mentioning Collin's martial arts training. He swallowed concerns about the possibility of her pursuing someone with black belt level training in martial arts. "Hey, whatever happened about the guy in the woods?"

"Oh yeah, didn't have a chance to tell you. After pestering the medical examiner's office repeatedly, they finally let me check out the body. I also ran over to the ballistics lab to see what they found out about the gun, belonging to the guy whose brains you bashed in, could tell us. You are never going to believe what I found out."

Dirk raised one eyebrow. "My guy was Mafia?"

Carrie instantly went from a smug smile to a pained grimace. "How in God's great creation did you figure that out. You've been cooped up in this hospital for days, and suddenly, you have a clairvoyant moment? Yes, Mafia, an Arrcado too. Don't say Victor told you, or I swear you will have a whole bunch of new injuries they will be treating you for."

"And I am guessing a fairly junior hit man too." Dirk ducked as Carrie swung a pillow at his head. "Sorry, darling, but they tied me up and forgot about my feet. That's a rookie mistake. Although I didn't hear the woman clearly, the guy spoke Mafioso like a pro. Probably from the streets of New York or somewhere around there, based on the accent. He didn't shoot me right there on the property which meant either they had a place in mind or they were afraid to do it on church property. Then there was the way that asshole entered the woods. Maybe a junior league hit man but not his first rodeo. The bastard took time walking into the woods, making it harder for me to take advantage of the situation. This guy was careful and measured. Good thing he didn't know about the bike lock."

Carrie sat down on the bed. "I have to admit, Dirk, when you get a good case, you sure do go all in. The only way you could ever top this one is like space aliens or something. Seriously though, this is the second time this week the Mafia became a subject of my discussions. If you are going to pick a fight, you sure do know how to pick them."

Dirk chuckled. "What can I say, some are born to greatness, some men find greatness, and some men beat a Mafia guy's brains out in a dark forest wearing nothing but his undies. You said Arrcado? What would the Arrcados want with low-level theft? Way below their weight class, to be sure. At any rate, I want to go home. I think I need to do a little prepping if I am getting myself into a Mafia war."

"I am reasonably sure that is against doctor's orders. And mine as well. No Mafia wars for you." Carrie frowned at him.

The doctor insisted on bringing him downstairs in a wheelchair although Dirk wanted to walk out under his own power. The doctor explained they used it as an insurance policy against patients hanging around the hospital trying to score some of the great culinary delights and ogling the staff's classically masculine physiques.

Carrie rebuked his complaints and admonished him to follow the doctor's orders. After a few witty suggestions about what she should tell him to do, Keith and Carrie helped Dirk into the car, and they headed for home.

After a quick stop at Del Rio Taco, for a taco deluxe meal for Dirk, they made their way toward Dirk's place. When they turned onto his street, Dirk's stomach clenched into a thousand knots. A large orange sign advised caution. A front-end loader sat off to one side, and four men, in no hurry to do much of anything, stood in a four-foot-deep hole in full view of Dirk's house.

Keith said, "For the past few days, this road crew camped out in that pit. They don't seem like they have gotten very far. "

"While you were in the hospital, Keith and I asked those workers how long they thought the work would continue. None of the men working in the pit could give us a definitive answer."

Dirk recoiled at their presence. "Wait, stop."

Keith pulled the car to the side of the road. "What's up, buddy?"

"Those are the guys who worked there all week?"

"Yeah, the same guys have been here every time I've been by. Why?"

"Do they see us?" Dirk continued.

"No, not yet. Dirk, what are you getting at?" Carrie asked.

"Do you remember me having to stay at your apartment two years ago because the water main burst in front of the neighbor's house?"

Carrie thought for a moment. "Yes, it took a week to fix, as I recall."

Dirk turned to Carrie, sitting next to him in the passenger seat. "There's no water main on that side of the street, all the utilities are joint trenched on the other side. Why are they working there?"

Carrie squinted back at Dirk. "Because they don't want anyone to call the legit water department, complaining about the lack of water. Keith, let's use the driveway behind us and turn around."

KEITH BACKED the car out of the driveway and drove around the corner. Another street backing up against Dirk's allowed Carrie to crawl through the underbrush to Dirk's backyard. She hopped the fence and quietly entered the back door. Carrie crawled up to the window and gazed through the curtains at the fake road crew. Dirk's house sat on a fairly steep rise from the street. He'd remarked it gave him great drainage, and she complained her car bottomed out every time she pulled into the driveway. Right now, the heightened position afforded a bird's eye view of the men where she wouldn't be noticed. She called for Keith to come up a side street and then turn away from Dirk's house to see how the men reacted to the sight of the car.

As soon as the car came to the corner of Dirk's street, a gruff man in a yellow road vest pointed and tapped one of the others on the shoulder. Three of the other men in the pit grabbed something below where Carrie could see. One of the men pulled whatever he carried a little too high, and another suspicious man yelled at him. The receiver of the verbal abuse quickly lowered an automatic weapon. Keith, after catching his breath, turned the corner and drove away from the house.

Dirk, although still recovering, demonstrated his instincts were as sharp as a tack. The team had learned to rely on those instincts. This time, it saved them all from a trap set for him and whoever stood in the way. Those men waited for Dirk to come home to finish the job the man and the woman at the warehouse could not.

Jesus Christ, Dirk, what the hell have you gotten us into?

DIRK STAYED low in the back seat, and Keith discerned the furtive actions of the work crew in the site the moment he turned the corner. "Yeah, buddy, I hate to say this, but you were right. Someone is watching your house, and I don't think they want to talk, sell you vacuums, or save your eternal soul."

Dirk's cell phone rang. "It's Carrie." Dirk hit the accept button. "Hey, babe. Uh-huh. Yeah, let's meet up somewhere. Maybe back at the station. What's that? No, not there. They are going to watch the shop if they thought enough to watch the house. Okay, see you then.

"Keith, head to the station. We'll meet up there." Dirk let out a sigh. "Sorry, buddy."

"What's to feel sorry for? We got into this together and we'll get through it."

THE BRIEFING ROOM of the police department sprawled out across the floor it shared with the Detective Pit. In addition to serving as a conference room, they conducted smaller training sessions in it. The other half of the floor held the Detective Pit. In one of the smaller rooms, Dirk sat, as the sole occupant of a huge black conference table built for twenty, fingering a half cup of coffee.

The feeling of powerlessness crushed his soul. He managed to drag everyone he loved into the crosshairs of a lethal criminal organization, and still the reason eluded him. Carrie ran off to brief the chief about the situation. Keith stood in the hallway making phone calls to the shop and the church. The chief walked off to make arrangements for what everyone hoped only would take a week or less. She declared their team under police protection for the moment and refused to let them leave the building without police protection.

The situation fell so far out of his control that now the three of them hid like cowards.

In the meantime, Dirk reviewed the crime scene photos from Vance's murder. Whoever did this—Dirk was still not completely convinced Collins committed the murder—did a particularly brutal job. Vance looked like a bag of meatloaf someone left out too long. With his head beaten in, the extra bullet wound to the chest added nothing. A needless gesture since the medical examiner determined the man was likely close to death when the shot was fired. There was also a hastily penned note in Italian that read "Così finisce per tutti i traditori," which translated to "Thus it ends for all traitors."

Dirk did what came naturally to him and offered a measure of comfort. Spreading out the evidence Carrie brought, he formed piles. A collection of crime scene photos, photos taken at the burglary scene, photos of the warehouse, and copies of the spreadsheets from the archbishop were all sorted. The activity was enough to keep his restless mind occupied and less inclined to obsess about the danger they found themselves in.

Putting the things aside likely having nothing to add to the question of why anyone committed these crimes, Dirk made copies of everything else and made notes on the photocopies. The case files contained little of interest with the exception of a few notes on Vance's house. According to the crime scene officer, the door wasn't smashed in. Likely, Vance let the assailant in. An equally good chance stood out in Dirk's mind that Vance recognized Collins from the interrogation.

One additional note caught his eye. A neighbor, walking out of her home to take out the garbage, noticed what she called simply "another fellow." According to her, a police officer, matching Collins's description, walked in the door and then one other person walked in moments later. Scanning the bottom of the report, he read the signature on the report from a tech named Rodriguez.

"Hey, Detective," Dirk said, glancing at Carrie, "can you have a crime scene tech named Rodriguez call up to the briefing room. I have a question.

"Sure, but why do you want to talk to Hector?"

Dirk frowned at the note in his hand and then looked up. "He talked to someone at the crime scene and made a note in the margins of the evidence report about it. I'd like to know a little more about the conversation."

Dirk went back to sorting, but his mind kept going back to Hector's note. It wasn't a loose end the police normally missed, and he ruminated over it for a while. If a witness came forward, why didn't a detective follow up on this?

The phone in the center of the large conference room let out an almost deafening ringing noise. "Briefing room," Dirk said matter-of-factly. He never answered one of the phones in the precinct before and guessed at the proper way to answer it.

"Detective, this is Hector Rodriguez," a voice answered on the other line. A moment later, the door opened and Carrie walked in and plopped down into one of the chairs lining the large table.

"No, not detective, I'm a private investigator, working with the department on a case, and I came across something you can help me with." Dirk expected the tech to voice concern over the phone call, but Carrie must have already told him to cooperate. "In your notes, you mentioned that a neighbor, Mrs. Flores, mentioned a third person entering Vance's apartment. I am curious, did you tell anyone about it."

"Yes, sir, I did," he replied in a thick Latino accent. "I told Detective Higgins."

Dirk pointed to Detective Higgins's name on the sheet of paper, and Carrie nodded her understanding. "I see, you told Detective Higgins?" Dirk repeated the information so Carrie could go out and ask. Likely, faced with a mountain of paperwork related to the case, Higgins just forgot to follow up on the lead. It was not uncommon that a lead with little or no backing fell through the cracks.

"Okay, thanks. I appreciate the information. I'll let you know if I need anything else." Dirk hung up the phone before saying anything to Carrie. Outside the glassed walls of the briefing room, Carrie engaged in an animated discussion with Higgins. He showed her a few notes on his desk and Carrie nodded.

Returning to the briefing room, she addressed Dirk. "Okay, well, they planned on talking with her, but it fell to a low priority. Apparently, the woman is hard of hearing and afraid of anyone not bearing a Latin-sounding last name.

They are sending Richard Ramirez over right away. It is his beat, and she'll talk to him. Is there anything you want ask?"

Dirk scanned the note from Hector again. "Yes, description. See if they can tell you anything about this guy. I wonder if Collins let him in. She might be hard of hearing, but it's her eyesight I am most interested in."

Dirk realized his mistake as pain played across Carrie's face. The last thing anyone needed to remind her of right now was that Vance died because of her. However, nothing could be done about that fact, and hiding from it wouldn't bring the boy back.

Dirk looked into her eyes. "Sweetie, I know you don't want to hear this right now, but you are blaming yourself for something that wasn't your fault. You are beating yourself up over nothing at all. The chief has forgiven you, the other detectives have all made mistakes before, I love you no matter what, and Keith is like your big brother. No one here is going to judge you except for you. And you will judge yourself far more harshly than anyone. You need to stop this self-flagellation and concentrate on the task at hand."

Carrie wiped a tear from her eye. The steely determination of Detective Pettygrew returned. "So, what do you have here? We arrived at arts and craft time with Dirk." She talked for the sake of talking at this point. She knew his methods and loved to watch him work.

"Okay, so we have two different things going on here which seem related by one event. My unfortunate run-in with that pipe or whatever they hit me with."

Carrie raised a finger. "Okay then, how does my church break-in link to all of this, or are we barking up the wrong tree? I mean, perhaps you are just really that unlucky."

"Oh no, I am definitely getting lucky. That is another matter though."

"Not if we don't get out of here, Dirk. I am pretty sure the chief isn't going to let us move into the station for the long haul. We need some sort of plan." Carrie's phone rang and she held up a finger, pausing Dirk. "Detective Pettygrew."

Dirk watched Carrie's face as her expressions changed from surprise to concern and back to surprise again. "Say that again," she asked the person on the other line. "Okay, thanks for letting us know. I am a little shocked, but that helps fill in a few of those missing pieces. Yeah, don't worry, I'll tell him he needs to pick better enemies."

Dirk registered genuine shock on Carrie's face. "What's the matter honey?"

"Dirk, does the name Bruno Scarpolo ring a bell?"

Dirk shook his head. "Not really. Should it?"

"I can't believe I finally have one on you. However, for the rest of your life, you are going to remember that name. I just hope we can make it a long life. You, my lover, have chosen to stick your nose in the business of the Arrcado Mafia family. Bruno is a cousin and hit man to the Arrcado family. That call came from our good friends at the FBI RICO squad in New York who flew down here to pull a little sting on the boys crawling out of the hole outside of your house. They used a remote-control version of your car and parked it right in front of your house. Bruno and his boys lit up the car. The FBI rolled up and arrested the lot of them."

Dirk raised an eyebrow and then scrunched his forehead together in thought. A surprised expression emerged. "Exactly what do you mean by lit up the car? My house is behind the car."

"Okay, so you are going to need new windows and paint. But, focus here, Dirk. They caught the guys and quickly identified them as Tony Arrcado's soldiers. The RICO guys send their thanks. They wanted a reason to nab Bruno. He doesn't get out much, spending most of his time drinking expensive Russian vodka and playing video games."

Dirk's eyes flew open wide, and his mouth opened slightly in shock. "Yeah, but my house?"

"Totally missing the bigger picture here, Dirk. We know who is behind the church thefts."

"I'll have to repaint." Dirk sat dumfounded at the idea of the house being shot up.

"Focus on the bright side, the FBI will gladly pay for any damage. Their sting operation netted a big fish they have had their eyes on for years."

Dirk thought back to them almost pulling up in front of the house. A wave of relief washed over him. Had they not noticed the oddly placed work crew, that could have really been his car and those bullets may have gone into them and not just an empty car and siding. In reality, this situation all worked out for the best, and Dirk smiled at the little miracle.

It still didn't answer the question about what connection the Arrcados could have to the church and why they would want to steal anything.

The next morning, Carrie went back to Dirk's house with a huge police escort and grabbed enough clothes to sustain them during the brief hiatus. After sleeping on an uncomfortable cot in the basement of the precinct, Dirk changed clothes and got as clean as possible. Taking an unused desk, he continued his quest to tie the ends of the complex case together. At the end of the day, a nun and an archbishop still hoped he would find answers, regardless of where they were currently hiding out.

He did a search through the police database for any of Tony Arrcado's known associates. Records for Tony Arrcado and family spread across the screen in front of him. Dirk scanned through all known Arrcado associates for anyone who had an ax to grind with the church or a reason to co-opt the church for their own designs.

Finding nothing, Dirk pulled up all known family affiliates making up the big fish in the relatively small sea of Virginia-based crime families. Very little information turned up, with the exception of a few photos of Tony as a child. Tony Arrcado's brother had wanted to hand over the reins of the family to his son, Jimmy, as he died of cancer in a hospital in Cleveland, Ohio. However, numerous reports indicated Jimmy not only did not want the responsibility but also proved to be a less than an adept criminal. When Jimmy's father passed away, the family control transferred to Uncle Tony.

Going to the internet, Dirk searched news articles about the family for any shred of evidence. Tons of news clippings about arrests, suspicions, murders, weddings, and funerals were presented at the top of the search results. Nothing the police database did not already capture. An online photo album from a wedding, which took place in the tiny Italian village of San Vito, carried tons of photos. Men stared back at them in fine suits while women made funny faces and struck comical poses in fine dresses. The photos showed a younger version of the family. Tony Arrcado, then twenty years younger, sported a full head of hair, lightly peppered with gray.

Carrie joined Dirk and remarked on the younger Jimmy

standing between two adults. The kid still had not done much changing, based on the picture in the album. Another child stood next to Jimmy, gazing at something off camera. According to the notes, the children were not his but belonged to his deceased brother. They were his niece and nephew.

Dirk's heart skipped a beat.

Dirk yelled over to Keith who was at another desk working on church things remotely. "Keith, come over here."

Keith pulled off his headphones with an annoyed growl. "What is so important you have to interrupt the Lord's work?"

"Look." Dirk pointed at the photo.

Keith just shook his head. "I don't see what you are seeing, mi amigo, you are going to have to—" Stopping mid-sentence, Keith backed away from the screen. "Holy shit."

Half of the officers in the room let out a chuckle because the majority of them were either Keith's parishioners or at least knew him as a pastor.

"I don't believe it," Keith continued.

A few moments piling through criminal records sent chills through them all at the same time. The little girl's facial features remained remarkably the same over the years. Although she lost some weight, there could be no mistaking it. Jimmy Arrcado's younger sister, the niece of Tony Arrcado, answered to the name Carolyn.

16

BOMBS NEVER DISCRIMINATE

As they excitedly relayed their story to Carrie, she listened impartially and tried to make sense of what the two most important men in her life tried to explain.

"Boys, I understand, you are super excited. However, I'm not a private investigator. I need proof before I rush in with the cavalry. So, we need something more than just what you two are thinking. Clue the rest of us in."

CLAIRE JAMES, or Claire Bentley, as she sometimes liked to call herself, rolled to a stop in the parking lot of Bentley Motorcycle Repair. After carefully spending her free time that summer restoring a 1972 Honda CB 250, it became her pride and joy. Every part came from someone she loved, the frame a present from her uncle Dirk, the gas tank from her mother, spokes and other items from Keith and Carrie. Completely restoring the cycle, she put an amazing amount of miles on it. Everything she needed to know she learned from her uncle, and she cherished the time with him. Spending as much time fixing motorcycles as she could, she dreaded the day high school ended and college, likely at a faraway university, would begin.

She eyed the parking lot and found it shockingly empty. Ordinarily, the head mechanic, Dirk, Keith, or any number of other people milled around. Today, she made up the only parking lot visitor. Pulling out her own key, she thought about the pieces of a transmission waiting for a customer before any new projects began.

She flipped out the kickstand, stepped over the top of the bike, and took off her helmet. Carefully hanging it off the handlebar, she made her way toward the building. She paused to dust out her hair, dyed auburn the night before. When her mother asked, she had told her she was trying something. Backing up, she admired the beautiful Honda, as it gleamed in the sunshine with its period accurate colors and markings.

Inside the shop, Victor paced back and forth through the office. He normally watched television while other people worked in the shop or the business sat closed for the night. Staring out the window at her, the specter appeared overly agitated. Something bothered the ghost and normally he avoided the door so people would not call the police to report an intruder in the building, something that happened at least once a year.

Victor got himself worked up over the smallest of things. Once he went on for a week complaining about her uncle's attempt to move the couch from one side of the room to another. Dirk relented to keep the peace.

As Claire approached the door, Victor became increasingly more agitated. Not knowing what else to do, Claire resolved to open the door and find out what put a bee in his otherworldly bonnet.

Years ago, someone broke into the shop, so Dirk and Keith put in a reinforced door and brickwork to make it harder for anyone to break in, and coupled with the tempered glass the previous owner installed, hearing any conversation inside the office was next to impossible. Victor's yells came through as nothing more than unintelligible babble.

As she twisted the key in the deadbolt, it struck Claire how easy the key turned. It felt like no one had locked the door, which she thought impossible since she locked the door herself the night before. After she stepped into the office, Victor instantly rushed her, enveloping her in a ghostly shield-like covering, and knocked her to the floor. Before she uttered a single word, Victor yelled, "Hold on, Claire, I've got you."

A fraction of a second later, the world outside of Victor's embrace became a ball of flame and indescribable violence. Shards of brick, mortar, glass, and Victor's new television flew in every conceivable direction.

The large garage doors on the building crumpled under the concussive force of the explosives wired deep inside the building with a trigger mechanism wired near the door. A thin aluminum structure, passing as the roof, launched over the walls and into the parking lot. Shards of wood, metal, and glass of the business's exterior pushed out in every direction, sending it flying into Claire's carefully restored Honda, knocking the prized possession over on its side, smashing the mirrors Carrie gave her.

Victor's spiritual energy surrounded Claire and took the brunt of the concussion from the massive explosion. Changing his own physical properties protected Claire from the worst of the blast. It did nothing to control the sound, but it protected her from the lethal effects. She would definitely be worse for the wear, but Claire stood the best chance of surviving the un-survivable.

As she sat up in the rubble of her first real place of employment and her uncle's livelihood, she knew Victor saved her thanks to his quick thinking. Claire only sensed a high-pitched squeal and a buzzing suggesting something was terribly wrong. She tried to stand, but waves of nausea overtook her. Grabbing a hold of the nearest thing, Claire collapsed into the shattered remains of her uncle's desk.

KEITH'S PHONE rang and he juggled it out of his pocket. "Keith here."

Dirk watched with sudden interest as Keith's face changed colors. Emotion was not something the normally unflappable man ever showed. Talking in hushed tones into the phone, Keith shot Dirk a panicked glance. Dirk felt ice water bubble up in his veins. He knew, without knowing, that something else had gone terribly wrong.

Carrie, seeing the exchange, also noticed the less than subtle change in Keith's demeanor. Getting to his side first, she grabbed Keith by the arm. "Keith, what's wrong?"

Keith mouthed nonexistent words, as if someone magically removed his vocal cords. Carrie gulped for air as something in her friend's face suggested that whatever it was that shook Keith to his core likely carried significant implications for them.

Dirk, read the alarm clearly in his lack of expression and slumped shoulders. Instinctively putting his hand on his friend's shoulder, he asked, "What's the matter, buddy?"

"It's ... it's Claire, Dirk. She went to the shop. The explosion destroyed the entire building. That was Helen on the phone."

Dirk fell to his knees in the little hallway. Seeing the commotion, the chief left her office and made a beeline for the trio.

Keith realized what he said and rushed to add the rest of the details. "Dirk, she'll be all right. She is pretty banged up right now though. They need us to go to the hospital." He pulled his friend from the floor, and the two embraced.

Carrie joined them, and for a moment, the three stood there and allowed the horror to wash over them like a tidal wave set loose by an unseen earthquake below the murky depths of the ocean representing their lives. The bad guys broke the unwritten rule stating you never targeted minor children. Dirk knew the target was him and not likely Claire —a fact that did nothing to lessen the sting.

The embrace was not of pity but one of support. In everything, Carrie and Keith supported him and, by extension, Claire. A private investigator, a police detective, and a pastor stood there holding each other. The group suffered a wound, not a mortal wound, but a wound never the less.

"The injuries are severe but not life threatening. They'll keep her in the critical care ward, for now. They think they will move her to the general hospital the day after tomorrow.

She lost her hearing, but the doctors are confident it will come back."

"I have to go." Dirk absently patted his pockets for car keys. "I need to ... go ..."

THE CHIEF PULLED Carrie away from the others. "I don't expect you to stay here after this, but I need you to be careful. These guys want Dirk dead, and that puts you in the crosshairs too. I can't stomach the idea of having something happen to you."

"I understand, Chief."

"You need to be strong, Carrie. Stronger than ever before. I will put every piece of this department at your disposal to protect the three of you, but you need to remember that I didn't train just another officer. You are mine, and I know you are stronger than anything they can throw at you. You have all the skill you need to do whatever comes next. I am assigning you a protective detail for now. Take care of those two." Melonie Dixon's eyes welled up as she looked over at Keith trying to console Dirk.

Chief brushed a tear from Carrie's eye. "It sucks when someone attacks your family. We are police officers and we take care of our own. Dirk and Keith are part of your family and, by extension, a part of ours. An attack on them is an attack on all of us."

Carrie turned from the chief with renewed determination. "All right, boys. Time to go. We need to see that girl of ours, she needs us right now." She ushered the two down the stairs and out to her car. From now on, they traveled only in a squad car. At the very least, Carrie's cruiser carried enough weapons for a small army. In the event of anything going wrong, the firepower to save themselves waited only at an arm's length. Anything short of a grenade launcher sat in the trunk or in the front seat in the gun lock.

As she drove, Dirk sat mutely next to her, letting out an occasional sob. Carrie knew how important Claire was to him and to her as well. Whoever was doing this almost killed a defenseless teenager, an offense begging for an answer. The dirtbags who did this would pay, and the fine would be costly. Carrie wondered silently if she could contain herself in the event she came face to face with whoever did this. For a moment, she wondered if she even wanted to control herself.

Running lights and siren, Carrie sped through the intersections with almost reckless abandon. Keith attempted to remind Carrie to slow down and take her time, but he stopped talking when she telegraphed a message through the rearview mirror. *If you value your life, shut the hell up.*

After they pulled into the parking lot, Keith moved to Dirk's door, opened it, and stood there waiting. Dirk stared at the dashboard, not showing any acknowledgment of the world around him. Something deep inside of him broke, and Carrie knew that piece needed repairing. He needed a little TLC and a pep talk to retrieve his fighting spirit. She needed both men on top of their game if things got bad.

Almost killing Claire stood out as a glaring strategic mistake for the perpetrators. Once Dirk came around, he would either make them pay or die trying.

Crossing in front of the car, their assigned escort parked across the parking lot, and one man stayed with that unit while the other came over to Carrie. She was relieved to see the wiry Deputy Smiles, or Smiley, as she knew him. He and Dirk were old friends, and she knew he could be counted on in a fight.

"Dirk, you need to step out of the car." Carrie put her hand on his shoulder.

"I failed, Carrie. I failed her. I made a promise to her dad and I failed." Tears streamed down Dirk's face.

"Dirk, look at me." She turned his head to face her. Staring into her longtime boyfriend's eyes, she wanted to ensure every word sunk in. "Nobody failed anyone. They just got one step ahead of us. Yes, we should have probably kept people away from the shop until it was swept for threats, but that doesn't mean we failed. It was them who failed.

"Look, Claire may seem all grown up, but inside, she is a scared little girl, and she needs you right now. You are her Uncle Dirk. To her, you are a superhero and she loves you more than anything in this world. If you don't get up there right now, you'll let these bastards win this round. You're the strongest son of a bitch I know. You feel bad right now, but I know you are going to rise up and find someone's ass to kick. When you do, I'm certainly going to look the other way until you take it out of their hide. Right now, a little girl is scared and needs you to put on your cape and fly to her rescue.

"You stopped a serial killer and led us to save a girl's life. A quitter doesn't do that. You are no quitter, and I need you to grab your bootstraps and give them a big pull. We have a whole other round to fight, and it could start any second now."

Dirk stared at the dashboard for a moment and then reached out with both of his hands, putting them flat on the faux leather interior. "My little girl is up there, and she needs her Uncle Dirk." He let out a sigh and exited the car.

Three minutes later, they stood outside the door of her room. A dizzying array of medical equipment lay around, most in its original packaging, thankfully indicating it was brought in but not necessary. The doctor explained the bruises were deeper than superficial and the full extent of the injuries might take days to manifest. Her internal organs received a terrific jolt from the concussive force. However, being a teenager, her body took the shock with resilience. Claire was extraordinarily lucky to be alive or even in one piece. It was the second time in a few days Dirk heard someone use the term "miracle."

After giving his sister a quick hug, Dirk entered the room without any prompting. Carrie knew he needed to reboot his system and understand that retreating into a pity party did not benefit anyone, least of all, his niece. He needed to take charge. Plenty of time existed later to replay every decision he'd made.

Pulling up a chair next to her bed, Dirk took her hand and rubbed it. Hanging his head low, he failed to notice the girl open her eyes. "Uncle Dirk?" she croaked, her voice raspy.

Tears filled Dirk's eyes anew. "Oh, honey, I am so very sorry."

Claire smiled through the haze of the pain medicine sedating her. "It's okay, Uncle Dirk, Victor took care of me."

Victor did a lot of that lately. This made the second time in a week he stood in between them and death.

"I think we owe him a lot, sweetie." Dirk shouted to her as Claire's hearing had only improved slightly.

Claire smiled. "Yeah, he's going to be simply impossible to

live with now." Claire laughed painfully at her own joke. "Ouch, laughing hurts."

Dirk smiled at the meek teenager. The brokenness of his insides healed slightly while gazing into her eyes. No longer afraid, anger took the place of fear. Knowing she would be all right went a long way. "I'm going to find whoever did this to you. I swear to God, I am going to make that son of a bitch pay." Dirk's face turned red.

"Beat someone's ass for me, will you?" Her voice came across so loud that several of the nurses in the hallway looked up from their paperwork with sudden interest at Claire's room.

Dirk laughed. "You got it, sweetie."

Claire looked over at the door. "Hi, Aunt Carrie."

Carrie smiled. "Hey, sweetie. Not aunt yet. That is up to your uncle."

"You have to basically scream, she can't quite hear you at normal volumes yet," Dirk said.

Carrie repeated herself in a much louder voice while holding the frail patient's hand.

"I think it's funny you don't see it," Claire said dreamily. Her eyelids dropped precipitously as the pain medicine kicked in and pulled her toward a restful sleep.

Carrie shot Dirk, who tried his best to stare at anything in the room other than Carrie, a curious glance. Unsure of what Claire referred to, she thought it could be possible something in the mail at his house caught her inquisitive mind. If she did see something, he didn't want her to spill the secret.

Keith stepped forward and grabbed her hand. Saying a short prayer reserved for the sick, he followed it up with a plea for a speedy recovery.

Dirk felt better with the doctor's assurances Claire would be okay. Bruising aside, she inherited her fight from her mother and it showed. The little girl he knew and loved lay in one piece, sleeping peacefully now. Still, things took a dark turn in an investigation that resulted in him dying and Claire being blown up. Victor had more than proven his worth this investigation. It was also true, they wore his luck thin. Right now, Dirk knew they could only be sure of one thing—the other team likely would try again.

Time to go on the offensive.

17

WHO KNOWS WHAT EVIL LURKS IN THE HEARTS OF MEN?

The next stop took them to the remains of Bentley Motorcycle Repair.

From the main road, Dirk reviewed the building from his normal approach. "Funny, it doesn't look too bad from here." When they turned into the driveway and made the steep incline toward the building, the reality became clearer. "Never mind."

A truck with Arson Investigator painted on the door was parked in the spot normally reserved for Dirk. Stepping over to Claire's motorcycle, Dirk picked it up and put it back on its stand. Not irreparably damaged, time and love should bring the classic motorcycle back into perfect running order. Her helmet, taking the brunt of the falling motorcycle, lay on the ground, a large crack in its shell.

Keith talked with the crime scene investigator near the building. Carrie stood with folded arms, surveying the wreckage of the repair bays, being careful to stay out of the crime scene. The arson investigator, an ill-tempered but competent man named Buck, got especially mean when non-arson-trained detectives went mucking around his crime scenes.

Dirk joined Keith. "Find out anything?"

"Buck said the explosive sat under the oil rack inside the main bay. Designed to go off when someone opened the door, it was to leave no one alive. The few remaining walls shifted off their foundations by about six inches around the entire perimeter of the shop. There is no way Claire should have survived this.

"The fire department found her over there. She was behind your desk which they think took an enormous part of the blast."

Carrie spied through one of the window openings left in the partial remains of one of the walls. "Wonder where that goofy spirit got off to?"

Keith picked up a bit of charred wood from the ground, examining it and then letting it fall with a thud. "From what I understand, we won't see him for a while, he is likely drained from saving Claire. Plus, Victor haunts the shop, not sure what having the shop destroyed does to him. Maybe we won't see Victor at all until the building is back up and running."

"All right," Dirk said in a voice louder than he intended, "what do we know?"

"We know you royally pissed off someone with a bad attitude," Keith said.

"Thanks, Sherlock." Dirk frowned.

Carrie took up the charge. "Dirk hit a nerve when he started poking around at the warehouse. We know a team was sent out to kill him, but we thwarted that. We also are reasonably certain my investigation and the hornets' nest you two kicked up are likely connected."

RICHARD RAMIREZ, a veteran of the police department, had walked a beat for longer than anyone could remember. A veteran by experience, a patrol officer by choice, he did everything possible, including threatening to quit, to forestall any promotion. The idea of walking off the beat for the last time painted an alien picture. And now, in the thirtieth year of active service, the unpleasant thought of mandatory retirement loomed heavily in front of him.

I'll retire on my feet the day they replace me, Richard thought, approaching the door to the apartment. He knocked three times and waited for the elderly woman to answer the door. As she approached the door, he heard what experience had taught him was a pair of old slippers shuffling along the floor. Removing his hat, he waited for her to make the mandatory inspection of her visitor through the peephole. In this neighborhood, they all did.

After a few moments of observation, the chain on the door and the deadbolt slid out of their normal places. The door opened slowly, due to the resident's age and not to any apprehension on her part. Likely she recognized the man in the peephole as she had watched him grow from a boy into a man. In these less than safe neighborhoods, the department maintained the old-style foot patrols of a bygone era to reassure the elderly residents.

A silver-haired woman wearing a blue housecoat and pink slippers stood in the doorway with a wide smile of recognition. "Well, Richard, how are you? Oh, perdoname, Officer Ramirez." She smiled at him coyly, the same way she had when he first became a police officer. Her hair sported mostly dark gray with a few flecks of raven black dotting the top. With wide-brimmed, thick bifocal glasses, she only made it as high as the middle of his badge in stature.

He'd worked the same beat, off and on, for most of his career and knew most of the residents by heart. "Hola, Abuela Flores. You are looking well."

"Gracias, little Ricky," she said, in deference to the use of the Spanish term for grandmother. "Can you stay a moment? I have a fresh pot on and some tea cookies. I have a few leftover from Anita's wedding. Which, by the way, you were not at." She turned from the door and shuffled over to the coffee pot. "I notice these things," she added with a little reproach.

Age stole none of this woman's resolute sharpness, he thought.

Wanting to avoid a prolonged discussion about why he missed her granddaughter's wedding, Richard decided the direct approach would be best. "I'd love a cup and a cookie. I have to tell you, I am not here on a social call. I have a couple of police questions for you."

"Tut-tut, probably about that nasty business up the way. I hoped someone would come back and talk to me. I wanted to call, but I wasn't sure how to go about it. Not really an emergency, and finding the non-emergency number is hard. Yet, I am glad they sent you, Ricky."

Richard knew she understood how to call the police, but it was more likely reluctance making that call difficult. Her upbringing in Mexico taught her to distrust most police officers. Ironically, the officers with Spanish-sounding last names earned her trust quickly. He sat down at her lovingly cared for Formica dinner table she and her long since deceased husband bought at a defunct department store.

"Si, Abuela. That is correct. I need to know what you saw. I got a call from my shift sergeant who asked me to follow up with you for the detective."

"Sheeesh, you should have been a detective."

"Took the exam and passed. I turned down the promotion because I like being on the streets too much. If was behind a desk, who would take care of you?"

She walked over to the table with a large silver tray containing the coffee pot, two cups, sugar and creamer, and a plate filled with a ridiculous amount of tea cookies. "That is true. These kids don't respect or care for their elders. It's okay, Ricky, someday they will be old and know what it is like to be abandoned and forgotten."

"True." Richard poured them both cups of coffee and then made up his own, knowing she preferred hers black. The advantage of working the same beat most of your life was that you knew everyone. "Tell me, in your own words, what happened the other night?" Richard moved a hand to hit the record button on his body camera to make a recording of the discussion. He knew the prosecutor would ask for a recording. He also took out a small notebook and made a show of taking notes.

"I did my regular thing that night."

Richard interjected, "And what night was that?"

"Tuesday, October seventeenth. I ate my dinner around five thirty and then settled down to watch the six o'clock news, as I always do. I remember an article about a home in Richmond which got overrun by rats because people just dumped their garbage into the alleyway. No one bothered to pick any of it up. Isn't that awful? I would just grab them by their ears and—"

"I remember you grabbing me by the ears as a boy. What happened next?" Richard asked. The old woman's mind held a sharp edge but needed prompting to stay on course from time to time.

"Well, I remembered that I needed to take my own garbage bag out. You know, that Mr. Bransford, such an angel, brings my cans down to the main walkway for me. He is on a business trip, so he moved them the night before. I walked down with this little bag of trash. It's not far, you know. This old woman may not have a ton of fire in the furnace, but I generate enough steam when I need it."

"Si, Abuela, you are as strong as an ox, I say. So, you took your garbage out?"

"I did, Ricky. Took it from the can and walked down the stairs, thank you very much. Didn't even get winded." The old woman smiled at her accomplishment. "Then I heard the ruckus."

"The ruckus?" He thought about a scene from an old movie before bringing his mind back around to the point. "Can you tell me exactly what you heard?"

"A knock on the neighbor's door up on the third floor. I saw a police officer I didn't recognize, standing at the balcony. My sight is way better than my hearing, so making out what they said was difficult. However, it seemed they both spoke cordially to one another. Like they were, you know, familiar."

Richard remembered reading in the case file where Officer Collins took part in the interrogation. If the officer standing outside Vance's apartment was Collins, then it explained why she said they were familiar. "Excellent, go on."

"The two talked at the door and then—"

"Which door exactly, can you point to it?"

"Why sure," she said. The old woman doddered to the door, opened it, and pointed to Deluca's door.

"I see," Richard said. "Go on."

"You remember, I stood down on the lower level, putting the garbage in the can and stopped to watch them. Then I noticed something move at the far end of the walkway."

The apartments on this end of town featured the block and stucco finish popular in lower-income construction. Criminals favored these buildings as people tended not to ask questions, and for a little hush money, the manager stayed quiet about most illegal activities. An old wooden walkway fronted each doorway, running the entire circumference of the building. The old woman indicated she stood on the lower level, watching the events of the evening up at the third story. The lower level contained a platform that residents put their garbage cans on for the truck to haul away. From her vantage point, she would be able to see it all, and no one likely saw the small elderly woman standing next to the dumpsters.

"What did you notice?"

"A figure in the shadows. When he stepped out into the light, I saw it was a man. He was ... sorry, I can't think of the proper word. Looked like a Guido."

Richard grimaced at the racial slur. People of her generation more likely used derogatory and outdated terms to refer to nationalities. "You mean the man looked Italian?"

"Yes, that's what I said. You know, a suit and hat on."

Richard thought about the ridicule he might garner by putting out an all-points bulletin for a Guido wearing a suit and hat. They would think he went insane. "Thank you,

Abuela. Is there anything else you can remember about him? That isn't terribly specific."

"Well, Ricky, my eyes are still pretty sharp with my spectacles on, but my hearing isn't what it used to be. Anyway, after the police officer entered the apartment, this other man sort of snuck up to the door and listened against the glass of the outside window. You know, these old windows don't keep out wind and cold, let alone noise."

Richard made a note about the windows being thin. "Okay, so how long did he stand outside like that?"

"I guess about five minutes or so. Then he did the most peculiar thing I've ever seen anyone do. The man reached into a jacket pocket with his right hand then opened the door with the left. It was so smooth I hardly believe it. It reminded me of one of the television shows, you know, like true crime stories or something like that. It only occurred to me the next day he might have had a gun."

"They stayed inside then?" Richard wondered how bad the woman's eyesight really was.

The old woman thought about it for a moment. "Si, five minutes or so. That's it though, no longer. Then two men, the police officer and the Italian man, came outside the apartment and walked down to the parking lot."

"Did they get into a car?" Richard asked.

"Oh, that is the interesting thing, Querido. You know, I am no busybody, but I did see another car pick the officer up. That Italian helped him into the car and it sped away. After that, I watched the Guido go back into the apartment. But that is all I can remember."

Richard poured himself another cup of coffee and freshened up hers. He resisted the temptation to point out she fit the description of a busybody perfectly. "Really, these tea cookies are amazing, did you make them yourself? They sure taste like yours."

The old woman stiffened with pride at his compliment. "Si, they are mine. I am getting too old to roll the dough, but my dear Maria comes over to help me. We make a day of it and bake enough for a few months. But the recipe is the same as back in Ciudad Victoria when my grandmother taught me to make them."

Richard knew that if he took her mind off the night and complimented her cookies enough, some detail she missed the first time through would surface. An old cop technique learned from his field-training officer a long time ago, it never failed to produce results. After a few more minutes of chatter about family matters, he put the notebook away and stood, taking the cups to the sink.

"Well, I appreciate everything you have told me. I'm going to head back to the station. Not much to go on, but I am sure we will figure it out. If you think of anything else, call me." If she held back any tidbit of earth-shattering revelation, this would be the time to spill it.

"Oh, one other thing I noticed that could be helpful. I am not sure if it means anything or not."

Richard put down the dishtowel he dried his hands on, smiling inwardly. "Oh, please tell me. No matter how insignificant you think it is."

"The man walked with a slight limp and used a cane. I don't think he needed it."

She now had Richard's full attention. "Really, why do you think that?"

"It wasn't one of those they give you at the hospital. More

of a dress cane, something you take with you to a fancy dinner or something. I remember a glass top. I only noticed that because the lights on the walls outside the apartments shone through it like a diamond would. It ... what is the right word ... refracted. I guess that's the right word."

Richard took one of the old woman's hands. "Abuela, you have been amazingly helpful. Maybe more than you know. I will let you know if we find out anything in another couple of days."

Richard left the small apartment with a belly full of coffee and tea cookies. Mrs. Ramirez would be furious at his limited appetite for dinner, but the visit was well worth the grief he might receive. Only one man, of Italian descent, who dressed that way, with a limp, who routinely carried a dress cane lived in town.

Back in the squad car, he dialed the desk of the on-duty sergeant. "Hey, McRae, this is Ramirez. I need you to send a couple of black and whites over to pick up Tony Carpolli on suspicion of murder." He waited a few minutes while the desk sergeant flipped out over the idea of sending a couple of police officers over to pick up a known Arrcado associate. "I understand how this sounds, Sarge, I really do. After I tell the detectives what I just found out, they are going to want to talk to this guy. I think I just found out who bounced Vance Deluca's brains all over the walls."

18

THE CURIOUSLY EMPTY OFFICES OF CENTER POINT

Carrie left Dirk and Keith at the shop and headed back over to the station. She wanted to write up notes and check her messages. She instructed their protective detail to keep a close eye on Dirk and Keith. Carrie wasn't about to take any chances with them.

At the station, a flurry of activity gave Carrie pause just inside the main entrance. The duty sergeant, an older, plump man, though not overweight, grabbed her by the arm as soon as she walked into the room. She'd gotten to know him and his family while pulling the night shift while still in patrol division. "Detective, I need a moment of your time. I talked with the duty detective, but he told me to talk to you. You got here before I could call you."

"No worries, what's up, Sarge?" Carrie briefly thought of all the times she sat behind that same desk pulling the shift as the duty sergeant. Not a fun job, but it gave you a taste of all strange things rolling in off the streets.

"Just got off the phone with the black and whites. They are bringing that dung heap, Carpolli in."

Carrie raised an eyebrow. "Sorry, did I miss something?" She found it a little annoying that the sergeant was essentially recapping events somewhere in the middle of the story. She remembered the instructors specifically teaching you not to do that at the sergeant's academy.

"You are going to want to talk to Ramirez. He's in the chief's office, filling her in now."

Carrie didn't need further explanation to which Ramirez he referred. Only one guy on the department simply went by the name Ramirez. Approaching the door, the wizened cop stood at a modified position of attention in front of the chief's desk. His seniority at the department exceeded even Melonie Dixon by about ten years, and standing at attention in front of the desk was not expected. At the end of the day, Richard loved the formality of it all.

Carrie knocked on the door and waited for the chief to yell for her to come in. Upon hearing the obligatory "Come," Carrie opened the door and Ramirez gave her a nod. She relaxed a little as something in Richard's smile suggested good things came from the activity currently taking place at the department. The officer usually put people at ease though.

"Ramirez, tell Detective Pettygrew what you just told me."

Ramirez relayed the story of his interview with Mrs. Flores, occasionally straying into unnecessary detail.

Carrie thought about the possibility of the murderer being with the Mafia and the men outside of Dirk's apartment. They belonged to the Arrcado family as well. "Chief, I think I have something." She turned to Ramirez. "Thank you, Richard, you may just have broken this case wide open.

Remind me to bring you a latte from The Beanapse. Hell, I'll buy you breakfast."

The chief interjected, "I'll buy you both breakfast if this is anything good. Ramirez, unless Carrie needs anything, you are excused."

Ramirez nodded to both women and walked out of the office, closing the door behind him.

"Jesus," the chief said. "I am going to have to write him another award for being an incredibly good cop. I'm going to hate to see Richard retire."

"Chief, I think he'll hate to retire more than we will hate seeing him go." Carrie nodded. "I think I know how those two cases are linked. If Carpolli really did kill Vance, then that means the Arrcado family ordered the hit against the guy they knew talked to the police. Vance was our guy in the church burglaries, but Dirk and Keith only worked the warehouse case, and the Arrcados seemed laser-locked on hurting Dirk."

"Yeah, hearing you say it sounds far less crazy in my head. I was kind of hoping you would say something that might make it sound less likely.

"Right, I am still bothered by Collins in all of this though. Based on what Ramirez said, no one actually witnessed him hurting anyone. Or, I am just having a hard time accepting it. Part of me wonders if he was a victim."

The chief took a drink of her coffee out of a mug emblazoned with the words World's Greatest Cop. "It's possible. And I think your logic is pretty sound. I trained you well." She smiled at Carrie. "Anyway, something to think about. Say, where is your police escort?"

"I left them with Dirk and Keith. So far, they need it more than I do."

"Good call. You know, the three of you are like family to me. I don't know what I would do if any of you got hurt. How's the kid doing?"

"Well. The doctors are sure she is going to recover completely. It could be a while before we know if her hearing is going to completely return. I am confident everything will work out all right."

DIRK KNEW LITTLE ELSE COULD BE DONE until someone took another shot at him. Alternatively, looking for trouble offered a compelling option. Preferring the offensive, Dirk bounded up the steps of the police department intent on solving another part of the mystery.

Center Point Security came to the forefront of his thoughts. Who were they and why would anyone deliberately build failure into a security system? Anyone connected with the company easily might know of the flaw and be able to enter the building with little to no problems.

After saying hello to a relieved Carrie, he sat down at one of the department's computers and searched for Center Point Security. Established in 2015, the company functioned primarily as a security firm. A construction branch of the company built things like barriers, security towers, and sheet metal buildings. According to the company's website, they also worked with several non-profits, including the arch-diocese.

The company's website appeared complete. However, as Dirk clicked on a few of the links, they led in a continuous loop back to the first page. One page offered a way to contact the office with questions, but with a few clicks, Dirk determined the form likely went to a random email account from a free service.

"Hey, Keith, check this out." Dirk clicked on a few of the links and showed Keith the endless loop of connections embedded in the webpage. "I am no expert, but if I hired someone to build a website for me, I wouldn't be a fan of this setup here."

Keith grabbed the mouse and clicked on a few links. "You know, I think a five-year-old could come up with a better site than this one. This thing is about as fake as a three-dollar bill."

Carrie filled Dirk in on the situation with the Mafia enforcer now positively connected with the Arrcado gang. Dirk hated to admit to himself he dragged them all into this swirling mess, and now he'd either have to solve the case or find someone responsible for almost killing Claire and make good on the promise he made to his recovering niece.

Although the site appeared suspicious, the internet offered plenty of examples of bad websites created by people who thought themselves webmasters.

But, no construction companies construct deliberately flawed security barriers like the one at the warehouse.

Evening and stress-induced fatigue snuck up on Dirk quietly and all at once. Carrie, still sitting at her desk, worked away with her customary gusto. Albeit, the stress on her face looked like a mask. No matter what, she never yawned or even complained about being tired.

"Carrie?"

She smiled at him. "Yes, love."

"What do you say we go to your apartment and spend the night? I would rather avoid the house as long as possible.

Your place is secure as far as buildings go. We can find a poor patrolman who wants overtime to keep us safe."

Carrie nodded and in a few minutes arranged everything. One officer, assigned watch over them and in need of overtime, would stand guard in the kitchen all night and listen for trouble so Dirk and Carrie could wash up and sleep. Keith took another officer with him to check on things at the church and spend time grading papers for an online class he taught at community college. As always, plenty of tasks divided his interests.

THAT NIGHT, Dirk and Carrie ate frozen lasagna they picked up from the store and drank a glass of wine. Neither one of them drank more as the alcohol might dull their senses. The patrolman helped himself to whatever remained of the lasagna while Carrie stood guard for him. After showering, Dirk made a flirty gesture, but both fell asleep moments after placing their heads on the pillows.

The next morning, Dirk woke up before Carrie as he normally did. In the living room, the patrolman sat at the table drinking a cup of coffee. The deep, nutty aroma of the coffee filled Dirk's nostrils.

"Good morning, Mr. Bentley."

Dirk hated the idea of anyone calling him Mr. Bentley, a title no one used since his father passed away a few years ago. The young officer, sitting at the table, reminded him of a kid who showed up at his door dressed as a police officer for Halloween last year. "Good morning. You know, you don't have to call me that, right? You can call me Dirk."

"Okay, Mr. Dirk, did you sleep well?"

Dirk shook off the Mr. Dirk comment. He would have to work on this guy. "Yes, thank you." Dirk walked over to the coffee pot and poured himself a cup of coffee. "Say, I'm going to run down to the mailbox. I'll be right back."

The patrolman frowned at the idea. "I don't know, Dirk. My instructions are to—"

Dirk put up his hand in a gesture to settle the overeager police officer. "Don't worry, I will just go the mailbox and grab the mail. Then I will be right back. I will bring my weapon with me. As a matter of fact, you can check the hallway first." Dirk motioned toward the door.

The patrolman scanned the door as if it proffered an opinion on the matter. "Just down the bottom of the stairs?"

"Yep." Dirk impassively poured milk into a coffee cup and stirred it with a spoon.

"Tell you what," the patrolman said, "why don't I go downstairs and grab the mail for you. No one knows me in this building and probably would not recognize me."

"Patrolman, you are an excellent cop. Thank you for that."

The officer grabbed the key from Dirk and headed out the door and down the stairs, and the patter of his patent leather shoes echoed off the cement walls of the apartment building. Dirk knew no police officer worth their badge would even consider letting their charges out into the unprotected world. He took a gamble, hoping the patrolman's inexperience might just allow Dirk to talk him into getting their mail. A gracious act giving him just enough time to pull off a stunt he would likely catch hell for later.

Dirk knew, from previous experience, it took about a minute to reach the bottom of the stairs at a leisurely gait. He also knew it took someone about two minutes to open the mailbox, grab the mail, scan out the front door to see if anyone kept a closer than normal eye on the building, and come back up to the apartment. It would take about three minutes for the young officer to leave the apartment and make it back. At least it would have if Dirk gave him the correct mailbox number. This would take the officer an additional minute to work it all out.

He judged four minutes were necessary to put the plan into action. The stairwell to the apartment building had three landings to access the bottom floor. At the uppermost landing, which lead to Carrie's apartment, one of the boards made a squeaking noise. The second Dirk caught noise of the officer's foot hitting the first landing, he ran to the bathroom and turned the shower on. On the way back to the living room, he tugged at the butt of his weapon to ensure it remained firmly secure in the holster.

Running back to the living room, he opened the window and stepped out onto the fire escape. The building's front door opened toward the other side of the street and the officer would not see him drop into the alleyway. Also, equally as likely, anyone watching the building would not have anticipated Dirk would leave the building by using the fire escape.

In the alley, Dirk skulked away from the main street and down to a short residential road. A few blocks up, he entered a rental car place which featured cheap, nondescript cars. Bentley Detective Services maintained a standing account. Ten minutes from the time he slipped away from the police officer, ironically assigned to protect him, he drove out of the rental lot and toward the next logical place to check for clues.

CARRIE WOKE to the sound of cooing outside her bedroom window. The winged rats, as she called all pigeons, reminded her why she preferred sleeping at Dirk's house. Her small apartment, less than a thousand feet, only featured one bedroom, a bathroom, and a small study barely larger than Dirk's walk-in closet. She mused his house made a perfect location to start a family.

Out in the hallway, she heard the shower running. Dirk must have decided to take a shower. Odd since he showered the night before. Given the insanity of the last two days, he simply may have forgotten.

Carrie put on her robe and made her way to the kitchen. The officer, sitting at the table, gave her a wave and returned to reading the morning paper.

"Did you bring the mail in for me?" Carrie asked.

"Yes." The patrolman put down the paper. "Mr—err, Dirk asked me if he could go get the mail, and I volunteered to do it so he wouldn't be exposed."

"Good thinking," Carrie said. Moving toward the counter, she eyed the coffee cup sitting next to the coffee maker. "Is this for me?" It struck Carrie as odd the patrolman would have made her a cup of coffee.

"No, Mr. Bentley's. I mean that is Dirk's," the patrol officer said with a self-satisfied smile.

"Yeah, don't let him catch you calling him Mr. Bentley. You will get a lecture." As she put her hand on the porcelain, its warmth radiated. It was unusual that Dirk poured a cup and then just let it sit. He always took the coffee cup into the bathroom with him.

Certainly not acting like himself. Something is up.

Turning from the counter, she walked toward the bathroom and pushed open the door to see an empty shower with the water running. "Damn you, Dirk!"

Moments later, the officer stood at her side, staring at the shower dumfounded. "I am so sorry, Detective. I didn't even realize he ... well, you know. I'm not even sure how he got past me."

"Relax, Patrolman, Dirk is sneaky. This means he decided to go it alone. I hate it when he does this crap."

DIRK SHUT off the ringer on the cell phone to lessen the guilt about ignoring it. There would be hell to pay but also things he needed to do alone. A little guilt bubbled to the surface of his consciousness for giving the patrolman the slip. Although the police tail was not mandatory, it would be highly suggested by Melonie, and Carrie would certainly insist. Being driven around in Carrie's squad car, being tailed by another squad, made him stand out like a sore thumb. Distance between himself and anything appearing to be a squad car ensured he could carry out the next step in his plan.

Finding a parking spot in the parking garage of the office building housing the headquarters of Center Point Security, Dirk made his way to the front. Sitting in the crowded center of town meant a lot of foot traffic to cover his movements. It also made it less likely anyone looking for him might take a shot. The noise would attract a lot of attention and provide a plethora of witnesses. Something the Mafia hated.

The address, Hennessey Building, on Waldon Street, Suite

301 could easily be forgotten as just another professional building in a seascape of other professional buildings. Someone walking up and down the hallways would easily blend into the background.

Dirk quickly checked his phone. Three missed calls and a text message from Carrie sent a clear message about how she felt. As a matter of contrition, he typed a short message reassuring her and promising he was only checking clues in the downtown area. He added "Love You" to the end of the message. In response, she sent an annoyed face emoji.

Stopping by a small coffee shop, he bought a coffee and a bagel before taking up a position on a park bench to observe the daily comings and goings of the Hennessey building. None of the workaday people coming and going gave the slightest impression they planned anything more nefarious than clocking in a few minutes late. Most were dressed in the ubiquitous slacks and button-down dress shirts of the lower end of the business world, and it appeared as nothing more than an average business day.

After a half an hour of observing, Dirk stood and crossed the street, which showed a marked decrease in both foot and auto traffic as many reached their offices to resume their cubicle existence. Initially, he worried about someone potentially recognizing him. That fear dissipated as a herd of oblivious, coffee-swilling employees returning from one errand or another swallowed up Dirk in a gaggle of people.

The lobby of the large office building offered a breezeway design. Double doors on the street side stood in mirror image to double doors opening into a courtyard. The inner area was exclusively staffed by an out of place gaggle of smokers trying to cling to coolness in a world that long ago decided smoking was decidedly uncool. The walls screamed of fake opulence with faux marble paneling covering off-white walls. Four elevators, flanking a seating area too small to be of any use to anyone, busily let people in and out taking them up to the heights of the building.

To Dirk's right, a security guard sat behind a desk made of the same faux marble. The guard, a portly and balding fellow with a bushy Fu Manchu mustache, ignored the entire world except for the *Guns & Ammo* magazine glued to his nose. Dirk glanced at the wall behind the guard, scanning the directory for the offices of 'Center Point Industries'.

Forgoing the elevators, Dirk took the stairs to avoid the chance anyone would recognize him. Surprised to find a bland white stairwell instead of the faux marble of the entry-way, it smelled vaguely of urine and cheap industrial non-slip paint used for the floors of commercial buildings. After opening the door and glancing down the hallway, the scene surprised and confused him as both directions yielded no activity. In fact, whole sections of the floor sat unfinished. Although, drywall hung precariously from small points of black screws. Several of the office spaces lacked doors, and floor spaces remained covered in plastic to protect the carpeting below.

Walking down the corridor toward where Dirk hoped to find office number 301, he came upon the only office on the floor even remotely finished from the outside. A small sign, printed hastily on a piece of computer paper and taped to the wall, declared Center Point Industrial Services. He peered through the skinny window running the length of the door, and the interior appeared ill suited for office work. In several spots, wires and phone cords hung down like tentacles.

Dirk tried the door handle and found it resolutely against permitting him entrance. He scanned the room again through the window, but little screamed out of interest.

Turning to leave, he froze as something behind him forced a cessation of movement. Reaching down, he put his hand on the butt of his gun and moved to face a would-be assailant. A man in overalls approached carrying a gallon of paint. Over the top of his pocket, the name Earl was emblazoned in red stitching.

"Hey there," Earl said. "How are you this morning? Strange to see people up here so early. Are you looking at the Center Point suite?"

Dirk thought quickly. If Earl suspected anything amiss, he could always call whomever owned the suite to tell them he had been nosing around. "Yep, I sure am. Trying to decide what furniture I need to order for it." Dirk took a stab at an improvised personality for an ad-hoc situation.

Earl put down the gallon of paint. "Well, it is about time. They rented this place a while ago and no one even visits during the day." Without interrogating Dirk any further, Earl dug into a pocket and pulled out a key ring. Unlocking the door, he said, "My name is Earl, and I didn't catch your name."

"That's 'cause I didn't throw it. My name is Jacob Stansfield. I'm with Center Point, sorry it took me so long. I usually just handle office spaces and the like, but I have been a bit behind with the cold season and all." Not wanting to allow Earl to process the fake name, Dirk followed up with "Unfortunately, the guy scheduled to meet me couldn't make it, and I don't have a key. I just hoped to look in from the window. Someone is going to have my ass if I don't get this done."

Earl, a white-haired man who sported a white mustache,

removed his hat and scratched at a stalwart forehead. "I sure don't want to see a fellow worker bee in trouble if we can help each other out. Most of the Center Point people are only here at night. Separate entrance in the back lets them come and go as they please. Not sure what they do here though, seems there isn't much to do. And, even if they worked in here, none of the fiber lines are active in this suite. They couldn't get a decent internet signal in here if they wanted."

"Well, that's odd. I wonder what the holdup is? Aside from the furniture." Dirk laughed to inject normalcy into his recently faked persona. Freestyling a narrative during an investigation like this always struck him as uncomfortable and disingenuous.

Earl chuffed at the question. "I'll tell you what it is. These kids show up with gobs of money, pay a ton for a one-year lease, in cash, and then party away the rest of their investor's money. Now you show up to bring in the furniture and they only have a month left on the lease. Yes, poor planning is what this is. Sure ain't the way we did business back in the day. A good business takes planning."

"Well, I am certainly much obliged, Earl. Did you say the lease only has a month left?" Dirk wondered about this for a moment. Why would anyone lease an office for a year and never actually occupy it? Earl could be right that their business sense lacked, or they never intended to occupy the space.

Dirk walked the length of the suite while they talked. He tried to keep Earl as distracted as possible while looking for clues by asking questions about the sizes of the space, carpet type, and how often he changed the light bulbs. As he had no idea what to look for, anything and everything could be of interest. At the end of a short hallway, across from a bathroom, stood a large office. Several pieces of plastic clung to the windows through the staying power of industrial tape.

The same plastic clung to the floor in one continuous roll. It suggested they wanted to either protect the interior from something or possibly obscure the view from the outside. Pulling up the plastic, thick enough to hide whatever lay below it, could lead to some questions from Earl he wasn't prepared to answer. He needed Earl to leave him alone for a few minutes.

Under the pretext of going to the bathroom, Dirk quickly opened the cabinet under the sink to find an ordinary bucket. Filling it with water, he dumped it on the floor at the foot of the sink being careful not to make any noise. Then he cut a small hole in the copper pipe supplying water to the faucet, which immediately sprayed water everywhere. Flushing the toilet, Dirk stepped out into the hallway, where Earl examined the drywall installation like an art collector admiring the works of the Louvre.

"Earl?" Dirk said. "I think you need to come quickly. You've got a leak in the bathroom."

Alarmed, Earl came to the bathroom door and almost slid across the floor on the water Dirk dumped there to give the ruse credibility. Opening the vanity doors under the sink, he was hit fully in the face with a spray of water. "Damn, I hate these pipes. Stupid things are always leaking." He turned the water off and stood up.

"Can you hang out here for a few more minutes? I need to run down the hall and grab a few proper towels and a mop bucket."

Dirk smiled at Earl. "Absolutely, I am happy to help out. Us worker bees need to support each other."

Earl, not waiting for another word, turned toward the door and disappeared. Dirk pulled up as much of the plastic as possible in what was likely only a limited amount of time before Earl returned.

Two gallon-sized cans of an industrial primer sat conspicuously under one piece of plastic. Dirk picked one up, shocked at the lack of weight. The can read "Covers-All, Industrial Paint." The floor under the plastic sported a fresh coat of the stuff, and whoever did the painting made sure the job was thorough, perhaps putting on more than a few layers. The paint extended up the walls in a haphazard fashion. It suggested they were covering stains on the wall and not just prepping for a future paint job.

About to give up and leave the room, Dirk paused when something caught his eye. Near the windows, something glinted in the sunlight. A metallic object caught in between the unfinished floor and the frame of the window beckoned for attention. He knelt and pulled out a length of chain. At the end, dangling by a small gold ring, a miniature cross featured the figure of Jesus dying for the sins of the world.

Across the face of the tiny figure, a dried splatter of something dark stood out. Unsure what the darkened stain consisted of, it reminded Dirk of blood weeping from the crucified man's face. If his intuition proved right, it could be the blood of someone recently in this room, and whatever happened here involved something someone desperately wanted to cover up, both figuratively and literally.

Noise behind him indicated Earl returned from his mission with the things he needed to clean up the spilled water. Dirk took this as the perfect cue to leave.

"Find everything you need?" Earl said.

Dirk smiled inwardly at the ironic choice of words. "I think I found exactly what I was looking for."

With renewed purpose, Dirk left Earl to clean up the mess he made in the bathroom. The next stop would be the police lab to analyze the blood on the cross tucked safely in a small plastic bag in his pocket.

19

CAT AND MOUSE

Keith continued working the case and established that, out of all the suspects, Edwardo definitely could be eliminated. Not only did he have an alibi, but he readily agreed he should be a suspect because of access. Usually, the guilty party was the last one to come forward.

Keith also managed to clear the archbishop as a suspect. Not only did Keith not consider him a viable suspect from the beginning, he was at a conference when at least two of the items turned up missing. It was still possible to hire someone to steal them. Still, Archbishop Weebley had no motive.

All roads led to one place. Carolyn grew up an Arrcado and retained full access to every system necessary to make stealing from the warehouse easy. She not only sat at the nexus but she literally controlled it, and that gave her all the power. Keith remembered the archbishop had said he relied on her for almost everything.

Once a criminal, always a criminal.

Keith hated thinking that way. As an ordained minister, he liked to think people deserved the benefit of the doubt, but in an investigation, the benefit of the doubt was generally hard to come by. Just because you were born into a crime family did not make you a criminal, but it certainly tipped the odds in favor of you engaging in a life of crime.

Keith found a way to grab Archbishop Weebley out of his office and voice concerns about Carolyn. He was thrilled at the news about Edwardo, but when it came to the matter of Carolyn, the pill proved more difficult to swallow. She served as church secretary for so long he depended on her. Keith pressed the matter, and the archbishop admitted her access was limitless.

Keith planned to call the archbishop's office and arrange a meeting to interrogate Carolyn when a buzz on his phone indicated a text message waited. Dirk urgently told everyone to meet back at the police department.

In twenty minutes, Keith pulled into the parking lot. The station occupied a large building, shaped like a V. On the first floor, persons entering the building could either go left to the city offices or right to the police department. What currently held Keith's attention was the very heated conversation between Carrie and Dirk, standing at the end of the hallway.

Not wanting to intrude on their discussion, he could not help but feel it looked one sided. Apparently, Dirk did something she did not approve of. He recognized the one-way conversation from any distance. Carrie's voice pierced the walls and easily passed through the glass doors. She used words such as thoughtless, irresponsible, pigheaded, and teamwork. Keith simultaneously held at bay an insatiable curiosity about the matter at hand and relief he had not participated in whatever garnered such a tongue-lashing. Carrie's wrath, once stoked, flowed easily and plentiful.

"Eh ... hem!" Keith almost shouted. "Sorry to interrupt your discussion. I received a summons from our king." Keith tried to lighten the mood a little.

Carrie turned on Keith. "And you! Please tell me you weren't involved in what this irresponsible ass did this morning?"

"Blissfully, no. As much as I am normally in-line with this ass's more interesting exploits, ironically I was at home writing a religion column about forgiveness for next week's edition."

Until this point, Dirk remained mute. Keith knew the many faces of Dirk, and the man always wore emotions on his sleeve. Something in his old friend's grin suggested this morning's adventure produced results and every word of Carrie's tongue-lashing was worth the reward.

"You had better thank your lucky stars you stayed home." Carrie pointed an accusatory finger at Keith before turning back toward Dirk. Tone suddenly softened, she said, "I love you, but you have to be more careful. I don't want anything happening to you, and someone wants you dead. Do you have any idea what that would do to me?"

"I do. Probably the same thing that would happen to me if something happened to you. Carrie, I have to investigate this thing till it is done. Someone tried to kill me, and until this case is solved, we won't be safe. I need to finish this. You have to trust me."

They spent a few moments in an embrace that left Keith wondering how long it would be until he officiated their wedding. Probably very soon.

Carrie admitted that Dirk must have the freedom to run investigations his own way. To Keith, Dirk's methods always came across as reckless, leaning too far forward. However, it worked for Dirk, and he never failed to unravel any puzzle given enough time. The methods employed sometimes bordered on the questionable, but always for the right reason.

Inside the Detective's Pit, Dirk showed off the crucifix he'd found in the office which supposedly belonged to Center Point Security. Someone went pretty far to set up a front company if they actually leased an office. Carrie, once again, admonished her boyfriend for the idiotic extents he would go to for evidence. However, the chief quickly pointed out no laws were broken since Earl let him in with little prompting. Dirk left out the part about him representing himself as an employee of Center Point. He secretly wondered how much the chief really understood the methods he employed. He secretly thought she knew more than she let on.

He also mentioned the paint on the floor. At best, it was very suspicious but hardly anything they could pin a search warrant on.

"Keith, we need to go see the archbishop. This time, we are going to show up unannounced. I want to see Carolyn's reaction when we walk in. Right now, she's likely sitting on pins and needles waiting for word of my untimely demise. If that is really the case and we weren't mistaken about that photograph, we should have no problem rustling her Italian feathers."

"Dirk." The chief raised an eyebrow and a finger in a way that could only be described as maternal. "It seems to me that if Carolyn is really who you think she is the entire Mafia will stop at nothing to stop you. Including shooting up the archbishop's office. I won't even begin to insult your intelligence by telling you what that would look like. We can't let that happen."

Keith chimed in. "No worries, Chief. First off, they won't make a move on Weebley's office. Way too risky for them. Plus, if we do this right, they will to come to us on our terms. Maybe we—"

"Keith, you are a genius," Dirk interrupted. "Behind the warehouse. We stage officers back there and arrest anyone who makes their way down the hill."

Carrie chimed in. "How do you know Carolyn will fall for it?"

Keith smiled broadly. "Simple, we give her the chance to finish what she started. When we went to conduct our initial interview, Carolyn told us to be careful down by the warehouse. It seemed odd to me at the time, and I just dismissed the comment. I thought we talked about it in the outer office or something, and now I'm sure we only talked about it in the archbishop's office. Which meant that—"

"That secretary of his has a way of listening in." The chief completed his sentence. "Nice work, boys.

Carrie folded her arms and glared at Dirk and Keith, cementing the idea her statement was not optional. "We need someone to stand in for Dirk. I want him out of harm's way if something goes wrong. And, before you argue with me, taking a risk like that with a civilian would put us in a bad spot."

"Agreed," the chief said. "I knew there was a reason I kept the three of you around." She turned to Carrie. "This is your show. Make arrangements, but I want to be clear. Any sign things are about to get out of hand, I want the aggressors taken down. Snipers posted at every vantage point and teams available to cut off every route. Am I clear?"

Carrie nodded. "Yes, ma'am."

Dirk attempted to voice concerns about using a stand-in for himself, but a quick scowl from Carrie shut down any further discussion. He shared her concerns for his safety, which was why he didn't like the idea of putting anyone else's life at risk. She also made a good point about any ill-advised move of putting a civilian, even a private investigator, in danger when a suitable stand-in could play a convincing stand-in.

They still must warn the archbishop of the situation. If this stood a chance of working, they needed to ensure Carolyn heard their entire conversation. Keith became more and more convinced she monitored their conversations through the intercom system in the office, but he could not risk her missing even a single word.

It took a day for Carrie to make the necessary arrangements. To make this all work, police officers needed to be placed in camouflage, hiding out in the woods long before anyone walked into the building. If they were seen by even one person, it would jeopardize the entire operation.

Dirk and Keith used the time to visit Claire who bounced back quickly and fought with the doctors to let her go back to school. Dirk arranged a security detail after she left the hospital to ensure her safety, paying an old private security friend to stay with her when he was not around. He refused to let anything happen to her again.

For the ruse to work, the officer playing the part of Dirk needed to look exactly like him. One officer in the department, Lance Williamson, easily looked like Dirk, even without identical clothing.

Dirk and Lance standing together in identical outfits led Keith to remark, "Wow, that's just creepy."

Carrie walked up to the two men and faked a turn to kiss Lance.

"Hey!" Dirk protested.

Carrie laughed and turned back to Dirk. "Sorry, hon, I got so confused. He's a younger, more handsome version of you." She nodded at Keith. "All right, let's go over this one more time. After the meeting between you, Dirk, and whomever is listening in on the conversation, Keith and Dirk will head over to the entrance with Lance in the trunk. Lance gets out and Dirk takes his place hiding until you all are clear of the area." Turning to Dirk, she continued. "After meeting me at the top of the tree line, you will both join me in the suburban. I want to be far enough away to ensure no one hears or sees us and still close enough to react if we need to. This is for real, so I want to make sure everyone plays their part. For right now, I need you three to head over to the archbishop's office to get the ball rolling."

After checking in with the chief, Dirk, Keith, and Lance all left for the archbishop's office. The police department motor pool removed the back seat retaining bolts so Lance could easily move from the trunk and trade places with Dirk the moment they disappeared into the trees. Dirk would stay hidden until they cleared the trees again and rejoined Carrie in the command vehicle to watch the situation unfold.

Driving toward the archbishop's office, Keith took it easy to avoid jostling Lance, safely tucked away in the trunk with a blanket, snacks, and a smartphone with several episodes of

Downton Abbey. This way, if the meeting took longer, he could ride the meeting out in relative comfort.

Finding a parking place that put the trunk in a shady spot so they wouldn't cook Lance, Dirk and Keith exited the car. Walking in as they did every other time, the security guard, who now knew them on sight, waved them through the turnstile and into the building.

Keith spoke up. "Are you ready for this?"

Dirk channeled an old movie line. "As ready as I'll ever be."

Carolyn sat dutifully behind her desk, glancing at something of interest on her ink blotter when they walked in, she turned to meet their gaze and fell silent as her eyes locked on Dirk. "Can you give me a few minutes? I will have to call you back," she said after regaining her composure.

"Good morning, Carolyn. It is still morning, right?"

A quality in the way she drilled into both men told a story which did not need an explanation. Her eyes closed halfway as the skin around her eyelids scrunched together and the skin of her cheeks tightened. Her lips curled into a sneer.

If looks could kill, Keith thought.

"I am so sorry, gentlemen, His Excellency is not seeing anyone right now, but if you come back later, you can—"

The archbishop's office door suddenly flung open and he walked out. "Carolyn, I need a—Oh, hello, boys. Great to see you again. To what do I owe this great honor?"

Dirk smiled at the archbishop, whose entrance could not have been timed any better. Perhaps too perfectly for Carolyn's tastes. "Your Excellency, we are sorry to bother you again. I need something from you. A small favor, I promise."

What Carolyn did not know was that Keith sent a text to the archbishop, instructing him to come out of the office. The archbishop knew the basic plan and agreed to go along if they promised to exonerate Carolyn if no link could be found.

"Well, sure, no problem. Do you want to speak inside my office?"

Dirk shook his head adamantly. "Oh no, that won't be necessary. We can talk out here. I only need your permission to go back to the warehouse. I'll have Keith drop me off, and I will take another look around."

"Are you sure Edwardo can't bring you down there?"

Keith said, "No, not at all. And, really, it's no problem." Carrie ensured that Edwardo safely remained out of the picture to avoid putting him in any real danger should things spiral downward. They also worried about Edwardo unintentionally interfering while going about daily chores.

Archbishop Weebley gave them a thumbs-up. "You boys know where you are headed. I would join you, but I have too much going on right now. Let me know what you find out."

Keith turned to Carolyn. "How about you, Carolyn, want to join us?"

"Oh, heavens no," she said. "I don't go down there unless I need to check on numbers or something. What would I want with a dirty building like that?"

"Fair enough," Dirk said. "Well, we'd better be off." Dirk and Keith shook hands with the archbishop in turn and then nodded to Carolyn before walking out the door and closing it behind them. They stood in the hallway, waiting and listening. The doors were surprisingly thin in the building, and any noise within an office carried well into the hallway. Inside the office, the unmistakable noise of a handset raised from a cradle made Keith smile. While unsure what Carolyn said, her voice came across as hushed and yet still very excited.

Dirk and Keith shuffled down the hallway. Although it would be impossible for them to estimate exactly how long it would take Carolyn to arrange things on her end, they needed to give her time to put a plan into action. If everything went as expected, she presently arranged for someone to finish the job they were unable to complete before. If all worked as well as planned, someone would take a shot at Dirk ... or Lance really.

Dirk knew Carrie took a bit of a calculated risk, and it made all the sense in the world. The odds of the same sequence of events repeating themselves again stood impossibly high. They expected something more forceful. Anyone with five hundred dollars lying around could buy themselves a decent hunting rifle and a high-end scope. Essentially, a civilian sniper rifle. The valley and trees would absorb the sound of the shot, and this late in the year, people easily could mistake it for a legitimate hunter.

Getting back into the car, Keith said, "All right, we threw in the line and bait. Time to see if this fishy bites."

A stifled laugh came from the trunk. "You private investigators really talk like that on investigations?" Lance apparently found Keith's comment too cliché.

Keith chuckled. "I dunno, felt right to me at the time. How you holding up in there, Lance?"

The police officer replied, "Pretty good. Anxious to get this over. I really hope no one shoots me today."

"So do I Lance," Dirk said.

A few minutes later, they drove down the dusty road leading to the warehouse. Counting on the Mafia hit men needing a few minutes to make it to the warehouse, the delay ensured Dirk and Lance could switch places. Still, this needed to work seamlessly. If anyone witnessed the activity in the car, it could raise suspicions. It didn't even have to be a Mafia person seeing them make the change either. Any security alerts of suspicious activity would be funneled through the archbishop's office ... and right through Carolyn's hands.

In addition to the large warehouse structure, small buildings dotted the compound. Smaller outbuildings dotted the secured area, which Edwardo said secured utility vehicles and lawn equipment used on the property.

The dirt road leading to the warehouse ran perpendicular from the parking lot in front of the administration area and then took a sudden turn to the south and down into the valley that contained the warehouse. On the other side of the valley, opposite where the road wound its way down, another road followed along the ridgeline and then descended toward a freeway. Carrie guessed the ridgeline presented the most logical location for any potential threats to set up. Countering this, she placed snipers along the hillside, offering them overlapping fields of fire. Deeper into the woods, behind a couple of cheap duck blinds Carrie bought at a local hunting supply store, three teams of officers sat in camouflage uniforms. Geared up and ready to go, the teams could cover any point in their assigned sectors of the forest in less than sixty seconds.

Coordinating it all was Sergeant Andrews. With a flair for this type of operation, he always made Carrie's list of logical choices for chief of operations. Seeing an old friend watching all their backs reassured her.

Halfway down the side of the roadway, Keith stopped the car. Lance pushed the back seat down and rolled out of the trunk. Dirk crawled over the passenger seat and into the trunk, pulling the back seat into place as he did.

"By the way, Dirk," Lance said, "don't drink out of the soda bottle back there. It isn't filled with soda."

"What? Why?" Dirk suddenly let out a yip, like a cat which had its tail stepped on. "Are you kidding me, Lance!"

Keith erupted into laughter and pulled away from their temporary parking spot. "Lance, did you pee in a bottle?"

Both Lance and Keith chuckled uncontrollably for a full minute and then yielded to a troubling silence. Laughter became a survival mechanism. The tension wore on each of them like a suit of ill-fitting clothing. Three men continued in silence. One driving, one hiding, and one being dropped off as a human target for people already demonstrating the desire to kill.

20

HUNTERS BECOME THE HUNTED

Carrie let out a long sigh as Dirk and Keith climbed into the command vehicle. The easy part over, if anyone could call baiting an organized crime syndicate into a trap easy, and they settled into their seats. Designed for undercover work, the darkened vehicle was more function than form. An old Chevy Suburban, it seated only four because of the overabundance of computer and communications gear.

From her position, just behind the driver, Carrie could check in with everyone's radio, monitor body cameras, and contact every emergency radio channel. The truck's exterior benefited from magnets allowing it to blend in with suburbia in any situation. On the back, they displayed a "Live to Hunt, Hunt to Live" magnet. The police department had a collection of other magnets designed to essentially give people any other impression they wanted. The resident department artists even went so far as to paint a series of rust spots to give the impression of age.

A block away, on a quiet residential cul-de-sac, another officer sat piloting a small quadcopter outfitted with special sensors to detect movement and body heat. A few blocks away from the pilot, two other officers sat in a car at a fast food restaurant. They acted as an insurance policy in case the perpetrators made it away from the woods and onto the main roads. They drove a police cruiser especially outfitted for high-speed chases.

Carrie stayed on scene most of the late morning, and now with early afternoon threatening to leave them, she itched for something to happen, and she hoped none of this would run into shift change. Additional vehicles into the equation made it difficult to keep the operation under wraps, and at this point, they managed to do just that.

Regardless, she could not leave this operation until its completion. Carrie's heart would not allow her to turn the operation over to anyone else. After a brief check of all the teams, she flipped through each of the cameras.

It was now or never, she thought, as fake Dirk made his way around the building, picking through the brambles and the brush the way Dirk did before. Lance carefully moved to his destination to give anyone watching the chance to identify him and make a move.

Panic welled up in her chest as she realized this operation was for real and one of their own now stepped into the crosshairs for the man she loved. She observed Lance's sleek form move through the woods on one of the cameras. The reassurance of the bulletproof vest under his jacket did little to assuage her fears.

"Hey, Charlie," Carrie said to the driver. "Take us to the rendezvous point.

"Yes, ma'am," the officer at the steering wheel replied, firing up the vehicle's massive engine.

"I forgot to ask, did everything go all right, boys?" Carrie glanced up at Dirk.

"Except for dingus here, thinking it was the Indy 500, he practically killed me. And, if that wasn't bad enough, Lance left a bottle of pee rolling around in the trunk."

Carrie laughed at the idea of Dirk being trapped in the trunk with a bottle of pee when suddenly her laughter stopped. Speaking into her microphone, she said, "Command to ten twenty-one, repeat." She listened to whatever the officer said in the earpiece. "Charlie, back to our position. Sounds like it could be showtime."

The officer running the quadcopter reported a vehicle slowing and stopping along the woods. The road along the ridgeline was little traveled most of the year with a small uptick in traffic during hunting season by hunters making their way to the state forests beyond. Two men exited and one of them grabbed an elongated case from the back seat of the car.

Both men wore hunting garb, not blaze orange as the law required, and stood about six feet tall. Neither of the men wore hunting boots but instead wore white tennis shoes. Coupled with the fact that only one of the men carried a rifle, they made an unlikely pair of hunters. Deer hunters along this stretch of road were common, but to have them enter the property of the church was unusual. No hunting signs every ten feet ensured anyone who could read knew hunting was out of the question.

Carrie switched on the speaker in the truck so Dirk and Keith could listen to the reports coming in. The teams worked flawlessly. Although the westernmost team could not see anything, the two other teams observed the men as they made their way into the valley. Three snipers reported in and only one presently could take a shot if need be.

For the first minute, the men stood near the vehicle at the tree line. The man with the rifle entered the woods and stood for a time, pretending to pee against a tree. The other man scrutinized the roadway in either direction, seemingly for any activity. Not wanting to spook the suspects, Carrie ordered all patrol cars to hang back. She could not risk someone sparking a firefight.

Carrie, Dirk, and Keith watched the action on the screen unfold until suddenly the camera went blank. The officer controlling the quadcopter explained it as a "small" momentary glitch in the system and worked to correct the problem.

"Well, I kind of see this as a big problem," Dirk remarked.

"What happens if we don't get the image back?" Keith asked Carrie.

Not responding to the question, Carrie picked up the handheld radio. "Command to ten twenty-four." Carrie, as if suddenly remembering Keith's question, said, "Snipers. Hopefully they have eyes on."

"Ten twenty-four, go ahead."

"Ten twenty-four, tell me you have eyes on the two men walking through the woods?" Carrie didn't have to tell Dirk and Keith the man behind call number ten twenty-four belonged to Officer Smiles, a close friend, the department's lead sniper, and easily the best shot on the east coast.

"Ten twenty-four to command, negative. Nothing yet."

"Damn," Carrie yelled. She gave the armrest a swat at her bad luck. Suddenly the camera on the quadcopter sprang back to life. The scene spread across the woods as before with the exception of the men who disappeared from view. "Ten twenty-one, get them back."

Scanning the woods for any sort of activity, the viewfinder lost the men completely. The officer controlling the craft switched the camera to infrared. "Ten twenty-one to base, I can't keep this up too long, the IR really wears the battery down."

"Finding them is priority. If you need to land, try to tell us where they are not."

Winds picked up making the camera jiggle slightly. Carrie knew the copter likely only flew on borrowed time, but finding the men could literally be a matter of life and death. Another gust of wind blew the copter across the tree tops, and when it stabilized, the camera showed two figures cautiously walking down the hill.

"Ten twenty-one, that's it. Just back out of there so we know where you are at." The copter gained altitude and reversed course back toward the officer.

"I think I know where they are," Dirk said. "In between Teams A and B, about half way down the hill."

Carrie breathed a sigh of relief. "Ten twenty-four, Smiley, tell me you see them."

"Wait one, command." A few moments painstakingly slipped by while the battle-tested sniper worked to pick up any visible traces of the men. "I got them. 'Bout halfway up the hill, between alpha and bravo."

The two other snipers reported in. One of them kept an eye on the area where Lance walked to address any close-in threats. The one remaining sniper reported having a partial shot on the lower half of the suspect's torso.

"See, what did I tell you?" Dirk said with a self-satisfied smugness.

Carrie keyed the radio connecting with the earpiece Lance wore. "All right, Lance, it's showtime."

Lance made his way out of a carefully chosen hiding spot and around the side of the building. The last thing anyone wanted was a situation they could not control.

"Team C, move to position two ... as quietly as possible." Carrie set three positions for every team. This way she could move them around the field as needed to adjust to the changing situation.

"Affirmative, Team C on the move," a female replied.

Carrie watched through the body camera of the leader of Team C as the team delicately picked their way through the trees and underbrush. Although the team could see the position they moved toward, the fall leaves made stealthy movement difficult.

Lance rounded the corner and proceeded toward the middle of the building, stopping at the fence to examine the unusually constructed opening. Carrie worked out the exact path he would walk and approximate pacing of movements so they could ensure everyone would be in the right place at the right time. Flipping the camera between Team C and Lance, she tracked both movements.

"Ten twenty-one to base, something is happening. Hold, Team C." Officer Smiles watched the two men on the ground shift their attention from their weapons to something in the distance.

Sergeant Andrews, nested with Team A, suddenly spoke up. "Talk to me, Smiley, what do you see." The two men in the woods turned toward Team C, frozen in position like mice fearing the impending pounce of a hungry feline.

"I think they hear Team C."

Carrie quickly thought through the situation and made her call. "Team C, stay put. Smiley, keep your eyes on the perps." She knew, based on how the perpetrators dressed, they could easily make an argument they accidentally stumbled into the wrong area and did not realize their mistake. In order to make a charge stick, intent to do harm needed to be present. Carrie balanced Lance's safety against the need to apprehend the bad guys.

Lance moved from the fence line to the building, examining the panel on the wall.

After a few moments, the two perps must have decided the noise was nothing more than a squirrel running from tree to tree or perhaps wind in the branches and resumed their deadly work. Finding a suitable place, one of the men dropped into a prone position while the other man dropped to a knee and leaned against a tree.

"Steady, everyone, keep your eyes open." Carrie tried to speak calmly into the microphone.

With no warning, the man in the prone position raised his rifle and fired.

A loud explosion sent the situation into chaos. Team C rushed the men's position as fast as they could while Team B moved into their secondary position in case the perpetrators made a break for it. A second shot rang out, and the man on the ground screamed in pain.

Carrie choked back the momentary wave of panic that overtook her as Lance's body bounced into the fence line and then collapse on the ground. "Lance, are you all right? Lance, come in!" Carrie shouted into the microphone.

"Holy fuck! That hurts like a son of a bitch!" Lance's voice came over the radio.

Dirk, Keith, and Carrie breathed a sigh of relief.

"Lance, are you okay?"

Lance sounded winded. "I think so. These vests may save your life, but that bullet still hits you like a truck. Think I'll need to take tomorrow off."

The other radio channels buzzed with orders and reports. Andrews took control of the situation on the ground, and Teams A and C converged to find the would-be assailant lying on the ground next to the rifle. Blood from his split skull seeped into the ground and painted the side of the tree. There was no mistaking the fatality of Smiley's shot.

"Andrews to base, one down, the other is on the run."

As soon as Andrews let up on the microphone key, two shots rang out farther up the hill with three shots returning in rapid succession.

Everyone held their breath as quiet retook the forest.

21

BURRITO NIGHT

The second assailant ran as fast as possible, putting distance between his fallen comrade and himself. Covered in blood and brain matter, the confused criminal panicked and ran with all the stealth of a charging rhinoceros. The moment the suspect saw Team B blocking the path, he fired two shots. One shot falling into the ground in front of the team, and the other went wide and hit a tree. The team responded with three shots, one of which hit its mark and sent the man crashing to the forest floor.

It took only a moment, and every member of the team trained a weapon on the man, who now screamed and held his arm. An officer stepped forward and flipped the man over. Grabbing a wrist, he pinned the man's arms behind his back and slapped on a pair of cuffs.

"Son of a bitch, try and be a little gentler. I was shot, you know." The gruff man yelled loud enough that his voice carried easily to Carrie's now open door. When she arrived at his side, he lay out on the ground, bleeding from an apparent shoulder wound, and the conspirator reminded her of one of her nephews faking an injury after accidentally running into the wall. After a quick inspection, she could tell the man's injuries likely only amounted to a flesh would and did not represent any permanent damage.

His screaming increased as the amount of people increased to hear him. Carrie waved off the growing assemblage. "Hey, scan the rest of the woods for others. We haven't secured the scene."

Carrie hardly blamed them. All were anxious to see what kind of man would attempt taking Dirk's life. Dirk joined Carrie from the truck.

As soon as the man stopped thrashing around in the now blood-soaked leaves he said, "Hey, you're dead. We just shot you." Realizing the error, he added, "I mean, on accident. Thought you was a deer. Sorry 'bout dat."

Dirk wanted to slug the guy for being so flippant about attempted murder. However, Lance was fine, and in reality, it was as good of an ending as they could have hoped. Besides, slugging a handcuffed man lacked a sense of fair play.

"Tell you what. Since I can see you are hurt, let's start with something easy. What's your name?" Carrie demanded.

"What's it to you, sweet cheeks?"

Her cheeks flushed with anger, and her fists suddenly curled into fists. "Let's just say I am an inquiring mind. And, while you're at it, why don't you tell me why you tried killing a man."

"My full name is"—the man suddenly smiled at Carrie —"Mr. I ain't saying shit until I talk to my lawyer."

Dirk worried she would beat the man senseless as he lay handcuffed on the ground.

The detective in her overruled her base instinct, and the color returned to her face. "Seriously, I would really like nothing more than to beat this guy's face in."

"I am pretty sure there would be a nice long line for that privilege," Sergeant Andrews said.

"No," Carrie said. "He wants a lawyer. So, we'll call whatever scumbag of a lawyer would represent him." She motioned to Sergeant Andrews. "Take this ... cooperative suspect ... to the hospital. Remember, he has an arm injury, so go as gentle as you feel necessary—or not. I want him under a constant double guard. The next time I see this fine fellow will be in an orange jumpsuit, facing down a charge to commit conspiracy to ambush and murder a police officer."

Walking away, Dirk gave into his curiosity. "Carrie, I don't think I have ever seen you so delighted to ensure someone will get their attorney before you question them. What gives?"

"True, I was mad as a hornet there for a minute, and then it occurred to me that him lawyering up could be the best thing ever. Soon, Mr. Arrcado is going to send a lawyer, and knowing who that is will be helpful. The bigger the lawyer, the bigger the fish." Carrie smiled to herself. "Don't worry, I'm going to grill this guy, but first, we will do everything by the books."

The next three hours, a flurry of activity overtook the police department. Dirk and Lance showered while the rest of the teams reconstituted. Officer Smiles gave a statement and then went home to rest and report back for a post-incident psych evaluation required after a shooting incident. Lance would require one as well.

Dirk understood the itch Carrie tried to scratch by waiting for any dirtbag of a lawyer the Arrcados would have on their payroll. One of three people would show up. One of them served as a glorified public defender making sure people didn't spend too much time in the slammer. Another lawyer possessed some clout and made a good career out of keeping thugs out of jail. The third attorney wore a Rolex watch and traveled to all appointments with a bodyguard.

Carrie didn't have to wait long. Silas MacGiven, the middle-of-the-road lawyer, walked up to the front desk and asked to see his client. He was shown to one of the interrogation rooms, where he sat and waited. While this happened, Carrie, Dirk, and Keith hid behind a wall and glanced over at him, like high school football players trying to catch a glimpse of the other team's quarterback. Carrie leaned back on the wall. "Great, MacGiven. I hate that asshole. Not the best lawyer they have but still pretty good. Basically, it just confirms our friend is important enough for the Mafia to care about him but not someone they are too worried about losing. This should be fun."

The chief came out of her office and walked up to Carrie. "You ready to do this?"

"I am. I'd love nothing more than to let this guy squirm a bit. I assume you must possess a soul in order to feel guilty enough to squirm about something. I doubt he has one." Carrie sneered in the direction of the Mafia's chosen spokesperson.

Carrie and the chief entered the interrogation room. "So, Silas MacGiven," the chief said. "Nice to see you again. I see they still have work for discredited lawyers. I would hate for you to be out wandering the streets. I am not sure it would be safe for our youth today."

"Well, if it isn't my favorite chief of police. How nice to see you again. Ruin anyone's career lately?"

The red-hot animosity between the two seared the air around Carrie the moment they laid eyes on each other. A veritable ocean of hostility washed over her so deep that she could barely find a pocket of air to breathe. They definitely had a history.

The attorney began. "I want to know where my client is. Either present him immediately or I'll file papers you are obstructing justice."

"Oh, Silas. You wouldn't know justice if it hit you in the chest and knocked you on your ass." The chief held a plastered-on smile in place. "Don't worry, your fine upstanding client will be along shortly. He suffered an arm injury, and we patched him up. Also needed a bit of a shower after getting his buddy's brains splattered all over himself."

"As long as we are just talking, why don't you explain to me what justified shooting a hunter just out looking for deer?" Silas sneered back at the chief in a pitched battle for who could deliver the most hate-filled glare.

"A little on the weak side, don't you think? I mean, seriously. Even for you, that is a stretch. Or that is what your handlers told you to say? Who's pulling your strings these days anyway? Oh, I am sorry, buckets of shit have handles, not strings." The chief leaned forward and glared at Silas with eyes that could melt steel. The simple act of viewing the exchange sent chills up Carrie's spine.

Silas leaned a little forward, causing the unflappable police chief to give a few inches. "You have the audacity to call me a bucket of shit when you went out of your way to ruin my life. You lesbian whore!"

Carrie did not have to be a psychic to see what came next. Under ordinary circumstances, she would have never grabbed the chief, but this situation's increasing volatility outpaced anyone's ability to control it. Carrie pulled her out of the interrogation room and into the hallway, which ran down the basement, separating the interrogation rooms from the storage and holding cells. The chief exploded in her rage and punched the nearby storage door, screaming out in anger.

Carrie, taken back by the sudden outburst, stepped toward the rearmost wall of the closet. Unsure if her friend's anger stemmed from her actions, the scumbag lawyer sitting in the interrogation room, or perhaps a combination of both, she said, "Chief, I'm sorry, I just—"

"Don't ... It's just that ... Look, Carrie, you didn't do anything wrong." The chief choked back a sob and wiped the tears in her eyes. "Let's step in here. She motioned to a storage closet holding paper products.

As soon as the door closed, the chief, her mentor and a close friend, melted into a puddle of emotions. Carrie held her oldest friend and offered comfort in an unknown situation. Melonie Dixon always offered support when things got tough, but now circumstances reversed themselves. Silas evoked something in her that pushed the normally unflappable woman over an edge Carrie did not even know existed. The chief sobbed into Carrie's shoulder for a moment.

Pushing back from the embrace, the chief grabbed one of the several hundred rolls of toilet paper off the shelf and pulled out a few pieces to blow her nose. "I'm sorry, Carrie, you really shouldn't see me like this. That fucking asshole gets to me in ways that no one else ever can. He's the physical embodiment of sexism and intolerance, and when I'm around him, he brings out the worst in me."

"It's all right, Chief. Every one of us has someone who gets under their skin from time to time." Carrie smiled and added, "I am just glad you didn't beat the shit out of him. What kind of headline would that have made?"

The chief laughed. "You need to deal with him. I hate that SOB more than I can even say. If I go back in there, you are going to have to pull me off him as I beat his head into the floor. For that, you need to know what kind of man he is. Silas is a dirty lawyer. Back in the old days, he used to hit on all the women and took it personally when I filed sexual harassment charges against him. Then, after catching him planting evidence at a crime scene, we arrested him."

Carrie raised an eyebrow. "But, why wasn't he disbarred?"

The door to the closet opened, and a startled janitor stopped mid-stride.

"Excuse us," Carrie said, glaring at the surprised man. "We're having a meeting in here."

The janitor backed up and re-read the label on the door before shaking his head in confusion and closing the door on the women.

For a moment, Carrie and the chief said nothing. Simultaneously, both burst out into laughter.

"Thanks, Carrie. I needed that." The chief dried her eyes on the remains of the toilet paper. "Let's just say he was really connected back then. Still has Mafia connections back to Tony Arrcado, even if his star has fallen somewhat as of late. Someday, over beers, I will tell you the story of what happened between me and Silas, but right now, I need you to go tear into that suspect. Just don't give Silas an inch. He'll take it and anything else he can steal. Best thing to do is isolate this little twerp and pretend Silas isn't even there. You can do this, I have faith in you. This is me, Melonie talking. Not Chief Dixon, but Melonie telling one of her dearest friends she can do anything."

Carrie never handled an interrogation this important before. The stakes were incredibly high, and one false move would let this dirtbag walk. Still, Melonie's faith in her was all she needed.

Carrie exhaled. "Okay, Melonie, I've got this. You can count on me."

The chief put her hand on Carrie's shoulder. "I know you do. Do you need anything?"

"Yes, can you bring Dirk and Keith down to the observation window? I want them to see this."

"I think that can be arranged." The chief opened the door, and both women exited the broom closet turned meeting room.

Carrie reentered the interrogation room where the suspect sat cuffed to the steel ring in the table. A wiry kid, he swam in the industrial orange cotton jumpsuit. With dirty-blond hair and gray eyes, he'd paint a handsome image cleaned up if his attitude was knocked down a few notches. Silas occupied the chair next to him.

Carrie weighed her options for getting this kid to break. With a lawyer sitting there, it made things a little difficult. Difficult but not impossible. She guessed his lawyer likely would make his client be as quiet as possible. The kid's self-generated swagger coupled with the slight hint of fear in his eyes told Carrie all she needed to know.

Silas cleared his throat. "I trust the chief is all right? She doesn't like good attorneys or the law for that matter."

Carrie shot back at him with daggers in her eyes. "Oh, yes, she is fine. She begs your forgiveness. She has other, more important, cases to work right now."

"More important?" Silas said with manufactured incredulity. "I am pretty sure a case involving the murder of an innocent man is far more important than anything else going on right now."

Carrie ignored Silas. "All right, when last we spoke, you didn't want to give me your name. How about now?"

"The name is Jimmy Arrcado." Jimmy leaned back in the chair with a plastered-on self-satisfied grin.

Carrie didn't even look up from her notebook while scribbling something down. "Jimmy Arrcado, is that with one R or two? As a matter of fact, spell it out for me."

"Detective," Silas interrupted, "is there a point to all of this?"

Carrie held up her finger as she continued scribbling on the notepad. "So, is it one or two?"

Jimmy scowled at her. "That is with two R's. Are you telling me you have not heard of the Arrcados?"

"Jimmy, shut up," Silas said.

Carrie glanced up briefly at him. "No, should I have?" Without letting him answer, she continued. "Address, please."

"Ten sixty West Addison, Chicago, Illinois."

"I see." Carrie studiously wrote it down. Of course, she realized the address was bogus, but played along. "Visiting from out of town. Ten sixty West Addison. Is that street, avenue, court ... or what?"

"Is this bitch fuckin' with me, Silas?" Jimmy shot a glance

over at the dirty lawyer who shrugged his shoulders in a dumbfounded gesture.

"So, Mr. Arrcado with two letter R's in his name. Can you give me a good phone number? Oh, and an e-mail address too?"

Silas suddenly spoke up, "Detective, what the hell are you doing? Are you interrogating my client or signing him up for the jelly of the month club?"

"In-processing. You know, as well as I do, we have to start with the correct information on our forms." She glanced back down to the papers. "Oh, yes, here is a great question, can you give me the name of your closest living relative?"

"Sure thing, doll. I'll give you the name of my uncle, Tony Arrcado. Maybe you know that name?" Jimmy leaned back in his chair and tried to resume a smug grin, this time a little less sure of its intended effect.

Carrie glanced up briefly from her notebook, remaining emotionless. "Sorry, no, that name doesn't ring a bell." Carrie made a notation on the piece of paper in front of her. "You have a good phone number to contact him?"

"You've got to be fucking kidding me." Silas slammed his hand down on the table. "Now you're just wasting our time. Tell me, Detective, what do you hope to gain by playing this little game?"

Carrie impassively studied Silas for a moment and then, cocking one eyebrow upward in a quizzical expression, said, "Counselor, I'm just trying to do the best job I possibly can. I need to get all the correct information from your client here in order to process him through the jail. I promise you, I'm going as fast as I can."

Carrie shifted her gaze back to Jimmy. "All right, how can I get a hold of this Donald Ar-cat-o?"

Jimmy slammed a fist down on the table in front of them. The sound reverberated off the cement walls of the interrogation room. "You fucking bitch. It's Tony Arrcado. You know perfectly well who Tony Arrcado is."

Silas waved his hand at his client. "Jimmy, be quiet."

"Hell no. This bitch is messing with me. And it is time someone messed back."

Carrie, in a volume just above a whisper and not looking up, said, "I assure you, sir, I am not messing with anyone."

Jimmy's face turned red. Carrie's plan going into the room, built around the chief's suggestion, leaned heavily on continually needling Jimmy—figuring out what buttons to press and then continually mashing them. She got the impression Jimmy liked being known. The way he said his name, with increased volume and a little bit of a lilt, Jimmy thought quite a bit of himself. The way he said his last name suggested he did it only to impress her.

She knew of two ways to handle a man like this. Either give the impression that having captured an Arrcado impressed her or pretend to not even know what the name meant and work him into a lather and let him say something stupid. In no mood to feed egos, Carrie realized Jimmy was the right kind of stupid to trip over his own tongue, given the right stressors.

Inwardly, Carrie was beaming as her plan worked perfectly.

"All right then, shall we continue. So, Donnie, oh, I'm sorry"—Carrie faked a glace toward her paper—"Jimmy, how do I get a hold of this Tony?"

Silas, finally seeing through Carrie's plan, spoke up. "Jimmy, don't answer that."

"Like hell I'm not going to answer. He lives over in the Glenn Fields part of town. Tell you what, cutie pie, take a ride over there and go talk to him. I'm pretty sure the guy at the front gate will be more than happy to see you. You might get your pretty hair a little mussed up."

Silas made another impassioned plea. "Jimmy, I really don't think—"

"Silas, shut the hell up. You're an idiot and always have been," Jimmy yelled. Red-faced, he turned back to Carrie. "You're telling me, you have no idea who Tony is? As many times as you pigs dragged him here, you are going to insist you have no idea who my uncle is and no idea who I am? I can tell you one thing for sure. Pretty soon, you're gonna pay for all this, and that isn't a threat, Detective, that's a promise. Nobody fucks with Jimmy Arrcado."

"Mr. Arcadia ... I assure you there is no need for—"

"Arrcado, you stupid bitch. The name is Jimmy Arrcado, and my uncle is Tony Arrcado of the Arrcado Mafia family."

"Jimmy, shut up." Silas yelled at the scrawny adult now. Increasingly more and more agitated with his inability to hold his tongue, the lawyer understood Carrie currently sat on the winning team. "As your lawyer, I have to advise you to keep your big mouth—"

Jimmy shifted toward Silas as far as the cuffs would allow. His bandaged arm strained to reach out. Silas jumped back a little in the stainless-steel chair. "Silas, you are a worm. Keep flapping that jaw of yours and I will make sure they have to wire it shut for you."

"Mister"—Carrie stopped to examine her paper as if

searching for a name—"Arrcado, you need to calm down so we can finish up here. I have a bunch of real criminals we have to deal with today."

Jimmy's eyes shifted from Silas to Carrie. His face showed the markers of stress brought on by severe anger. Red skin, beads of sweat on the forehead, and eyes bulging out of their sockets made Jimmy appear to be in the throes of a heart attack. A small vessel in his temple bulged out so far that Carrie wondered if he would need a paramedic before too long. "What do you mean real criminals?"

Carrie knew Jimmy sat precariously on the ledge between where she wanted him and his comfort zone. A slight nudge in the right direction easily would send him right over the edge, and the only thing left would be to deliver the recording to the transcriptionist for evidence. "I mean, Mr. Arcadia, you didn't pull the trigger, so I just assumed you are nothing more than a lackey."

Carrie thought he would explode. She could almost feel his temperature rise. The whole scene reminded her of a cartoon character blowing steam out of their ears. She smiled innocently back at the young man, waiting for what she knew surely must come next.

Once again, Silas tried to interject. "Jimmy, I am giving you one final warning that—"

Jimmy, ignoring Silas, stared at Carrie across the table. "You ain't shit to me. Nothing more than a glorified jailer, and I have them on my payroll. I am Jimmy Arrcado. Get it right. That guy you iced is nothing more than a stooge and does what I tell him to do. He don't shit without me saying the word and only pulls the trigger because I tell him to." Jimmy suddenly trailed off, a look of panic suddenly replacing the previous self-sure demeanor.

Carrie glanced at Silas who simply sat in begrudging appreciation of the game she played exceptionally well. Silas underestimated her. Carrie's good looks and deceptively petite frame proved a deadly combination with the cocksure underworld types used to shoving women around and getting their way. She loved taking them down.

His red face suddenly turned a gray color. Jimmy silently turned toward Silas and just stared as if the counselor hid a magic button allowing them to go back in time ten minutes.

Carrie smiled and stuck her pen in her shirt pocket. "Thank you, Jimmy. That will be quite enough. I appreciate your patience. I'm formally charging you for attempted first degree murder and conspiracy. By the way, stay tuned because I think there could be federal charges coming soon."

"You fucking cunt, you tricked me." Jimmy's color changed from a deathly gray to more of a puke-colored green.

Silas, who hadn't said a word, deflated like a balloon. He slumped over in his chair. "For the love of God, Jimmy. Shut the hell up."

Carrie smiled at Silas. "I quite agree. Time to end this. And no, Jimmy, I never tricked you. You said everything of your own free will. We have the entire conversation in a digital recording if you want to see the playback. Although, we will probably just save that for court."

Jimmy suddenly struck a more conciliatory tone. "I said all of that in front of my lawyer. Isn't that, like, privileged or something?"

"Not quite how that works, Jimmy. Silas, you can come with me if you want a cup of coffee or something. Or you can sit in here with this guy. Either way, we're done for the day." Carrie turned toward Jimmy. "Just hang tight, and a nice gentlemen will come around and take you back to the jail for the evening. If I were you, I would get comfy. You are probably going to hang out for a good long while before trial. But after that, they'll probably inject chemicals into your veins. Then you will go to that place all bad people go."

"I want a plea deal. I have information to trade," Jimmy stuttered.

"No thanks, I think we're good here. Have a nice evening, Mr. Arrcado. I think you're in luck, it's burrito night at the jail." Carrie left the room and Silas walked after her. He didn't say anything and reminded her of a lost kitten. Surprisingly, a pang of sympathy hit her for the dirty attorney. Tony would likely have him killed after letting his nephew come up on charges. At the very least, this exposed the family to considerable bad press. Silas essentially became a walking corpse the moment Jimmy opened his mouth too wide.

The chief met them in the hallway. As soon as Silas went into the waiting area to call Tony with the bad news, she ushered Carrie into the office.

"I swear by all that is holy and right in this world, I have no idea how you pulled that off. You were amazing in there. Like watching Picasso work."

Dirk and Keith joined them in the room for the mini-celebration. "Great job, sweetie! I think you just nailed an attempted murder conviction for that guy."

"Yeah, thanks. I am so thrilled I just gave myself a bunch of paperwork to do." After hugs all around, Carrie left the group and stepped into the hallway. Taking a quick glance into the break room, she saw Silas was nowhere to be found.

Desperate to rub it into Silas's face, she expected the attorney to stay long enough for the official paperwork on his client. An equal possibility, he realized the gravity of the situation and decided now was the perfect time to go into hiding. Maybe he would turn and go into witness protection against the Arrcado family. Running promised the only way to avoid a bullet to the temple. Then again, the Mafia could be very persistent.

Making her way down the hallway, she walked past the desks allotted the uniformed officers to do their paperwork. She turned left and opened the door into the Detective's Pit and the offices for the department's senior officers.

Approaching her shared desk, she noticed a piece of yellow paper folded in half lying on her keyboard. The pen she used for taking notes lay on top of the yellow legal pad on the corner of the desk, and the paper matched the one used to write the note.

She unfolded the slip of paper and stared at the odd message. "11378 Boston Lane. Compare to the church warehouse."

Carrie folded up the paper and tucked it into her jacket pocket. A noise caught her attention in the corner of the room. Charlie, the department's janitor, rustled a trash can while going about his duties. "Hey, Charlie, did you see anyone in here leaving me a note."

"Yeah, some guy in a brown suit came in and asked where your desk was. He wrote a note and then left."

22

UNFATHOMABLE COLD

The chief eyed the yellow piece of paper. "Yeah, that is definitely Silas's handwriting. I've seen it enough to know what it looks like. Why would he do this though? Seems a little odd for him. He's a devoted servant to the Arrcado family. Giving us a tip signs his death warrant."

"My guess is that the death warrant was signed the second we charged Jimmy. Not sure what is going on behind the scenes, but if Silas turned on the family and is making a run for it, this tip could be his way to throw the family in chaos while he makes a run for the hills. Maybe Dirk knows something. Let me grab him." Carrie got up from her desk.

"Don't bother. Lover boy went home. He figured the coast is clear enough for now since the Arrcados are likely going to lay low until this either blows over or Jimmy serves a life sentence." The chief handed back the little piece of paper to Carrie. "Did you look up the address?"

"I did, the old satellite photos show an old dock house by

the river. One of those late-1800s places. Sitting vacant for a long time. An angler on the internet complained building at the location ruined the fishing. I remember answering calls to there once or twice. I did find a reference to the Bureau of Engraving and Printing buying the property."

Carrie eyed the yellow piece of paper. "Well, I want to hide from paperwork, so I'll run over there and take a quick look when I am ready to take a break."

AS FAR AS loose ends go, Dirk really hated them. A bunch of unanswered questions swirled in his mind. First and foremost, why did Jimmy Arrcado want him dead? All Dirk did was investigate a low-level theft from a church warehouse. Not something that would normally even register on the Mafia's radar screen. Certainly not enough to warrant them sending out two different hit squads.

The tie between the cases sat unresolved. Why would a construction company building a ready-made back door into a place be of any consequence to the people who stole trinkets from a church? It just did not make any sense. Then there was the crappy front company, Center Point Security. What did that have to do with any of this?

The warehouse also bothered Dirk. One hundred percent sure he'd seen the layout of the warehouse before, he couldn't put his finger on it. The building gave off the same vibe he'd gotten while visiting a former military installation.

Keith admired the numerous bullet holes in the walls. "Wow, they sure did a good job on this place. There must be a thousand holes in the walls."

"Yeah, must have been a sale on ammo or something." Dirk and Keith took an inventory of the things in the house, making a careful list of everything broken. The insurance adjuster already came out and approved the outside work but wanted a more comprehensive list for the inside.

Then the matter of the motorcycle repair shop weighed heavily on Dirk's mind. Since it was effectively destroyed, Dirk decided to make internal changes to the layout. As long as the insurance paid for the major expenses, he wanted to put a little of his own money into the project and make a few improvements. Dirk briefly thought about walking away from it entirely but knew Victor would likely never forgive him. The ghost saved Claire, a debt never repayable. Dirk knew he could not leave the shop the way it was and find a new location. Risking the specter if his only tie to this world was whether the repair shop stood was a price too high for him to pay. Dirk wanted to see Victor back, if only to thank him.

Keith picked up a photo of the two of them fishing in Colorado a few years earlier. "Hey, Dirk, what do you say we head out to the mountains for a few days. Bring the poles with us and do a little fishing? We could use a break."

Dirk snickered at the idea. It would be great to just slough off all responsibility and head down to the river for fishing. He recalled a great spot right along where the old port facilities operated back around the turn of the century when they still relied heavily on the river for transportation.

There was so much to be done, with the house still in need of repairs and the shop in need of rebuilding, it would be a bad time for them to run off. Even if Dirk could go fishing for a few days, he needed Keith around to help redesign the repair bays in the shop. For years, he had wanted to do that but could not justify the layout of money. The bomb took care of all of that.

Fishing would be so much fun, but I think they were doing construction down by the river the last time I drove by.

"Holy shit," Dirk exclaimed.

"Dirk, you know I don't mind a little bit of swearing, but come on now." Keith gave Dirk a parochial grimace.

"Keith, look on the computer for the name Center Point, and I will give you an address to cross-reference."

Not questioning his friend's sudden change of attitude, he sat down at the computer in the office in the back of the house and typed in the name. "Okay, got a few hits, not a ton, but some references. What are we searching for?"

Dirk scrolled through a series of maps on his smartphone, identifying street names. "Okay, cross-reference Boston Lane and any mention of a permit for construction."

Keith's knack for using the internet always impressed Dirk. A few strokes of the keyboard and a couple of right clicks brought them to a listing for a permit, filed two years ago, for work on a new federal building being constructed at 11378 Boston Lane. The particulars of the construction were more or less irrelevant to anyone without a background in federal contracting, but far more interesting was the name of the person signing for the company. All the permits were signed and accepted, on behalf of the contractor, by Silas MacGiven, Esquire.

"Okay, I forgive you for swearing. How on earth did you connect those dots?" Keith leaned back in the office chair.

Dirk placed a finger on the tip of his nose. "You actually connected the dots, you just didn't know it. Your suggestion we go fishing jogged my memory. From the first moment I set foot on the grounds of the warehouse, that building felt familiar to me. Like I'd seen it before. The memory sat just out of reach, taunting me. Driving me a little nuts."

"Crazier than you already are?" Keith interjected.

"Indeed, but a different kind of crazy. It was a nagging sensation, like when you thought you remembered everything when you left for the house that morning but then realized you left your coffee sitting on the roof of the car. Kind of like when you forget to write your sermons until the last second."

"Get on with it." Keith turned on the printer, and pages spewed forth from a website featuring all contracts for government-related construction.

"Again, I knew I'd been there before. But, that couldn't have been possible because there is no reason to set foot on the property until you brought me that case to work. Still, the building is so familiar I could almost see it in my head. Even the placement of the fence lines and security cameras felt familiar.

"You, my fine feathered friend, put the last piece of the puzzle in place for me. When we were kids, we used to fish at that old abandoned port facility. Remember the place with the old concrete docks?"

Keith raised an eyebrow. "Oh, you mean the Port of Tetanus?"

Dirk smiled at Keith's recalling of their pet name for the place. Back then, the buildings fell and disintegrated right in front of their eyes. They called it the Port of Tetanus after Keith sliced a hand open on a piece of rusted rebar one afternoon.

"Two months ago, I worked one quick case without you,

remember? It was that guy who suspected his wife of cheating on him."

"What ever happened with that anyway?" Keith asked.

"Totally screwing his boss, but not important to the story. I drove by the Port of Tetanus multiple times that week and would eat my lunch out there sometimes. I watched them put the finishing touches on a new warehouse. Do you want to guess whose warehouse it looks exactly like?"

Keith's eyes widened, and he pursed his lips. "And Center Point constructed them both?"

"Exactly. Keith, stick with me here, what if the construction and thefts from the warehouse are nothing more than practice runs for something larger. Maybe something bringing in a much larger payday? Or possibly just a distraction?"

Keith, already ahead of Dirk's thought process, typed furiously on the keyboard. "That doesn't explain what numbnuts was doing. You know, the guy Carrie got to confess to attempted murder. What could they be storing in that facility the Mafia could want?"

"Sheesh, numbnuts, huh? You gave me a hard time about my language?" Dirk smiled.

Keith continued his search while Dirk watched over his shoulder. He would have to call Carrie and let her know what they discovered. Before making that phone call, they wanted to know more information about what sat inside the warehouse. What could possibly be that valuable to warrant this much trouble?

CARRIE'S BINOCULARS focused in on the sign hanging on the wall indicating the facility belonged to the Bureau of Engraving and Printing. The building itself felt strangely familiar, but she could not quite sort out why. The size and layout screamed at her for attention but only teased her memory for the moment. In front a lonely guard post controlled access. A perimeter around the building lay flat and stretched out like a road around the building in either direction.

A small parking lot provided spaces for a couple of cars, three forklifts, and a small golf cart with the word security on the front. It bore a remarkable resemblance to any other federally run warehouse in Virginia. Reaching down into the cup holder of her squad car, she pulled out a bottle of soda and took a long drink. While she was not on an official stake-out, she always carried enough snacks in the car to cover any contingency.

She was unsure why Silas pointed them to this particular address, but he must have had a good reason. A connection between the government and the Mafia seemed implausible. Something happened which crossed a red line even a snake like Silas was unwilling to cross. An old informant from her patrol days mentioned the local Mafia family sat in the throes of inner turmoil as the old guard retired and the new kids took the reins.

Carrie could not shake the feeling of familiarity with this building. Years ago, she came here on a call when a bunch of homeless people took up residence in the building formerly occupying the space. Ordinarily, the department turned a blind eye to squatters, preferring not to force them to move from place to place throughout the city. However, the building could barely hold itself up let alone who knew how many squatters wandering the abandoned hallways. They needed to force them out or risk having to rescue people in a building collapse.

As she took her eyes off the computer screen, a flash of metal in the rearview mirror momentarily caused Carrie to shield her eyes. A vehicle pulled up behind hers. Guessing it to be a security car sent to find out why an unmarked squad car sat watching the building, she intended to wave the rent-a-cops off with a flash of her badge.

Carrie stepped out onto the roadway. "Good afternoon, my name is Detective Carrie Pet—"

Carrie only processed the noise of the gunshot and the muzzle flash before everything went dark. A sudden eruption of her own weapon narrowly preceded the sensation of razor-sharp metal ripping through her body before the world succumbed to unfathomable cold.

23

THIRTY FEET OF HOLY ROPE TO HANG YOURSELF WITH

When Dirk and Keith showed up at the station, the chief asked them to join her in the basement to participate in the interrogation of Carolyn.

Surprisingly, Carolyn waived her right to have her attorney present during questioning, and for the moment, the three of them sat together in the cold interrogation room.

After a few perfunctory questions, Keith asked, "It was the intercom, wasn't it?"

Carolyn fingered the cuffs holding her in place through the steel ring welded to the table. "Can you blame a girl for a little eavesdropping? Besides, it isn't a crime to eavesdrop, is it?"

Dirk considered it for a moment. It was so easy for her to just listen in on the intercom system in the office. Likely, that was the main reason Carolyn decided to eliminate him and also how she knew where to find him the day he got hit over the head. "No, eavesdropping isn't a crime, but conspiracy to commit murder is."

"You have to prove it first," Carolyn said with a smile.

"Probably only a matter of time before they subpoena your cell phone records and find out who you called the day I was injured," Dirk said.

"Yeah, how is your head, anyway?" Carolyn said.

"I never said my head," Dirk shot back. "Okay, let's say we just assume you are only in this for a small-time crime. Let's just say, for argument's sake, you are going to spend as little time in jail as possible with the understanding that I really have no say in the matter. Then there should be no harm in you telling me what part you played in all of this."

Carolyn dropped her good Catholic girl guise and took a less charitable tone with Dirk. "Wow, you are as stupid as you look. I am not even sure how you are such a famous private investigator. Do you really think I am going to tell you that?"

Keith, who sat stoically in the corner of the room, spoke up. "Actually, we kind of assumed you wouldn't. We are more interested in what you know about the building at eleven three seventy-eight Boston Lane? What can you tell us about that?"

Carolyn opened her mouth to say something, but stopped short of forming intelligible words. Keith continued. "We already know a lot. People on their way over there right now to check the place out. We also know of the connection between the warehouse and that property. Dirk discovered the fence line and built-in back door, and I am assuming there are more than a few more surprises in store after we peel back the onion a little."

For dramatic effect, Keith transcribed the address on

another piece of paper and slid it across the table so she could see it.

Carolyn's face drained of any color. "I ... I ... don't know anything—"

Dirk slammed an open hand down on the steel table. "Damn it, Carolyn, I don't care what you have done or what you think others have done. The game is over. You lost. We know it all and we are only sewing up a few of the loose ends. And you are going to help tug at the loose threads."

"Immunity, I want immunity."

Dirk rolled his eyes. "First off, I can't give you that because I am not a lawyer. Even if I could, you hit me on the head. Then, you tried to kill me. You actually shot another guy dressed up to look like me. How much sympathy do you really think I have for you?"

"The church robberies were all Jimmy's idea. I didn't do anything."

Dirk raised an eyebrow. "Jimmy came up with this plan?" Dirk considered the idea the plan came from Jimmy. From what he understood of the little dirtbag, Jimmy was nothing more than a worm of a person. As far as criminals went, Jimmy lacked even the rudimentary skills to be a criminal mastermind.

"Why was Jimmy out knocking over churches? It seems a little beneath what the nephew of a crime boss should be occupying his time with."

"Wow," Carolyn said, "you don't know much, do you. Here's a freebie. Jimmy was out there breaking into churches mainly to give himself something to do. My brother always wanted to be the big man but thought too small. Honestly, Jimmy came from the shallow end of the gene pool. Kind of a dolt, always has been. Uncle Tony understood the kid's violent tendencies and sent him out in the world to steal, rape, and pillage. More importantly, to stay out of everyone's way while something larger was being planned. Jimmy's little circus is nothing more than a convenient distraction."

The chief pulled a small brown envelope out of her suit coat and placed it on the table in front of her. For the moment, the four of them just stared at it. Dirk expected something to crawl out of it with the way Melonie placed it on the table. Wordlessly, she slid it across the table toward Carolyn. "Open it."

Carolyn let out a sarcastic laugh. "Why? Is it going to kill me or something?"

Melonie stared through Carolyn, her face reddened. Dirk could feel a seething hatred come from his friend's usually calm demeanor. Whatever that envelope contained carried critical importance. That small manila envelope contained the answer, and only Melonie knew its contents. "I said open that envelope."

The fear in Carolyn's eyes read like a book to all in the room. Something about the envelope suddenly repelled her. If the handcuffs and the table suddenly vanished, she'd jump out of the seat and run through the door, and no one would ever see her again. All because of a three-by-two-inch envelope. "This is stupid, but I'll play along."

Dirk and Keith held their breath as she painfully opened the envelope and let the contents slide out onto the stainless-steel interrogation room table. The glint against the fluorescent lights told Dirk in an instant what it was.

Before them all lay the small cross, now clean of the blood, that Dirk found inside the offices of Center Point. For a few seconds, no one said anything. Carolyn's brows knitted together in confusion. "I'm supposed to know what this means?"

"Do you know whose cross that is?" Melonie, never diminutive, rose to her full height. Dirk shared in the respect Carrie had for her boss. The scene reminded him of a teacher about to correct an unruly student.

"How the hell should I know?" Carolyn relaxed a little at the seemingly insignificant piece of evidence now lying before her.

"I am going to give you the short version of the story. That cross belonged to Sister Mary Rebecca. We can confirm this. On it, we found blood. You'll never guess whose blood. Or maybe you can?" Melonie stepped forward and leaned on the table between Dirk and Keith. "Your blood, Carolyn. We found your blood on it."

"I work with these penguins all the time. There is no way you can possibly pin murder on me because my blood is on a piece of junk jewelry."

Keith's mind flashed to the first meeting in the office with the archbishop. He remembered her arm bandage. Perhaps an altercation between her and the nuns left a wound?

Melonie glared at Carolyn who shrank into the back of the chair in an attempt to disappear. "That is the holy cross and not a piece of junk jewelry. It meant something to someone. A young woman placed it around her neck when her parents gave it to her as a simple gift when she undertook a life of service to her God. She never took it off. A life of service you decided was yours to end. By the way, no one ever said anything about murder. But I'm so glad you did."

"You can't possibly ..." Carolyn trailed off as she realized her line of logic would never hold.

"Now, here is where things start sounding really interesting. Guess where we found this piece of jewelry?" Melonie let a few seconds of silence pass for dramatic effect. "The offices of Center Point. But you already knew that, didn't you?"

"But, you can't really think that I know anything about them?"

"Carolyn, right now, I have a warrant on its way for a judge's signature. When she signs it, I'm going to have every single forensics tech at my disposal tear that place apart. Do you think there is even a chance I won't find evidence linking the Sister Mary Rebecca to that place? How about your DNA?"

Carolyn relaxed in her chair and glanced around the room as if the walls, floor, and ceiling materialized out of thin air or she had never noticed them before. It was the relaxation of someone resigned to total capitulation and a fate no long under her control.

"As I said, my brother pulled the strings. Can't be a crime boss in the Mafia if you don't have a dick and a pair of marbles. Jimmy ordered all the hits. My uncle told him to stop, but Jimmy refused. And, for the record, I didn't kill anyone. I told you the truth. That drunk Sully pulled the trigger. He'll do anything to keep the booze flowing."

The news hit Dirk hard. Until this point, he still held out hope the nuns would be found alive and well. Now that hope vanished with Carolyn's revelation.

"This is the one conciliation I'm going to throw you. How did your blood get on the cross?"

"Sister Mary Rebecca was actually a charity boxer back in

the day and still had one hell of a right hook. I defended myself, but she scratched the hell out of my arm. My blood is everywhere in that large room in the back. My nose bled for hours."

Dirk, who remained silent until then, cleared his throat.

"Yes, Dirk?" Melonie said.

"I am wondering. Why did the sisters have to die? What sin could they have possibly committed to make Jimmy mark them for execution?" Dirk spoke to Melonie with the words clearly intended for the ears of Carolyn.

"Well, Carolyn, it isn't polite to keep Dirk waiting. Why did those servants of God deserve whatever happened to them?"

Carolyn drew in a deep breath. "The three of them figured it out. They realized things went missing from the church and wanted to talk with the archbishop. They didn't know I was involved and called to make an appointment. Naturally, I called Tony, and a few of the enforcers came over and ushered them away. When we got over to the office, Sister Rebecca decided it was time to go all George Foreman on me. I was told to leave, and then Sully apparently did what he is paid to do. According to what Jimmy said, they took the bodies, wrapped in construction plastic, to a disposal location. I went back to the office to make sure the paperwork on them disappeared.

"No one told me where those penguins were dumped, and I never asked. They thought it better that information remained a secret from me. Tony himself actually hatched the plan to set up Center Point, offer to do the church's warehouse construction for next to nothing. After being too much of a thorn in my uncle's side, he let that lunkhead Jimmy try out his own new crew on a few thefts. He even forced a few of the more senior guys to help out so Jimmy wouldn't go too far."

Melonie interrupted. "So, are you saying that Vance and Carl were really there to keep an eye on Jimmy?"

"That's right. Sort of like babysitters for the maladjusted. Anyway, the sisters were just victims of being too clever and in the wrong place at the wrong time. And, once again, for the record, I was against killing them. I don't make the rules."

Carolyn broke down, less in remorse and more because the enormity of everything suddenly lay at her feet in a smoking pile. "I was all in, you know. We needed a big score, and that would be it for some of us. I'd leave town until things simmered down, and then we'd be on easy street. At least until those damn nuns showed up and ruined the whole thing."

Dirk almost forgot that at the end of all of this, one nun passed away without ever seeing her friends again on earth. However, he took inner solace in the idea of the three reunited in the afterlife.

Carolyn continued talking well into the night. Satisfied Carolyn filled in as much of their blanks as she possibly could, Dirk and Keith left for the evening to sleep. A little unnerved that Carrie had not returned, Dirk reassured himself that she knew how to take care of herself. At least he told himself that.

A DESERTED STREET with derelict buildings gave the impression of a post-zombie apocalypse world where homes sat abandoned. A gray-haired woman plodded her way down the pavement. Dressed in bright pink running pants and a purple cold-weather running shirt she juxtaposed her colors on the world to great effect. In her younger days she knocked the guys dead. After a marriage and becoming a widow at far too early an age, she learned to love life and long-distance running.

Her friends warned her not to run in that abandoned part of town, but with a ten-mile race coming up, she needed the empty streets and culs-de-sac. This little neighborhood no longer served the needs of residents, as a company planned to tear it all down and rebuild. The company folded, leaving the buildings derelict, waiting for a new buyer to surface.

The morning was chilly but perfect for an extended run. Passing a forlorn intersection, the time-worn runner noticed something out of the ordinary. A flash of color where none existed before during her previous runs through the deserted neighborhood, causing her to slow and then stop.

Having run this route fifty or more times over the past year, she knew the lonely Oxford shoe made a conspicuously new edition to the landscape. Slowly approaching the fence line, she stepped through an opening which once held a gate. The green water in the pool, collected from rain, stewed in a discolored soup with the tinge of algae left to grow undeterred by pool chemicals. A red slick of color tinged the green in striking opposition.

The woman let out a scream that a few years earlier would easily attract attention. Now in a completely abandoned part of town, her scream echoed through the streets, living rooms, and garages of a 1960s housing development left to rot and awaiting the unceremonious appointment with the blade of a demolition company bulldozer.

Over the lip of the pool floated the figure of a man in a brown suit. Blood streamed from a gaping head wound, leaving rivers of crimson blood reaching out from the body like red tentacles in search of another host.

Face up and just barely readable were random papers floating in the water, an airline ticket, and a small business card. The card read "Silas MacGiven, Attorney at Law."

DIRK WOKE with a start that morning. As if someone kicked him, he instinctively reached for his weapon.

His phone, lying on the nightstand, displayed a series of text messages. To his dismay, none of them were from Carrie. Three of the messages were from the chief and two from Keith. Dirk cursed himself for not remembering to turn on the ringer.

Instead of replying to the messages, he pushed through the grogginess and called Melonie back. "Hey, it's Dirk, what is going on?"

"Dirk, come down here right away. Something went wrong. No one has seen Carrie since last night when she failed to check in. They found her car parked along the side of the road with the keys locked inside. They found blood, a lot of blood."

"I'm on my way."

Dirk made it to the police station as quickly as possible. Forgoing a normal stop at The Beanapse for a cup of coffee, the thought of Carrie missing woke him up more than any coffee ever would.

The station resembled a swirling mass of controlled chaos. At its center, coordinating the chaos, stood Deputy Chief Duffley. A man with wings of gray hair at each temple, he reminded Dirk of his father who always carried an air of authority. Not the most fit man in the world, Duffley was born with the gift of being an amazing tactical commander. What the man lacked in strength and physical stamina, he made up for in organization.

Chief Dixon popped her head out of her office door and yelled, "Get in here."

Dirk, doing as told, fought to keep swirls of emotion in check. Something bad happened and it potentially involved the most important person in the world to him.

CARRIE WOKE to the deeply conflicted warm sensations of a hand on her chest and the ice cold of the floor. For a moment, she wondered if she fell asleep in an uncomfortable position in her own bed and the hand belonged to Dirk.

She tried to move, but sudden pain rang out in protest through her body. "Oh, Jesus," Carrie said.

"Detective, I need you to remain still. I am holding your wounds closed. They are, I fear, severe, and my first aid is only marginally successful."

"Collins?" Carrie managed to say under a ragged breath.

"Indeed, you are correct, Detective. I fear I may not have been as good of a police officer as you thought I was. My arrogance put us all in danger, and letting my pride guide my principles ended up—"

"Collins ... shut up." Carrie's head screamed, and his self-deprecating lecture struck at her nerves like a mallet to the forehead. "I need to think for a moment. Why are you grabbing my boobs?"

"Indeed, I am. It is to keep the bleeding to a minimum. I feared you would not wake up."

Carrie tried to move her arm in the dimly lit room, but the pain overwhelmed her. In addition, her stomach presently auditioned for the acrobat performance in a circus. The nausea was a clear sign of shock. Collins might have slowed her bleeding, but her situation remained far from stable.

"Collins, listen to me. We need to crawl out of here, and I don't know how much time we have." She scanned the room. A single source of light hummed somewhere above them. All four walls around them rose up to impossible heights. None of the walls gave any indication of a door or a ladder.

As if answering an unspoken question, Collins remarked, "I believe we are in a pit in an industrial area. I cannot tell where."

"Do you have a gun?" Carrie knew he probably didn't, but asking could never hurt.

"No, they stripped me of my weapons and broke both of my legs. I cannot move easily, or I might have saved us by now."

Carrie let the statement go. She really needed to try talking to this kid about not being quite so arrogant.

They needed to find a way out, signal for help, and do it all with Collins's hand exerting enough pressure on her chest to ensure she didn't bleed out in the process.

"How did I end up here?" Carrie asked, while scanning the walls for anything to better their situation.

"The individuals threw you in here with me, and I acted unconscious. Then I pulled myself over to you and assessed your situation and took action."

Carrie hoped for something more useful than that, but it did answer the question of why most of her body felt like someone beat it with a baseball bat.

In the dim lights floating into the would-be tomb, a pile of something in the corner caught her attention. The pile reminded her vaguely of human forms with a black piece of cloth thrown over the top of it. "What are those, Collins?"

"I hoped you wouldn't ask, Detective. I am reasonably certain those are the nuns your boyfriend searched for. Judging by the stage of putrefaction, they have been here for a while."

Carrie said a silent prayer. At their ages, the fall likely killed them instantly, if they even were alive at that point. Remorse hit her hard. They investigated the disappearances, and although Dirk lost faith in finding them, she and Keith pressed on in the investigation. At least now, the families could have closure. That was, if they could get out of there.

Carrie instantly chided herself for thinking that way. Negative thoughts were of little use in this situation. It would be a tough thing to accomplish, but escaping could be done. While Collins had his legs broken, likely he could still pull himself up if they could find a rope or something.

"Collins, can you move?"

"I can."

"Okay, here is what we are going to do. I can still use my feet, and I think I could probably stand. The first thing we are going to have to do is check on our friends over there. They may be dead, but I think they could still help us."

Working together, the two pulled themselves over to the stilled corpses. As they got closer, Carrie noted the change in smells. Fans running somewhere in the building kept the stench of the rotting bodies at bay, and as they approached, the smell became apparent.

The bodies were at different stages of decay. Carrie tried to make out each nun's face under the rotting visages. A task she quickly gave up on. Each wore a traditional nun's habit, a cincture at the waist, and one of the nuns wore a heavy golden cross around her neck which could double as a weapon should the need arise.

Removing one of the nun's habits and putting the gold cross in her pocket, Carrie tore the cloth, and Collins fashioned a bandage that could, at least temporarily, staunch the bleeding. She needed his hands free if they were going to climb from the pit. Next, she tied the cinctures together in a rope totaling about thirty feet in length. It would be enough to try hooking something at the ground level. A long shot, but at this point, few other options remained.

Carrie handed the rope to the young officer, and he tied a stiff knot on the end. "Collins, if we get out of here alive, I am going to make sure you receive a commendation for saving my life."

"I don't deserve it, Detective." Hefting the monkey-fist-sized ball he fashioned on the end of the rope, he threw it up and over the side of the pit. "I disobeyed your direct order, and it got me here."

"Okay, you made a stupid mistake. You are a young patrol officer and you have a long career filled with plenty of mistakes ahead of you. Follow orders next time. However, you likely saved my life. Sometimes, it's the actions you take after you screw up that shows your true character. Don't worry, if we make it out of here, I will make you pay for disobeying me, but for now, we've a job to do."

"I think I understand."

Carrie thought about how easy it was to forget that putting on a police uniform did not automatically make you wise beyond all reason. In times of trouble, people turned to the police for answers and forget that behind that uniform was a living, breathing human being just as capable of making mistakes as the people they tried to protect.

Carrie could feel, as she tried to move, the effects of the blood loss taking its toll. Although the dim light made the amount difficult to discern, the last thing she remembered was the muzzle flash and the smell of burning gunpowder outside the car.

Collins made a few more throws up the side of the pit and connected with a few things on the other side. Neither one of them had any idea what potential items sat up at the top, or if they could even grapple anything to help them. Carrie also worried silently about the possibility of someone seeing the rope thrown over the lip of the pit. At this point, inaction translated into a death sentence.

24

OFFICER DOWN. I REPEAT, OFFICER DOWN.

"Chief, you have to let me come along," Dirk begged.

"Dirk, I'm sorry, if there was any way I could make it work, I would. You know the rules. You are a private investigator and, therefore, a private citizen. I can't run the risk of you shooting someone on the scene. What happens if you accidentally shot one of my officers?" She got stoic. "What happens if you take a bullet? Dirk, do you think Carrie will ever let me live that down? That is a risk I'm not willing to take."

Keith, watching the exchange from Carrie's desk, offered a solution. "What about this? We hang tight off the scene until you decide it is all right to let us in? That way, we are out of the line of fire, and we are still technically within the scope of the law since we are really only entering the scene after the police think it's secure."

Chief Dixon eyed the men warily. She knew, given the right set of circumstances, they'd easily overstep their bounds.

She let Dirk do that before, and he got into a shootout. However, in that instance, he showed good judgment, and it likely saved a life. "Fine. You guys stay out of it unless you or the lives of others are threatened. I don't want you running in guns blazing. Do I make myself clear?"

Dirk took a more somber tone than normal and nodded in agreement. "Fine, I promise. We will stay back on perimeter until you give us the all clear.

Thirty minutes later, every police officer at the department, every deputy they could pull from the county, and every federal agent they knew descended on the warehouse along the river. During Keith's research, they found the facility was paid for under a contract from the federal government and contracted to Center Point Contracting, a division of Center Point Industries, Incorporated. Outside of the federal employee paid to visit the site once a week, everyone else was a contractor. Although the warehouse didn't hold anything of high intrinsic value, it did house drums of the ink used to print currency. Dirk and Keith quickly surmised what the Mafia wanted.

Stealing anything from a federal property always came with inherent risks. Since Center Point constructed, staffed, and administered the operation, the theft proved to be the easiest part of the operation. After anyone became wise to what they were doing, they could cut their losses and run from the project. One drum of the special color-shifting ink used to dye U.S. bills would fetch a pretty penny on the black market to more than cover the initial outlay of the project and make everyone filthy rich.

After Carolyn admitted her part in the operation, an expert combed through her computer and found all the records she attempted to delete. Carolyn forgot the golden rule of database work—there were always copies of everything somewhere. The evidence sealed her conviction.

Dirk watched the police gearing up for the assault beside a grove of trees effectively keeping them out of the line of sight. Thinking back over the years, he remembered his private investigator mentor telling him about a case he worked where the building at this location was being used to hold a kidnapped man in an extortion scheme which went horribly wrong.

After the snipers gained a useful perch, the chief gave the order to advance. The order, through the radio, startled Dirk. At the moment, the facility remained too quiet for such an operation. Outside of the guard sitting in the security shack, no one came into or out of the building. Even the normal smokers, common to a warehouse such as this, were conspicuously absent from the equation. Dirk could not shake an unsettled feeling in the pit of his stomach, but he remained in place.

After the group advanced on the small security shack and secured the lone guard, the police made their way inside. With the help of the FBI, they gained quick access without alerting anyone. Dirk listened to the radio as each team reported a litany of clear reports, indicating they found no suspects.

Soon the chief called for Dirk and Keith to come up. What they found surprised them. With the exception of a few lone federal forms lying on the ground, the warehouse sat completely empty. Every box, barrel, or government-issued pen was missing. Almost as if no one ever inhabited the building at all.

Dirk found the spot where the false wall remained closed and pushed it open to the outside. He also pulled up the fence, just like the one at the church's warehouse. His suspicion proved correct, and the diocese warehouse stood as a convenient proof of concept for a more lucrative operation—only he didn't realize it until it was too late to stop the theft from taking place.

Checking out the rest of the building, he found more of the same, nothing. The worst part of it all was Carrie remained unlocated.

A HEAVY THUD of something wooden indicated the rope knot connected with something substantial. The noise it made as they pulled it across the floor suggested something of wood. As tough as Collins tried to be, she could tell the stress and injuries made continuing this work increasingly difficult.

In her own weakened state, Carrie prayed silently they hooked something useful enough to help extricate themselves from the pit. Time clearly grew short.

Over the top of the pit, two slats of wood appeared. A few tugs of the rope revealed a long wooden pallet. Not exactly a ladder, but beggars couldn't be choosers. He would not be able to stand on his legs, but Carrie might be able to climb out with her remaining strength.

A few more pulls of the rope and the wooden pallet fell into the pit with a deafening thud. What she lacked in strength, Collins made up in their partnership. While unable to stand on two broken legs, his upper body strength worked well enough to move the pallet around, allowing him to lean it up against the wall in a makeshift ladder.

Carrie noticed the amount of blood on Collin's uniform, or what remained of it. He'd lost far more blood than she had. Whoever threw them down here never intended for them to regain their freedom. By throwing people down here, half dead, it allowed time to elapse between the initial assault and actual death. A smart move as it established plausible deniability and allowed for plenty of cross-contamination of evidence.

"All right, Detective. I need you to climb up there. I am afraid my legs won't carry me."

Carrie considered the reach necessary to make the lip of the pit. In perfect shape, it would be easy enough to jump up and pull herself to the top without the pallet. In her weakened state, she wondered if she could do it and if it was possible for her legs to carry her far enough away from the building to find anyone to help them.

"Okay, but I need you to help me as much as you can. It isn't going to be easy. Once I am up there, can you pull yourself up to sit on the top of the pallet to let me climb up on your shoulders?"

"I will do my best, Detective. It is all I can give." With a stoic frown on his face, he added, "Detective Pettygrew, I am sorry for not following orders. I am afraid I have done-—-"

"Quit with the pity party, already. You took a chance and made a mistake. Life is full of those kinds of things. It won't be your last if I have anything to say about it. Now, put on your big boy panties, and let's do this."

"I am more of a commando man myself," he remarked with a smirk.

"Wow, he makes jokes. Hey, there is one thing I need to know. At the door of the Smiling Orchid, you said something to the man to let us in, what did you say?"

"Detective, that is simple. I recognized the man spoke Mandarin. In English, the translation might be: Come on, buddy, let us in."

"Oh geez." She smiled and shook her head at the youth while hoisting herself up the makeshift ladder. Her arms screamed out in pain and cramps formed in her legs, begging her to give up, and still she persisted until she stood on top of the pallet with her eyes just clearing the top of the pit. Thankfully, the small empty building, reeking of fuel oil and grease, sat empty.

The bullet wound in her chest burned with pain with every move she made. Carrie knew that with every movement she risked a chunk of lead severing something necessary for life. Nodding at Collins, she put one foot on his shoulder. He grabbed her by the ankles to help steady her.

"One, two, three, and go," Carrie said. With the word go, Collins pushed as hard as he could, making a horrifying groaning noise as he gave everything. She pulled herself out of the pit and onto the floor of the warehouse. The cold of the concrete floor pierced her shirt, but the feeling proved at least one of them escaped their prison.

Pulling herself around, she hung her head over the side, preparing to help him up. "Hold on, I am going to find something to help you out of there." In sharp contrast to a few short moments ago, his demeanor changed completely. He sat impossibly motionless with his shoulders hunched over, and panic welled up inside. "Can you hear me?"

His body shifted to the left and crashed from the improvised ladder to the floor.

"Collins, answer me!" Carrie shouted. The young officer lay on the floor, like a marionette whose strings were cut. The boy gave all to support her escape attempt, and if she could save him, time would be a limiting factor.

Grabbing the handle of a broom, she used it to brace herself. Carrie made her way to the door and pushed it open. A wave of nausea washed over her as she scanned the horizon. Less than one hundred feet away sat five squad cars with their lights flashing. She recognized the industrial building that had led to her current predicament.

With no warning, the lack of blood and abundance of exhaustion caught up with Carrie, melting the world around her in a lack of focus. The scene descended into a pinprick of light, and just before the last bit of light faded from her consciousness, someone yelled out, "Officer down! I repeat, officer down! We need an ambulance!"

25

YOU CROSSED THE WRONG MAN

Loving someone in law enforcement could be difficult under the best of circumstances, and the dangers Carrie faced loomed like a wraith waiting to swoop in at any moment. He, above others, understood the reality of what befell her on a daily basis. For years, the stories from the more dangerous aspects of her job became a backdrop to their lives.

None of that prepared him for the words "Dirk, they found Carrie. She is in pretty bad shape."

Keith, having known Dirk longer than almost anyone, stood at his side and awaited the inevitable implosion that would likely follow.

An officer, scanning the property, looked at an old building which was used for servicing train locomotives at the turn of the century. Shocked to see Carrie suddenly standing there, he ran to her as fast as his legs would carry him. The paramedics found a heartbeat which only trended strong enough to sustain life. It kept her in life's warm embrace, if only barely. The paramedics improved her situation slightly on the ride to the hospital.

Dumbfounded, Dirk stood motionless. Around him, squad cars moved from one place to another while crime scene techs worked to find evidence. Noises, voices, and even the birds in the trees took on an oddly monotone quality reminding him of a radio in the next room. The world fell into a slow-motion pattern around him, and for once in his life, he was unsure what to do next.

Deep in the pit, they also found the bodies of three nuns and the recently deceased Officer Collins. The paramedics hinted that he had lost far more blood than one person should and still live. For now, Dirk only cared about Carrie.

Driving to the hospital, numbness overtook Dirk like nothing ever before. If anything happened to her, nothing could ever repair the hole left in him. She made up the best parts of life, and losing her was a future he refused to accept.

As he merged onto a short stretch of highway leading to the hospital, something caught his eye. A convoy of trucks negotiated a cloverleaf onto a major highway out of town. He only caught the side of the truck briefly, but the words Center Point Industries clearly screamed out to him. Dirk hit the brakes and spun the car around in the grassy median in the divided highway. The moment his tires touched pavement again, he hit the gas pedal, driving like a man possessed.

The needle of his car hit ninety miles an hour before slowing down to negotiate the cloverleaf heading north. As he merged back onto the highway, the car's speedometer bounced back quickly to eighty miles an hour before leaving the acceleration lane. Ahead, the convoy of trucks continued their lumbering movement to their unknown destination.

Thoughts ran through his head. Dark and demonic, they ended with Dirk making them pay. They tried to kill Claire and might yet succeed in ending Carrie's life. Thoughts of nudging the trucks into the ditch, one by one, and shooting everyone inside filled his head. The law became unimportant, justice became an abstract concept, and, right now, revenge controlled his actions.

None of them deserved to live. They lost that right the moment the Mafia declared war on Dirk and his loved ones.

Then an innocent thought entered his mind. What would Claire think of all of this? What he contemplated easily fell under the umbrella of cold-blooded murder. Granted, murdering those who would think nothing of killing him, but murder never the less. The idea of Claire visiting him in a prison visitation booth shamed him.

Then his thoughts turned to Carrie. Primarily, she identified as a police officer. She valued justice and the imperfect system they lived under. Some small part simply could never forgive him for cold-blooded murder. Carrie would say she understood but not really. He loved her, and her disappointment would be crippling.

While the brake lights and the backs of the trucks grew brighter and larger, Dirk pulled his foot off the accelerator. It occurred to him that he did not want to slow the car. However, Carrie, Claire, and Keith stood out as the most compelling argument against giving in to his impulse. Hurting these men would be therapeutic and, no doubt, they deserved it. No matter what evil they undertook, Dirk was not a cold-blooded killer. He thought about the Mafia guy he'd killed in the forest. An act of self-defense. Running these trucks off the road would be murder, plain and simple.

"Phone," Dirk said, starting his hands-free device. "Dial Melonie Dixon."

"Dirk, where the hell are you? Someone called you in cutting across four lanes of traffic on the highway. Are you all right?" The chief's voice barely hid her shock and relief.

"Send me a ticket, Melonie. Listen, I'm Northbound on three seventy-one at mile marker ... ummm ... sixty-four. I am following three trucks from Center Point. We may have just missed these guys by an hour or so, and I found them by accident."

The chief shouted out something to a few people. "Okay, you need to come to the hospital to be with Carrie. She's out of surgery and appears stable. In rough shape, but they said her heartbeat is improving against all odds."

"Excellent, but I can't come back. Carrie would never forgive me if I gave up this chase. I need to stay on these guys until you can get here. If we lose them, we may never find them again and these sons of bitches need to pay. I'm not letting them go."

"Okay, backup is on the way. Promise you won't do anything."

"Chief, you know me, I—"

"Yes, I do know you. Again, behave yourself." Chief Dixon ended the call.

The trucks continued down the road at a curiously legal speed. Dirk recalled a study of criminals discovered because they essentially broke common speeding laws, causing them to be pulled over just before they could make their getaway.

These guys are almost being too careful.

Keeping a safe distance, following three large industrial trucks down the highway at the posted speed limit posed little challenge. Still, the drivers likely came heavily armed—even if the cargo was nothing more than barrels of printing ink.

Dirk's phone rang. "Dirk here."

"It's Melonie, I have news. Carrie has slipped into a coma, but all her vitals appear stable. Are you sure you don't want to turn around?"

"I'm sure. Tell Keith to stay with her. Call me when someone else has eyes on these guys and I'll turn around and come to the hospital." The words just about killed Dirk inside. The urge to turn the car around in the middle of the interstate and rush back to the hospital almost overwhelmed him. In his heart, he knew sitting with Carrie he'd only be a huge slobbering mess. Here, on the open highway, he could be an asset. Carrie and Claire both needed him to see this through.

Hanging up the phone, he almost missed the trucks coming to a stop along the roadway. If Dirk hadn't looked up, the car would have rear-ended the last truck in the convoy. Thinking fast, he turned into the next lane and drove ahead as if nothing happened. He would need to find the next overpass and hang out until the trucks passed him again.

A few miles up the road, one of the county highways crossed the freeway and he exited. Calling into the department, he relayed the new information. The patrolman he talked to gave him the number of a U.S. marshal who just happened to transit the area and could participate in the search.

Fifteen minutes later, a government vehicle pulled up behind Dirk's car on the overpass, and a man stepped out wearing blue jeans and a University of Iowa sweatshirt. "You Dirk?" the man asked.

"I am," Dirk responded.

"Marshal Jones. I didn't see the convoy when I came up from the city. Maybe they slipped past you?" The marshal frowned skeptically at Dirk. He did not have to say what he thought, but the condescending tone indicated he hated working with private investigators.

"No way, I have a pretty clear field of view, and if those trucks continued north, they would either have to drive past me at the exit or drive under the overpass. I would have seen them."

"Well, you can leave this to the professionals. I will take over from here. You can go home or wherever you people go."

Dirk instantly hated this guy's pompous attitude, but he didn't have time to worry about it. Wordlessly, he drove off. Turning south on the highway, back toward the town, he wondered if he missed anything. Some detail about the trucks themselves? The marshal was right, between where he stopped to watch from the overpass and where Dirk knew the trucks stopped, turning around or turning off the highway seemed impossible.

It bothered Dirk that three large moving trucks could essentially vanish in thin air. Turning the car around in the middle of the highway, Dirk resolved to check the area where the trucks stopped. Three trucks, weighing about ten tons a piece, could not just vanish into thin air.

At the place the trucks stopped, Dirk got out and examined the shoulder of the highway. Nothing specifically interesting stood out about the area. Dirk walked the length of where the trucks stopped and made out the faint indents in the dirt along the side of the road left by the tires.

The divided highway offered no easy place for large vehicles to turn around, and the marshal would have certainly noticed the trucks going the opposite direction.

Along the northbound lane, an old farm fence made of barbed wire formed the barrier between the highway right of way and private property. Largely intact, the wire would have to be taken down if anyone attempted to drive cross-country into the farm field.

Holy crap! That's brilliant.

A road led off across the farm field that was nothing more than an overgrown patch offering a flat path easily allowing trucks to pass. He walked up to the fence line, and the barbed wire gave way. In his hands, Dirk held movie-prop-quality rubber barbed wire. At a distance, it passed for the real thing. A brick lay near one of the posts which Dirk suspected served to hold the fake wire down to allow the trucks to pass.

Wasting no time, Dirk jumped in his car and headed down the farm road. Now easily twenty minutes behind the trucks, catching up in an open field would be difficult without being seen. At the very least, he could expect the owner of the field to call the police because of an idiot driving a car through the fields.

Dialing the phone again, he updated the department on what happened. Unfortunately, the marshal continued so far down the road, convinced Dirk lost his mind, it would be a long time before any backup arrived. A helicopter, procured through a favor the local FBI office owed the chief, still wouldn't be in place for another thirty minutes.

At a rise in the hill, the scrub brush gave way to a more substantial road, and Dirk clearly made out the tracks of the tires. At least he headed in the right direction. The road wound across an open field and into a ravine with bluffs on either side rising up in both directions. Trees filled the ravine as if a celestial being poured them onto the landscape and decided to leave the rest of the area bare.

Stopping the car, Dirk pulled out a set of binoculars. He scanned for any sign of movement. He realized any haste may result in barging into the middle of the group doing whatever they were doing. Stumbling onto the scene might result in him being on the wrong end of a rifle. He thought back to the men outside of his house, and that experience suggested the group in the trucks outgunned him.

In the unnaturally still grove of trees, anyone could develop the flawed opinion nothing sat inside the impenetrable tree line. As Dirk's eyes adjusted to the murky depths of the forest, a set of brake lights from one of the trucks flashed. Needing to close the distance, Dirk planned a route that brought him as close to the gang as he dared. The land between Dirk's car and the trucks lay out in an open field. Any attempt to cross it would gain unwanted attention.

He scanned the field for a way to approach and retain his cover. Grabbing binoculars from the glove compartment, Dirk prepared to make a low dash toward the buildings when a noise just below the rise sent him for cover. As if answering prayers, a herd of cattle came up from the bottom of the hill to Dirk's left. Moving in with them, he kept low. The mass of moving hamburger cooperated, and only three of the oblivious bovines showed any interest in the non-hooved creature in their midst.

Exiting the other side of the mass of odorous leather, Dirk took cover behind a pile of rocks where a farmer must have deposited them. Raising the binoculars again, Dirk made out five men off-loading the drums of ink and moving them into three waiting rental trucks from three different companies.

Dirk found himself oddly impressed by the plan. The moving trucks would become impossible to track and as ubiquitous on the highway as the asphalt itself. The large and conspicuously marked Center Point trucks outlived their purpose. Once they took to the road again, the moving trucks would be nearly impossible to track if Dirk was not in place observing every facet unfold.

Dirk's jeans pocket vibrated with an incoming call. This time, the caller ID read "Keith."

"Yeah, buddy, how's Carrie?"

Keith spoke unnecessarily low, matching Dirk's attempt to be quiet. "I just left the hospital. Claire and your sister are sitting with her. No change in her condition, I'm afraid. The chief wants me back at the station. Where are you?"

Dirk watched the men working at the trucks through the lenses of his binoculars and grimaced as one of the men walked over to a tree and dropped his pants to relieve himself on a tree. "I am off the highway where I told the chief I would be. I am guessing two miles from the fence line there is an abandoned farmhouse and buildings tucked in a small grove of dense trees. I am pretty sure you can find it on a satellite map search."

"Okay, just stay where you are at. We're getting you backup."

"Good, thanks. Hey, Keith, can you stop by my house and check the mailbox? I'm expecting a small package in the mail today, and I need it."

"Are you kidding me? You are tracking the Mafia, Carrie is

in the hospital, and you are worried about a stinking box in your mail?" Keith sounded beside himself with disbelief.

"Just do it, okay? I promise you I'll sit tight and wait for the cavalry to arrive, but I need that box."

"You are a mystery, my friend. We are going to leave the station soon. I just stepped out to check on Carrie." Keith hung up the phone.

Dirk wondered to himself how any of this would play out. If the cavalry did not show up soon, none of it would matter, and the trucks would surely slip into the anonymity of the interstate.

26

THE CAVALRY ARRIVES TO A POOL OF GREEN MUD

Only risking occasional glances over the top of the rock at the men, Dirk could tell it would only be a matter of time before they would complete the transfer and the trucks would likely disappear. Although Dirk knew it would be possible to track real moving trucks, these were likely stolen, had the tracker removed, and were given a new vehicle identification number along with a fresh paint job complete with decals good enough to fool just about anyone.

He occasionally sent Keith status updates, and after twenty minutes, the telltale sound of the rolling door of one of the trucks closed. Two of the men leaned up against the side of one truck and smoked a cigarette while waiting for the other trucks to finish.

The trucks bearing the security company's logo moved into a large pole barn on the other side of the property. The condition of the farm suggested visits came only infrequently so the trucks would have remained in the pole barn for quite a while before being discovered.

Overhead, and just out of Dirk's vision, a helicopter came over the horizon. One of the men sitting on a long-forgotten crate by the truck stood in sudden surprise as if someone kicked him. He reached inside the fake moving truck and pulled out a small portable radio. Dirk could see, through the binoculars, the small handheld radio appeared eerily similar to the one Carrie used to carry before she became a detective.

Oh crap, they will hear everything.

While the police maintained radio silence while moving the team to the farm, likely they would use the radio to coordinate movements closer in, giving the Mafia enough time to set up a trap. Dirk pulled his phone out and sent a group text to the chief and every detective or police officer he knew: Don't use the radios. Arrcado's men have a radio and will hear everything you say once you are in position.

Too late for a more elaborate warning, the men ran for cover as soon as the helicopter approached. Likely the pilot said something spooking them.

Cursing the bad luck cutting his observation time short, Dirk sent another text to the group: 8 men, machine guns, small arms. Perhaps more men in the house, cannot confirm.

Dirk got back an immediate response from the chief: Keep the intel coming, copy all.

Each man brandished some type of assault rifle or Uzi. Dirk hoped the helicopter made a full report of the men before they scrambled for cover. Between his report and the choppers, the picture might be as complete as possible until the shooting started.

At least Dirk could be confident information made its way

out to the team. Dirk glanced up at the helicopter, which now took a somewhat conspicuous location, hovering above the farmhouse. Through his binoculars, he observed one man sitting in the jump seat beside an open door. He carried a rifle and a pair of binoculars. He waved at Dirk, who waved back. Although in a gunfight, Dirk would be as good as dead, at least another good guy sat nearby, watching his back.

His phone buzzed in his hand again, and he looked at the glowing text: Two minutes out. Stay low when the shooting starts. Dirk wondered why anyone thought it necessary to tell him that. Generally, Dirk avoided getting anyone shot during an investigation, especially himself.

The eight men took off running. Each took up a position of cover behind a boulder and the front of one of the trucks. If the assault team was only two minutes out, there would not be much time before the good guys found themselves facing a wall of bullets.

Dirk typed another text: Chief, they moved to intercept you, ambush.

Dirk waited anxiously for a sort of response, hoping the volume on the chief's phone allowed her to hear the phone and she would read the message. Anxiously, he glanced down at the phone hoping and praying for some sort of acknowledgment.

Clouds of dust over the horizon rose up in the fall air. Dirk knew it could only be from the approaching team of police vehicles. The only access roads into and out of the area sat either where the police came from or where Dirk currently hid. The Mafia decided to stay and fight although Dirk could not figure out why. Although the Mafia certainly carried better weapons than the standard issue police armament, they usually ran when faced with the police. They preferred to live to steal and extort another day if possible.

Dirk glanced again at the helicopter, and the man sitting in the jump seat held up his hands, indicating he could not see anything from his post.

Since the Mafia gunmen held ambush positions, they maintained an upper hand in the initial fight. The police would win the engagement, but with the element of surprise and automatic weapons, the first volley would result in a blood bath. Dirk needed to do something quick to warn everyone.

One remaining truck sat open. Inside, several barrels of the ink sat in a row. Through the iron sights of his semi-automatic pistol, Dirk aimed into the back of the truck. A well-placed shot would likely put him into the crosshairs of the Mafia. It also could tip the odds back toward the police since responding to Dirk meant they had to leave their ambush positions.

It was a difficult shot under the best of circumstances, but he only needed one of the rounds to hit its mark for its intended effect. Dirk took careful aim and fired three shots into the back of the truck. One shot went wide and disappeared into the trees. The next shot sent the right turn signal cover of the truck spinning off into a thousand directions. The third shot hit its mark with shocking results.

Not knowing the exact contents of the barrels, or how full they were, the results were better than anticipated. The barrel exploded with the pressure of the round hitting it, sending a spray and a tidal wave of dark green liquid out the back of the truck, forming a river of deep green.

Two more shots barked from Dirk's weapon with similar

effects. One of the bad guys running for the back of the truck to try and close the door slipped in the ooze of quickly combining ink and dirt. Another man rushed to his friend in crime and ended up slipping in the soupy mixture as well.

The first man, now comically trying to regain his footing, fired a single shot which flew well over Dirk's head. Then he threw his weapon down in disgust as it refused to fire another round. The second man also tried to take a shot, but his weapon failed. At the very least, the mud and ink took their weapons out of service.

Another gunman, watching his friends struggle, took off running toward Dirk. Firing at him, Dirk's shots completely missed, and trees made another clear shot impossible.

Dirk watched helplessly as a man slowed and raised an automatic weapon to his shoulder while he closed the remaining distance. As he was only armed with his pistol, Dirk needed the man to come as close as possible if he stood any chance of hitting him. This left only moments before one of them lay dead in the dirt of the pasture, and the odds were firmly stacked against Dirk.

A crack issued from above, but Dirk was unable to process the sound in any meaningful way. The would-be assailant's head exploded, sending a crimson spray away from the body along with a sizable portion of the man's head. The body skidded to an unceremonious stop on the ground fifteen feet from Dirk. Blood oozed from the wound, forming a puddle under what remained of his head.

Dirk glanced up at the helicopter and saw the man in the jump seat, still holding a rife on his shoulder, wave and continue scanning the woods for movement. He would owe the agent a beer when this ended. Whoever the agent was, he likely saved Dirk's life.

The police, reacting to Dirk's shots, formed a perimeter and exchanged gunfire with the men. Two more Mafioso squatted behind a truck, waiting for someone to come within range. Dirk took the opportunity to move up after ensuring the police knew his position. He hated the idea of being gunned down by his own side.

Dirk ducked behind another clump of trees and watched the two men in the growing ink puddle try to stand and fail. The scene would have struck Dirk as hilarious if not so deadly at the same time. One of the two men ducking behind the truck recognized him and fired two shots that buried themselves into a tree. He returned fire and incapacitated one of them. The other man made a break for it and quickly fell in a barrage of police gunfire.

Chief Dixon appeared next to Dirk, who remained behind the cover of the large tree. "I can assume you fired those first shots?"

"Yeah, I needed to warn you before you got here. I tried to warn you in a text message, but I had no way of knowing if you got it or not."

Melonie glanced down at her cell phone. "Hey, check it out. We are walking into an ambush. Thanks, Dirk." She smiled at him. His actions likely saved a lot of lives, and she knew it.

"That ink sure made one hell of a mess. You are going to have to fish those guys out of there. I don't think they can get out on their own," Dirk said. The men who now sat in the green-tinged mud, resigned to their slippery fate, held their hands up in the universal sign of capitulation.

Dirk counted five of the assailants down, which meant three remained if his initial count proved correct. Several officers, still avoiding the radios, motioned they observed three men fleeing into the house silently bearing witness to the firefight from the shadows. As the police fished the two ink-stained men from the green lake of ink, Dirk scanned the windows for any sign of the rest of the assailants.

The house stood quiet, eerily so. None of the windows showed any movement, and the front door remained resolutely closed as if expecting someone to come up on the porch to ask for permission to come in. Entering the structure presented the most dangerous task, and everyone knew it.

The chief gave instructions to the entry team using hand signals as the suspects still likely monitored police communications. Sergeant Andrews nodded and brought the team up to the building and after clearing the windows, they shouted for the assailants to come out.

The lack of any discernible noise became deafening as the house stood grave silent before them. The old colonial fixture rose up two stories with a peaked attic window that leaned forward giving the impression it watched the goings-on with extreme interest. Wind swaying the trees lent an eerie noise as the branches clicked against one another.

Several squad cars moved up to provide cover for the officers as they waited for either side to make the next move. Keith sidled up to Dirk. "I have your box. So, what is going on?"

"Good." Dirk took the small, plain cardboard box from Keith and tucked it in his pocket. "Five bad guys down, at least three more in the house. Right now, we seem to be at a standoff."

The chief, having moved back toward incident command, suddenly overpowered everything with a loudspeaker. "Inside the house. We have you surrounded. Too many people have died already. Let's end this now, and no one else has to get hurt."

The stillness again gained its hold over the scene. Wind in the trees resumed the clattering of the browned leaves waiting to take their final fall to the ground. Birds, which sat in silence when deafening gunfire ruled the air, returned with a few tentative chirps.

"We have terms!" a gruff voice shouted from inside the house.

"All right, I am ready to hear them. But I need a show of good faith," the chief said through the megaphone.

"Send in the private investigator," the man inside the house said. "He can keep his gun. We need to talk."

The chief shot Dirk a quizzical glance. The response was unexpected and was far from the show of faith she'd hoped for. "I'm not going to make you go in. This sure seems like a setup to me. Do you have any idea why they specifically asked for you?"

"Not a clue. Although, he did say I could keep my gun. Maybe there is a reason they want to talk to me." Dirk glanced alternately from the chief to the front door of the house. "But, if I can end this, we should give it a shot."

"I can't let you do this. A civilian going into an active standoff. That's not going to work." She understood Dirk's innate curiosity made him naturally want to go inside.

Keith continued to scan the windows of the building. "I have an idea. Why not hire us? Not on retainer, but make us police officers."

"I would love to, but I can't without going through the board to make a hiring decision. They would have my badge if they knew I did that. But, wait a minute." The chief motioned to someone in the distance, and around the corner of the truck, the U.S. marshal who previously dismissed Dirk appeared. The marshal plastered a forced grin on his face, clearly understanding Dirk outclassed him by figuring out where the criminals went.

"Marshal, can you still deputize people?"

He frowned at the idea. "Yes, in extreme circumstances, I can. Why?"

"I need you to deputize Dirk and Keith."

His face issued a stern objection to the idea, but practicality got the better of him. "Okay, but understand this is only good as long as we are on this active crime scene." He turned toward the chief. "You are my witness of this act."

The marshal quickly administered the oath of office, which sounded made up, sounding as official as they could under the circumstances. Chief Dixon turned back toward the house. "All right, Dirk can come in. He brings Keith with him."

Keith shrugged the idea off as only being natural. "Hey, Dirk," Keith said. "We're federal agents. That's kind of hilarious."

Dirk snickered at the oddity of the idea. Out of all the jobs Dirk had over the years, federal agent was never one of them. The U.S. marshal sneered at the men. Dirk added the marshal to his list of people to buy a beer to mend the relationship after everything was said and done.

A voice called back from the house. "All right, he can come

too. But I swear if I see anyone make a move on this house before they leave I will kill both of them."

Keith never carried a weapon, preferring to use negotiating skills rather than shoot things out. His counseling skills often made the critical difference on many an investigation. Failing that, he held his own in any fist fight. Dirk suddenly wished his friend wore a gun.

Both men approached the house, feeling the tension behind them rising with every footfall. Alongside the worn walkway to the house, a small rusted tricycle sat under an old flowering bush blooming in spite of not having regular humans to appreciate its beauty. Peeling paint of a bygone era, sagging window sashes, and the remnants of green outside carpeting suggested years of disuse and neglect. Dirk wondered if he would ever see the outside of this house ever again.

Weapon or not, if this is a trap, we are dead meat.

As they stepped up the wooden stairs to the front door, the dust and mildew of disuse overwhelmed all other smells while the floorboards let out a squeak of protest. For a moment, the whole thing reminded Dirk of a haunted house.

Moving to the side of the door, Keith and Dirk knew if someone wanted them dead, shooting through the door presented and enticing option. It would be the perfect way to initiate an escape because it put the police in recovery mode before pursuing the criminals.

To Dirk's surprise, the front door opened, and a short woman stood just inside in the dark. She bore a striking resemblance to Carolyn, and he wondered if the secretary really remained in custody or not.

"Come in," she said.

Dirk and Keith entered what used to be a front room. The walls wore ancient strips of wallpaper, hanging down in places where water and mildew took its toll on the glue holding it to the wall. An ancient fireplace in the living room stood unused. The remains of a bird's nest sat in it.

"Head upstairs, gentlemen. The boss wants to talk to you."

Dirk and Keith ascended stairs squeaking a protest underfoot, suggesting they might give out at any minute, which delivered them safely to the top landing in spite of themselves. Unsure where to go, Dirk glanced into one of the rooms, and a collection of abandoned dressers and bedframes told the story of a home unoccupied for years. A calendar, tacked to the wall, showed a picture of a black cat standing on a pumpkin with the year 1995 carved into it. At the other end of the hallway, a man suddenly appeared in a lab coat and glasses. "Gentlemen, in here." They entered the room to see a sight stopping them in their tracks.

An old man lay in a supine position with a few dirty pillows lifting his head up from the bed. A needle stuck in one arm connected him to a bag full of liquid hanging unceremoniously from a nail on the wall. An EMS kit, likely stolen, lay open on a table nearby, obviously rummaged through to find anything to help the man.

"Mr. Arrcado, we finally meet." Dirk smirked.

Keith's mouth dropped open in genuine surprise. "You knew he was going to be here?"

"Mr. Bentley, please"—Tony coughed and took a raspy breath—"please come here." The Mafia kingpin held an oxygen mask to his chin. Occasionally grabbing it, Tony forcibly inhaled like a drug addict in desperate need of the next fix.

"Elementary, my dear pastor." Dirk turned from Tony and faced Keith. "Carolyn provided the final clue. I kind of guessed that Jimmy Arrcado is too much of an idiot to pull off a plan of this size, and she confirmed it. Only someone at the top of the Mafia architecture would have the funds to not only set up a fake company but build two complete warehouse structures. There were all these crimes that Jimmy was pulling; there is no way any self-respecting criminal from an organized crime family would pull off these minor heists. Unless, of course, they were meant to redirect the police from what was really going on. After seeing the church they burglarized, I knew there was more to the story. Employing Vance Deluca was another solid clue. Tony wanted to keep him on some sort of payroll. Partially to babysit his nephew. The person pulling all these strings naturally had to be the top of the food chain. And that is Tony."

Keith assessed his best friend's recap of the small items which taken out of context proved little but altogether painted a clear picture. Tony, for his part of this conversation, sat in silence smiling at Dirk's summation.

Dirk turned back toward Tony. "Mr. Arrcado, there is something I don't understand. Why did you ask me here? By the looks of things, we need to get you to the doctor." The man, lying before them, had a genuinely sickly appearance. Although a crime boss known for countless murders and suspected in many others, Tony appeared frail and harmless. Dirk didn't need medical training to understand the crime boss's life measured in minutes rather than hours.

"Dirk, my boy, let me introduce you to Doctor Lithowitz. He's a Jew, so you know he's a good doctor."

Dirk shot the doctor a confused glance, and he just shook his head at the obviously racist remark.

Tony laughed. "He hates it when I say shit like that, finds it insulting. I find how much money I pay him to be my personal physician insulting. A good doctor though, I have to give him credit where it is due. Why are all the good doctors either kikes or curry niggers? Anyway, Dirk, we both know there is no way I'm making it out of here alive. I had a good run though. I just wanted to meet you before I died. You are somewhat of a celebrity. Don't worry, I'm not holding any grudge against you. I lifted the execution order I put on your head. No one will touch you after this." Tony coughed uncontrollably and then wiped a little blood from the corner of his mouth. "You won, in a sense."

Keith stepped forward. "I don't understand, Mr. Arrcado, what do you mean?"

"It was your friend's investigation," Tony said, indicating Dirk, "that led to the demise of our empire. If this took place a few years ago, we would have been strong enough to make it through okay, but I needed this heist to work out for us. It led your girlfriend"—Tony pointed to Dirk—"the detective, to my warehouse."

"Carrie?" Dirk pursed his lips together in confusion. "What does she have to do with all of this?"

Tony coughed a little more and then laughed for a moment. "I wanted to see the look on your face when I told you this part." Tony laughed to himself for a moment. "I shot her."

Dirk turned white hot with rage. He wanted to wrap his hands around the old man's chubby throat and choke the remaining life out of him. Keith, sensing the rising confrontation, held Dirk back.

"You bastard! How dare you lay there with a smile on your smug fucking face and tell me you shot Carrie. Did you know you also almost killed my niece? She was in that building when it blew up. I should shoot you myself!" Spittle flew from Dirk's mouth as his vitriolic hatred of the man quickly became apparent.

Tony held up a hand, which took a considerable amount of effort. "My dear boy, I am truly sorry about that. I never intended to hurt the child, and I would have called off the bomb immediately. Rest assured, I got the worst of it. From what I understand, your niece, Claire, I think I recall, is recovering well, and Carrie is alive. With the one shot she returned, the same cannot be said for me, I assure you. You are seeing me at my last hurrah, as it were. And your girlfriend brought me to my end."

"Good, I am glad you are laying there dying. If anything happens to her, I swear to you —"

"You'll what? Kill me? My dear boy, you are not listening. She already did that. You've won. For what it is worth, I hope she recovers completely. As we both lay there bleeding on the road, she muttered something about telling Dirk she loved him. Touching, really. I am a sentimentalist at heart. There is no need for both of us to die."

Suddenly a rack of coughing hit Tony and blood spurted from his mouth, coating the blankets and the pillows. His eyes flew open with terror as something deep inside must have gone terribly wrong.

Doctor Lithowitz pushed Keith out of the way, running to the failing patient. Putting a stethoscope to the old criminal's chest, he listened to his lungs. Tony pushed the doctor out of the way and grasped alternately for the blankets and then something in the air that no one could see. The man let out one fitful scream and then fell back into the bed, ceasing to breathe.

"Doctor, what's going on?" The woman who let Keith and Dirk into the room pushed her way forward. Falling silent, she witnessed Tony's final struggle for life, and then he succumbed to the inevitability of mortality.

"I am sorry, Sophia. Your father is dead." Dr. Lithowitz put the stethoscope back into his lab coat pocket and stepped back from the warm corpse.

Sophia turned toward Dirk, and in her hand, she brandished a revolver. "You! You did this. If you hadn't meddled in our affairs, he would have never died."

Dirk understood her anger and pain. She just watched her father breathe his last. The professional in him weighed the volatility of the situation. One false move and this all turned deadly. "Sophia, you heard your father. He did not hold a grudge because of what happened. I am sure Carrie just returned fire on instinct."

"Shut up!" Sophia barked. "This is all your fault. You and your damn investigation." She ran to Tony's bedside and picked up one of his hands. Rubbing his stilled knuckles against her cheek, she stared into his eyes bearing silent witness to the events playing out before him. "Now my daddy is dead. You killed him!"

Dirk's mind put the pieces of the puzzle together. Carolyn and Sophia were cousins, which explained why they shared similar physical characteristics.

Keith held up a hand. "I know you are in pain right now.

Believe me, I do. Another person dying today won't change anything. We can still all walk out of here. Just put the gun down. Think this through, Sophia."

"No, he can't be dead. Daddy, please don't leave me."

"Sophia, listen to me. I want—"

Sophia's gaze locked on Dirk. "You killed him. My daddy is gone. You are going to pay for this, you son of a bitch!" Sophia turned on her heels and pointed the revolver at Dirk, who backed up reflexively. Keith, in contrast, took a step forward and was about to utter some eloquent statement guaranteed to defuse the situation, but an explosion stopped him while a puff of gunpowder threw the world into a hazy chaos. Keith, having becoming the object of her aim, fell to the floor in a howl of pain.

Dirk, not wasting any time, pulled out his own weapon and fired a round into the woman, knocking her to the ground in a spray of blood. The close-range shot cut a devastating hole in her chest.

Outside, the scene descended into chaos the moment the two shots went off. Three of the men left downstairs became so confused by the commotion they put down their weapons, eager to show the police they didn't fire the shots.

Dirk ran to Keith. "Buddy, are you all right? Talk to me."

"Ouch," Keith said. "I need to stop hanging out with you. It is proving hazardous to my health.

Dirk tore open Keith's shirt and assessed the wound. The bullet from Sophia's gun went far to the right and only grazed Keith on the side. With the exception of losing a good amount of blood, he would be fine. "Geez, one day on the job as a federal agent and you get shot. You should go back to being a pastor and learn not to jump in front of overly emotional women pointing guns at people."

Keith hobbled over to Sophia and checked for a pulse. An unnecessary gesture since anyone could tell Dirk's instincts and training meant his shot easily found center mass, ending any possibility of a second shot. Or, even another breath. Keith, ever the pastor, said a silent prayer for the woman over her fresh corpse.

Dirk helped Keith into a chair in the corner of the room just as the chief yelled from downstairs. "Dirk, are you all right? Keith?"

"Up here, Chief."

Chief Dixon ran up the stairs and gasped at the sight of Keith holding his side. "Keith, are you all right?"

Keith draped one hand over Dirk for support, and the other held a makeshift bandage on the wound. "I got shot, but I think I'll be all right."

27

IMPASSIONED PLEAS FALL ON SLEEPING EARS

Dirk watched in silence from the doorway as Carrie's chest rose and fell with each breath. No longer on a respirator, she remained unconscious. His fingers nervously tapped the box in his pocket. Claire, holding vigil with her mother, joined him at the door.

"She's going to be all right, Uncle Dirk."

"How do you know that, sweetie?" Dirk said quietly. "This case, it almost wiped us out. It still may. I died, Carrie might die, Keith got shot, and you got blown up. I can't handle the idea of losing any one of you. And the shop ..."

Claire grabbed his hand and held it. "But, it didn't. Victor saved us, and Keith is just too stubborn to die. My Aunt Carrie is a fighter, and there is no way she is going out this way. You know that's true. Besides, you still have to propose to her."

"Really, Miss Smarty Pants, how do you know I'm going to propose to her?"

Claire gave her uncle a smile. "You know, I am not a little girl anymore. I notice things. I see it in your eyes every time you talk to her. This is not just a springtime fling you two have going here."

"Springtime fling, huh?"

"Yeah, you two are meant for each other, and there is nothing you can do to change that." She kissed his hand. "I'm going to head over and see if Keith needs anything. Likely, he will tell me to fetch a laptop, a *Bible,* and the notes for next week's sermon. He's so lame. I'll see you later."

Dirk watched her walk down the hallway toward Keith's room in the next corridor. In the light, she appeared so much like her mother it would be easy to confuse the two. He smiled at the sight of seeing her up and walking again.

Stepping into the room, Dirk pulled up a chair and sat down next to Carrie's bed. As he took her hand, the warmth of her skin radiated into his. Just the other day, he kissed her lips and told her to be careful. Now, she lay in bed, appearing to cling to life by a thread.

"Carrie, I ... I need to tell you something. When I heard you had been shot, I almost lost it for a time. I wanted to reach out and hurt the people responsible. The opportunity sat right in front of me. All I had to do was keep going, and they would all be dead. You brought me back from that edge. I don't know much of anything really, aside from repairing motorcycles and a few things about finding people, but that doesn't make me who I am. It's you. You make me who I am.

"You, Keith, Claire, and even that goofball Victor make me complete. I can't function without any one of you but mainly you. I need you. You can't leave me, not now. There is so much left for us to do. Remember that little trail we saw last summer when we went hiking over the weekend? You wanted to go see it, but I needed to get back to the shop. We need to go back there, I promised we would. And, how about that trip to wine country? Do you remember? We need to go, you and me. I can't do it alone. That is the one thing I know, I can't do this alone. I need you. I need you to wake up. I need you to be my wife."

Dirk sobbed uncontrollably for a minute when shuffling of bedsheets caused him to crane his head toward the pillow. Carrie watched him, and a partial smile played across her face. Weakly, she said, "Are you proposing to me?"

With tears still streaming down his cheeks, he said, "Yes, I am. Carrie Pettygrew, will you marry me?" Dirk fumbled to open the box. Inside a diamond ring refracted the overhead fluorescent lights.

She smiled at him. "I swear you have the shittiest timing of any man on earth. I just accepted a marriage proposal from some half horse and half elf guy. Although, it could have been the narcotics they are giving me. Of course, I'll marry you."

Claire, having returned silently to Carrie's room, squealed with excitement at Dirk putting the ring on Carrie's finger. "See, what did I tell ya? Women know these things."

28

TEARS AND BLOOD FLOW FREELY

A week later, the hospital released Carrie, just in time for her to attend the funeral of Patrolman Aaron Collins. The department awarded him the Public Safety Medal of Valor, as well as other citations. Carrie sat in the first row next to his mother. On her other side, Sergeant Davis sat crying almost uncontrollably. When it came time to give a eulogy, Carrie stood and straightened her dress uniform.

Walking slowly with a cane up to the podium, she scanned the crowd and nodded toward Dirk and Keith. She adjusted the microphone just as the pitter-patter of raindrops reported the opening salvo of Mother Nature's barrage which scored direct hits on the large tent covering the assemblage. A cold wind drew up, matching the mood of the somber event. Before speaking, she glanced down at her engagement ring.

"They say that life is like a river. No matter what you do, or how hard you fight it, the river is going to win. Just like in a river, there are things that float into our field of view and are gone in the next instance. People can be like that sometimes. No matter how quickly they appeared or how quickly they left, they still came and went. They have an impact on us. Some impacts are profound and will never be forgotten. Such is the impact of Aaron Collins. Patrol Officer Collins made a commitment to serve and protect. For those of you who didn't know him that well, you missed out. I can tell you that.

"You see, wrapped up in that shell of a kid was an amazing soul who understood what it means to serve. Beneath the Goth style and the heavy metal aficionado beat the heart of a true hero. Even to the last moment, he gave his life, saving mine."

Carrie choked back the sobs forcing their way to the surface. Carrie cleared her throat and recomposed herself. She wanted to avoid making eye contact with Collins's mother sitting in the front row and failed. His mother was entirely too young to have a son die in the line of duty. For a moment, she thought about the hollow pain the young mother felt. Carrie thought about how she would feel sitting there watching the funeral of her son or daughter. What would it be like if her own mother or father sat watching Carrie's memorial service?

"I wouldn't be here today if it weren't for the quick actions of your son, ma'am. He saved my life and in doing so earned a spot of honor and respect that police officers seldom attain and no mother ever wants her child to earn. I am, and forever will be, a part of your family. His courage allowed me to live.

"We give Aaron baubles and awards, but the real legacy he leaves behind is all of us. We will never forget his sacrifice, and shame on us if we ever do, for even an instant. I know I will never forget the sacrifice Patrolman ... no, the sacrifice Aaron made for me."

Coming to the position of attention and taking two measured steps to the right of the podium, Carrie issued an order. "Funeral Commander, report!"

Sergeant Davis, dabbing weeping eyes, stood, and placing a uniform cap upon his head, he stepped forward in front of Carrie. After exchanging a salute, the suddenly stoic police sergeant stepped into the space Carrie previously occupied and said, "Pallbearers, to your posts. All rise for the final shift of Patrolman Aaron Stephen Collins." Turning to face the casket, he said, "Patrolman Collins, you are hereby promoted to the rank of Senior Patrolman and relieved after completion of your duties with honor and distinction. You bring great credit to yourself and the uniform."

Six pallbearers, in dress uniforms, sidled up to the coffin, lifting the casket from the catafalque, and turned it around to face the horse-drawn hearse waiting to take the flag-draped coffin to his final resting place.

With the pallbearers in position, Davis ordered, "All non-uniformed members of this assemblage, please remove head-gear and stand. Police Officers, attention!" With tears streaming down his cheeks anew, Sergeant Davis continued, "Pallbearers ... forward march."

THE COLD RAIN slid through the city in a relentless deluge. A mile away from the burial services of Patrolman Aaron Collins, a metro station hunkered down as waves of cold rain pelted it. Three men stood on the platform, huddling for warmth and what little dryness they could find. The day provided little of either. One of the men wore a silk and cashmere coat over the top of a business suit. Another man wore a long duster, pulled tight around himself, and the rain fell off it in sheets and immediately found purchase into a pair of black oxford shoes. The third man was dressed in blue jeans and a thin secondhand leather jacket. Wearing a thin pair of work gloves, he pulled a black hat over the top of his ears.

All the men gave the others a cursory glance and a nod of acknowledgment at their presence. If misery truly did love company, this day would find new friends everywhere. The man in the blue jeans, Mr. Rodrigo Hendricks, waited for the train to take him into the city to work. The new job as a nighttime maintenance man at an automobile warehouse suited his need for quiet and to work with his hands in a trade he learned as he served his sentence at the state penitentiary. A good of a job for a recently released ex-convict.

Rodrigo did not bear any ill will toward his capture. In fact, he smiled at the irony of it all. Born to a poor family, Rodrigo learned to live by violence early on. Drugs and alcohol became a crutch to deal with the world around him. The night the police busted him in his car with an underage hooker he marked as the beginning of his second chance.

Standing on the rain-slicked platform, he thought about the strange turn of events leading to this point in life. Before the police caught up with him, he ran a crew of thirty and commanded money, power, and cars. Now, he rented a room for two hundred fifty a month and used public assistance to afford food and the train.

The trade-off for losing everything was another shot at life. Now sober, optimistic, and thankful, the two years in jail with psychological counseling for anger and addiction issues forced him to take a different approach to life. After registering as a sex offender, Rodrigo left prison life behind him. A parole officer worked a few angles to secure his new job. The job kept him out of trouble and helped rebuild a life.

Rodrigo pulled his jacket up tighter. One more week and his first full paycheck arrived. Then it would be off to a secondhand store to buy a better coat for the winter. The parole officer graciously offered to check around to see if anyone at the station had an extra coat that fit. If the officer came through, part of the paycheck could pay for a pair of work boots at the secondhand store.

Off in the distance, the light of the train appeared around the bend in the track. Rodrigo examined the nylon lunch bag, a present from his sister, in his hand and thought about the contents within. A sandwich, a bag of carrots, and a chocolate soda.

It's funny how we never got chocolate soda in prison.

The train pulled up to the platform, and after a few seconds, the doors opened and Rodrigo slipped onto the train. Warm and dry, the vinyl and plastic train seats made him feel comfortable even in wet clothes. At least it would not rain on him anymore.

Looking out the window, Rodrigo marveled at the abandoned houses across the tracks from where the train sat. He briefly glanced at all the windows and wondered how many homeless people lived in them and how many more people hunkered down to stay out of the elements. It could just as easily be him.

Yes, getting arrested was possibly the best thing that ever happened to me.

The crack of the rifle from the upper story window of an abandoned house and the subsequent smash of the glass broke the otherwise dull silence. The last thing that went through Rodrigo's mind before the bullet shattered his skull, sending brain fragments and blood over the interior of the otherwise empty car, was *I sure am looking forward to my chocolate soda.*

SERGEANT ANDREWS PICKED through the crime with great care and attention to detail. Resisting the temptation to take anything from where it lay, he let the crime scene technicians process the scene while he stood back trying to piece together the plausible sequence of events leading to the grizzly site.

Based on the fact the glass fell into the car, the location of the body, and the damage to Rodrigo's head, the initial assessment suggested the shot came from the abandoned houses on the other side of the tracks. A police officer, sent to search the structures, could not find an expended shell cartridge but found where the shooter likely took the shot. The shooter took the step of building a platform to rest the rifle on.

What bothered Sergeant Andrews most of all was the feeling this was not just the work of a random shooter. Cold and calculated, this assailant took the time to be precise.

This was an assassination.

"Sergeant Andrews?" a patrol officer said.

"Yeah, what is it?"

"I found something you are going to want to see." The patrol officer handed Sergeant Andrews a pair of latex gloves and motioned over to where the medical examiner examined the body. "Doctor, show the sergeant what you just found."

"Certainly. Pocket litter we removed and cataloged." He grabbed a bag out of the box marked Victim's Belongings and handed it to Sergeant Andrews. Reading the small slip of paper, he let out a gasp. Someone scribbled a note on the piece of paper and a phone number which read "Contact Dirk Bentley, Private Investigator."

THE END

ACKNOWLEDGMENTS

I say it often, but I can't possibly say it enough—thank you, dear reader for choosing to read *The Reverent Dead*. As you may or may not know, this is the second book in the Dirk Bentley mystery series, the first book being *The Dramatic Dead*.

None of this is possible without the support of my dear wife who supports my obsession of writing; although, I am sure there are nights she just stares at me and wonders what the heck is wrong with me! Once again, her love and understanding helped this project take wings. I also have to thank my children for putting up with all of this.

It took me a long time to write this sequel. The reason is that I simply couldn't figure out how to end the story in a way I found satisfactory enough. Years of turmoil led me to finally come up with the idea of what happened to the nuns from the first book in the series.

I have to thank the wonderful beta readers who gave me such amazing feedback on *The Reverent Dead*. They stood at the literary anvil and shaped the written steel until it approached the intended form and function.

OTHER BOOKS BY BRYAN NOWAK

No Name

The Dramatic Dead (Dirk Bentley Mystery Series, book one)

Riapoke

Crimson Tassels

Visit Bryan online:
www.bryannowak.com

facebook.com/Bryanthewriter
twitter.com/Bryan_TheWriter

Made in the USA
Middletown, DE
05 November 2023